THE TWAIN
SHALL MEET

JOHN FRANCIS HART

The lives of two people born on the same day

in cities fifty miles apart become

tragically intertwined.

ISBN: 9798654871350

For Winefride

PART ONE

1

Sarah Watson came from Edinburgh.

Now, for the inhabitants of Sheffield or London or Bradford or indeed any other British city this would be unexceptional information. But for the inhabitants of Glasgow, this immediately set her apart as being something different, someone to be treated with caution. As her fellow law apprentice, Alastair Clarke, said to her on the first day of her apprenticeship, the popular Glasgow myth was that when Edinburgh children were conceived their parents remained fully clothed throughout. And Sarah was aware, as she was shown round the office on this first day, that she was treated, by the partners and by the secretarial staff, and even by her fellow apprentice, like a rare exhibit in a zoo – not to be approached too closely. Even with Pat McLaughlin she felt at a distance as she had to remember to call him Mr McLaughlin and not Uncle Pat, which made him seem more aloof.

The only person with whom she felt comfortable was old Mr Shaw who was long retired but happened to be in the office. He was seated behind the desk in what Sarah understood was Pat McLaughlin's office, but he stood up when she was ushered in by her Uncle Pat (no: *Mr McLaughlin*) and came forward to shake her hand. He had obviously been tall but was now stooped, and there was a twinkle in his eye.

'A female apprentice,' he said. 'That'll shake them up. And a good thing too. You will have to be twice as good as the men but, from what Pat tells me, you will be. You'll take time to get settled but if ever I'm in, which isn't often nowadays, I'd be delighted if you looked in for a chat.'

And, with that, he escorted her to the door and saw her out, with his final good luck wishes sounding in her ears.

Apart from that, Sarah was feeling deflated. She had had misgivings when she first arrived at the building which housed the office that was to be her place of work for the next three years. The entrance was framed in red sandstone, with the words 'Atlantic Chambers' carved on the stone. Just inside the heavy street door there was a framed sign board indicating that the offices of Shaw McLaughlin & Co were on the fifth floor.

The entrance hall of the building had been reasonably grand but now it was showing signs of wear. There was a lift to the upper floors with double, telescopic wrought-iron gates, operated by a lift attendant with a pronounced limp. He was also the caretaker of the building he told Sarah; adding cheerfully, when she went to enter the lift, 'I'm afraid you'll have to walk up today, Miss, as this lift has a mind of its own and it's having an off day.

The steps on the stairs to the first floor were marble and the walls were nicely tiled but as Sarah climbed higher she found that either the money had run out or the original builders felt that enough of an impression had been made, because, after the first floor, the marble gave way to stone and the tiles gave way to plaster, both showing clear signs of needing repair.

Sarah's only previous experience of legal premises was the grandeur of Parliament House in Edinburgh, where she had been taken by Uncle Pat, a partner in the firm of Shaw McLaughlin & Co., Solicitors and Notaries Public, to whom she was now apprenticed. She had imagined herself in an office of her own, obviously not very big (she was not silly) with legal textbooks lining the walls. In fact, having been introduced to the staff, she found herself in a small room with one small window opening out not to the open air but to the stairwell of the building. The only furnishings were a large double desk, one side of which was occupied by the other apprentice, with a rickety chair for each of them. Behind Sarah's chair (her colleague had taken the favoured seat) was floor to ceiling shelving jammed full of files which, judging by the frequent interruptions, required constant perusal by other members of the staff who had to squeeze past her to get to them.

Her first impressions of her fellow apprentice, with whom she would have to work in such close proximity, were also not favourable. Alastair Clarke was probably about her own age. He was above medium height, but his powerful build made him appear smaller and almost a bit menacing as he filled the chair opposite her. Sarah was also unhappy that as soon as they were. he made that reference to the sexual habits of people in Edinburgh. Was she going to be exposed to sexual innuendo whenever she was in his company? She found herself almost panicking and, wanting to be alone to gather her thoughts, she excused herself and made to go to the toilet. It turned out that the ladies' toilet was outwith the actual office premises but further along the same landing, access gained by picking up a key from the office receptionist. The tiled floor of the lavatory was chipped and the white fittings were basic: the toilet itself, which had a shoogly wooden seat with a split in it served by a high-up cistern with a pull chain; a wash hand basin (like the toilet, somewhat stained) and a cheap mirror, marked where the silvering had been scraped off the back. There was no heating and the room was cold, even now in the early autumn. It was not a place in which to loiter.

Sarah's thoughts were confused as she sat on the toilet seat, trying to make sense of her emotions.

Was this the refuge she sought, having determined to flee from Edinburgh?

2

It had been in Edinburgh that Sarah's mother, Maureen Johnston – or Molly Johnston as she was generally known – grew up.

Molly was the second of four daughters, who lived with their parents in genteel poverty on the outskirts of the city. Her elder sister, Sadie, was sensible, as elder sisters tend to be, and from an early age she had set her sights on marriage to a suitably sensible partner.

After Molly came Annie. She was of medium height, she had medium coloured hair and her skin was medium clear. Unfortunately, the only aspect of Annie which was not medium was her weight. She had developed from a plump baby into plump maturity and had no particular inclination to change. As Annie grew up, she listened while her friends told of their difficulties with boys, but she had never been involved herself. She had never been brushed against or had her bottom fondled and she sympathised when her friends confided their experiences to her without feeling that she was missing out. Although she read a lot, her reading was confined to film magazines and magazines like The People's Friend, a local weekly with stories of well-behaved men and women who coped with not-very-trying setbacks before surviving to live happily ever after, with no more reference to sex than might be found in Jane Austen. If asked (which would never have happened because Annie was the type of person who didn't attract any real interest) Annie would have said she had no ambitions. What she did have, was an inexhaustible well of compassion, which remained unplumbed until troubles beset members of the family or friends, when she absorbed herself night and day in providing succour. She came alive when her aid was required and, unconsciously, welcomed the distress of others as an opportunity to be helpful.

Annie was, inevitably, the one who cared for the girls' parents, which she combined with working part-time in a shop. The youngest sister, Betty, was the only other one still at home but, although very fond of her parents in a vague sort of way, she did not see herself looking after them in a practical sense – Annie could do that. Betty was the liveliest of the girls and was determined to have a good time. She had little patience with those who did not share her outlook, which included, most of the time, her three sisters.

Molly Johnston, herself, was not particularly pretty, although she had a shock of bright red hair, which caused her some distress when she was young as it made her the butt of bullying schoolmates.   Later, as the colour died down a bit, she became quite proud of her hair; she thought made her stand out as different, something she secretly longed to be. Neither was she particularly tall and she didn't do particularly well at school, perhaps because, in her eyes and in the eyes of her family, a secretarial job, one up from working as a shop assistant, was the extent of ambition.

Having started as an Office Junior in the small office that J & P Coats, the international threadmakers, had established in Edinburgh, she quickly moved to become a typist and was highly regarded in the firm for her dependability.   But she still thought there was something missing in her life.   Her family were dedicated Catholics and her social life largely revolved round Church activities that were enjoyable, but at the same time dull and routine.   Despite this, it was through the Church that she came to know James Watson, who attended the same church and whom she recognised vaguely from her office, where he also worked.   He was different because he had come through from the Paisley Head Office and also because he was an accountant.   In truth, he wasn't a real accountant, but he worked in the accounts department, which him gave some status in the office, raising him in the eyes of Molly and making her overlook the fact that although he was just under six feet tall, with jet black hair and brown eyes, he was a little diffident and more than a little dull. He was also, at thirty-two, twelve years older than Molly which, at her age, felt like a different generation. They started by exchanging a few words and going out together from time to time but, with James' lack of drive, the relationship might have gradually petered out, until news came through that he was being posted to the mill which the firm had set up about a decade earlier in Shanghai.

Now, *that* was different. Molly started planning. Over the months leading up to his intended departure, James was the unconscious target of a concerted campaign, which Molly brought to a successful conclusion when James, somewhat to his own astonishment, found himself proposing to Molly, a proposal which, with a suitable show of reluctance, Molly deigned to accept. There was just time to arrange the wedding ceremony (and Molly was aware that there were some who would gossip about the reason for the rush) before the happy couple left to take up married life together in China.

Expatriate life in pre-war Shanghai was a pleasant affair. The young couple was able to enjoy a standard of living far higher than they could have hoped for back home. They rented a substantial detached house, commensurate, in the eyes of the company, with James' staff position, with both indoor and outdoor servants to look after them. James' work was not too demanding and Molly, once she became accustomed to having servants at her beck and call, was able both to luxuriate in a life of freedom totally unlike her former existence and, unfortunately, to develop a lack of consideration towards the servants.

At first Molly was keen to explore, to take in the sights and sounds of the city. In this she was always accompanied by her maid, both from a practical point of view as she knew none of the language and could not make sense of the Chinese characters on the signs, but also because the maid took care that her mistress did not stray into areas where she might find unpleasantness, if not danger. Molly loved the exotic smells of the city from the open-air fish shops where the fish were kept alive in buckets until they were sold, and from the barrows heaped with vegetables freshly brought in from the country. And then there were the street vendors selling bowls of bean curd, yuanxiao dumplings broiled in rice wine, and sesame-coated shallot pancakes. The smells from these were so appetising but Molly heeded her maid's advice not to sample them.

The big difference was the sheer press of people. Coming from Edinburgh, Molly felt she knew about living in a large city, but in Shanghai the numbers were unbelievably higher. Not only that, but in Edinburgh, people, on the whole, were polite and well-mannered, and Molly decided it might just be a question of different customs because in Shanghai, the Chinese shoved their way to the front and pushed others out of the way. Furthermore, although Molly was of medium height she towered above most of the women she encountered and her red hair and blue eyes made her an object of amazement to the Chinese, whose black eyes and black hair were almost universal. It finally became so irksome to have people pointing at her, and children cowering away in half terror that she avoided, unless totally necessary, going on foot in the town.

The lives of the native Chinese were very different but the international community formed a totally separate cosmopolitan enclave within which they operated both commercially and socially, with remarkably little contact with the ordinary inhabitants. Provided James and Molly abided by their appropriate place in the social hierarchy, they were warmly welcomed into expatriate social life. James remained much the same as he had in Scotland, but Molly blossomed like a flower in the warmer eastern climate. She had time on her hands and started to enjoy reading the books the expatriate community exchanged amongst themselves. She managed, without being consciously deceitful, to convey a slightly fanciful account of her former life, even regretting she had become known as Molly.

'I'd like to be known as Maureen,' she said to James one day. 'Molly is a maid's name. It's a bit common. Do you not think so?'

James looked up from the paper he was reading. 'But Molly is your name. Everyone knows you as Molly.'

'I know, but I was baptised Maureen. It's more dignified don't you think?'

'I don't know about that,' said James with a puzzled frown. 'You're Molly to me and I like 'Molly'. I can't change that.' And he went back to his paper.

So, while in most things James followed where Molly led, in this he could not be moved and 'Molly' she remained although sometimes, posing in front of the mirror, she murmured 'Maureen' to herself; perhaps in James' next overseas posting she could try again.

In any event, helped by a previously hidden spark of life possibly related to her now auburn hair, she had a new confidence to relate to people more openly and show a sense of humour. It made her an entertaining companion, although she was intuitively aware that her exuberance should not lead her to trespass into a level of social relations higher than was her right. Molly did, however, gain the confidence to tease the great and the good, leaving them feeling greater and better in themselves. (*Not,* of course, the ladies. Great and good ladies were too aware of their own dignity to take kindly to teasing).

If she sometimes wished that James would show a bit more social drive, she did not allow his plodding to interfere with her own rise in society. James could add up three columns of figures in his head but was not capable of sustaining a meaningful conversation at a social level, possibly because he suffered from slight social deafness in a crowded setting.

What with the group of young people of her own age working in the settlement area and the number of sailors from ships both merchant marine and Navy visiting the port, an active social life opened up for Molly. There were many men who were unattached and many more who were temporarily separated from their attachments and they all found Molly a ready companion for their leisure hours. She was generally regarded as good fun. But no more than that. The combination of her Scottish Calvinistic background, her Catholic upbringing, and her striving for middle-class respectability meant that there was a barrier she unconsciously had in place and of which her companions were consciously aware.

The delicious past-time of flirting was just not for Molly. She sometimes wondered why? She knew her marriage to James had grown out of a wish to better herself rather than any of the passion described in the novels she had just started reading; her marital relations were loving rather than intense. Was she just a prim Edinburgh matron? But when Molly dressed, she did do so to be attractive to men, enjoying her bared arms and deliberately adjusting her blouse to disclose the first sign of her separated breasts. She had been so thin when she was younger but following her marriage her figure had filled out and she was proud of her bust. In place of her weekly Edinburgh bath, Shanghai's weather demanded a daily shower, during which she found herself lingering over soaping her breasts and enjoying spraying them clear of suds. And afterwards, she knew she took longer than was necessary patting herself dry between her legs. But this pleasure was something she kept to herself.

The social position of James and Molly was further cemented, and their marital happiness completed, by the birth of a daughter, Sarah, on 4 October 1936. However, their idyll was not to last. Confrontations between the Chinese and the Japanese had become increasingly serious, with the Japanese attacks leading to the Battle of Shanghai, not long after Sarah's birth, further de-stabilising the whole region. Head Office in Paisley was also acutely aware of rising tensions at home and, following on the Munich Agreement, made the decision to repatriate all European staff. So, there was no new overseas posting for James and by the beginning of 1939, James, Molly and Sarah had exchanged the comparative cold of a Shanghai winter for the piercing cold of January in Edinburgh.

3

It was not just the cold that made Edinburgh so unattractive to Molly. On their return, the family set up home in a small flat, a grey sandstone tenement in a not very attractive part of the town. Molly felt totally enclosed within its three rooms with no access to a garden, comparing it unfavourably to the spaciousness of their Shanghai villa and extensive grounds, lovingly – or at least diligently – tended by two gardeners. They were, of course, welcomed home by Molly's family, but the life of Parish Socials for entertainment, which was all the future seemed to hold out for her, made Molly almost scream in frustration as she thought back on the garden parties and drinks receptions with the brilliant, glamorous people (as Molly now thought of them) she had left behind her. She was back to where she had started. She was no longer different.

In truth, although she was not aware of it, she seemed very different to her Edinburgh friends and relatives. The mousy, diffident Molly had been replaced by a much more confident woman who did not fit back into her previous role. Human nature makes us unconsciously set others in a hierarchy of infinitely small ranks; some are slightly below us; some are entitled to respect; some we enjoy their stories, others we don't pay much attention to; some are the centre of a group, others are always on the periphery. Molly, on her return, upset her previous ranking, forcing her friends and relatives to adjust to the change – and some did not relish having to do so. Even the clothes she wore set her apart. To be fair to Molly, clothes rationing gave her no alternative but to fall back on her Shanghai wardrobe, but it was noticed and held against her by those who were looking for resentment. Nor did they relish her, perhaps too frequent, references to the glamour of her Shanghai life.

James did not seem to share the same problems. He was back doing much the same job as he had done in Shanghai and, if anything, he rather liked not having to attend the parties their Shanghai life had made inevitable; he had never felt totally at ease in that environment. Provided he could come home of an evening and have a pleasant meal and thereafter read his paper while puffing on his pipe (a habit he had developed in Shanghai) he was perfectly happy. A more sensitive man would have realised his wife's discontent but, as a couple, they had never talked much, and James lacked the imagination to pick up Molly's non-verbal signs. Having another child might have made a difference, but James, while loving and caring, was not physically passionate. In any event, Molly's labour at the time of Sarah's birth had run into difficulties and they had been told it was unlikely she could have any more children.

Molly reconciled herself to that, but she was determined that the one child would have all the chances she had missed. 'Sarah is going to go to university,' she announced to James one evening shortly after they returned from Shanghai.

'She's only two,' said James mildly.

'I know, but she's a bright girl and she's different. We must make sure that we encourage her, young as she is. My time in Shanghai opened my eyes, James. When I was young I thought no further than getting a job as a secretary in an office. Sarah is going to do better than that. She's going to go to university.'

James was happy to go along with Molly's dreams without doing more than his fatherly care of his daughter. But Molly persisted in her ambitions even murmuring to Sarah as she drifted off to sleep at night, 'You're going to go to university.'

By the time Sarah was four she was beginning to be old enough to understand her mother's wishes for her. She even had a vague notion of what a university was.

'Where will I go to university, Mummy?' she asked one evening as Molly brushed her long hair.

'Why, here in Edinburgh,' said Molly, whose grand ambitions did not for a second extend to another Scottish university, far less further afield.

'But will I be clever enough? What if I'm not clever enough?'

Molly smiled as she hugged her daughter. 'You'll be clever enough. No need to worry.'

Sarah, of course, did not fully understand her mother's plans for her but Molly was delighted to see (or possibly to imagine) that, although she was under two when they had to leave Shanghai, Sarah's time there had left a mark on her. She seemed more at ease with adults than any of her Scottish cousins. She had been a favourite with the Chinese servants and, in the normal expatriate way, had been allowed to spend time with them, especially with her amah who had been heartbroken when they had to leave. Sarah had even picked up some words of Chinese but whether they were Mandarin or Cantonese or from some other dialect, Molly did not know – knowledge of the native languages was not something the expatriates bothered to acquire.

It was at least two years before Sarah would start primary school but, once the family had become re-settled in Edinburgh, Molly made it her duty to teach Sarah to read and write. It did not trouble her that Sarah naturally wrote with her left hand. Her letters were beautifully formed, a reflection of her facility in drawing, which seemed to come to her naturally.

'That must come from James' side,' said Molly to herself. 'No-one on our side can draw a straight line.'

Molly also had the common sense not to force Sarah into formal sums. She merely played lots of games with her in which simple calculations were involved and, much to her delight, Sarah not only made quick progress but also seemed to enjoy what she was learning. Her reading developed to such an extent that when her father came home of an evening she would sit on his knee and, with his help, read to him extracts from his newspaper, enjoying trying to pronounce the funny German names, like Hitler and Himmler and Goering.

Unfortunately, the newspapers had begun to make unhappy reading. The German armies had swept through Western Europe and by the middle of 1940 even the heavily censored reports of the evacuation from Dunkirk made depressing news.

Molly was, accordingly, not alone in feeling low at this time but, unlike the other people in Edinburgh, she had her memories:

'Remember, James, in Shanghai – the terrible bombing? It completely flattened part of the city. There were thousands killed. And there's bound to be bombing here. Do you think we should send Sarah to stay with my cousin in the Free State?' She and James agonised over the decision, but they were reluctant to part with Sarah and eventually did nothing.

Apart from this, the family was not affected by the war as James, partly because of his age and partly because he seemed to be in some sort of reserved occupation, was initially not called up to serve in the Army. Eventually, however, he was called up, but even then, he was fortunate, as his basic training took place at Redford Barracks in Edinburgh, meaning he was able to come home at times of leave.

With his shy nature, James made few friends in his unit but did become close to one man called Pat McLaughlin, who came from Glasgow and who was a solicitor in what Molly came to understand as Civvy Street. From time to time James talked to Molly about Pat. 'He's very quiet and unassuming,' he mused.

'Is that all?' said Molly. 'What does he look like?'

James paused for a moment – men are not good at describing other men. 'I suppose he's not very tall, he wears glasses and his feet are as flat as his hair, which is always parted neatly in the middle.'

Molly thought, a little treacherously, that he sounded the sort of uninteresting person who would appeal to James (but at least he was a solicitor which was the type of friend Molly would want for her husband). 'Is he not a bit dull?' she said.

'Oh no,' replied James. 'That's the thing. He's the most interesting person to chat to. And he brings you out in conversation because he is interested in you.'

On another occasion James smiled as he puffed his pipe. 'You know, Pat is totally unco-ordinated. Despite all the bellowing from the NCOs he's incapable of marching properly. He seems to swing his right arm forward at the same time as his right leg. And he is completely unable to ride a motorbike – which even I can do. You can imagine the ribbing he gets and even the bullying he might attract, except for one thing. When it comes to football, Pat is far and away the best player in the squad. That gets him by.'

A little later James added, 'There's another thing about Pat. You can imagine the noise and racket in the barrack room just before lights out, Molly? Pat ignores that and kneels down by his bedside to say his night prayers. I wouldn't have the guts to do that. He's just a lovely man.'

When Molly and Sarah had the chance to meet Pat, they agreed he *was* a lovely man. And he very quickly became Sarah's Uncle Pat.

4

After James completed his basic training he was, because of his accountancy background, ordered to serve in the Royal Army Pay Corps. This suited Molly as it meant he would not be involved in combat but, to her disappointment, he was posted to work in the London area for the duration of the war with only occasional visits back home on leave. If Molly were brutally honest, however, his absence did not create an enormous hole in her life, because their life together was quiet and uncommunicative, but she did find time on her hands with only Sarah to look after and for company. It was fortuitous, therefore, that, shortly after James' departure for London, the curate in the parish she attended – he had taken a liking to her which she returned – told her that the Polish Consulate in Edinburgh was looking for a part-time assistant, preferably with some experience beyond Scotland. He wondered whether she would be interested? Whereas the old Molly would have been too cautious to think of such a job, the new Molly jumped at the chance and applied.

29 Coyltonbridge Crescent

24 April 1942

Dear James,

I hope you are well and keeping warm in this cold weather we are having. I was so pleased when you were posted to the Pay Corps because I thought you would be far from danger but now with the blitz I am terrified that you will be hit by some of those terrible bombs. I hope you are being sensible and staying in shelters whenever there is a raid on.

Sarah and I are both well. She is missing her Daddy very much and is looking forward to your next leave. I, at last, have some news of my own. You know Father Mitchell, the new curate? He came to me last Sunday after Mass and said that the Polish Consulate was looking for a part-time secretarial assistant and he thought of me. Wasn't that nice of him? Anyway, the upshot was that I applied for the post (I hope you won't mind) and they gave it to me. It's only four hours a day, three days a week, and I have arranged for my sister Annie to look after Sarah when I am there.

I am working with the Consular Assistant, Mieczyslaw Grzeskiewicz. I have no idea how to pronounce his name and have great difficulty typing it but fortunately he is quite happy to be known as Mickey and that makes it easier – although Mickey makes me think of Mickey Mouse and he is by no means a mouse, being quite big. I am coping easily with what is required of me and am enjoying doing something worthwhile again.

Please do look after yourself. I keep hearing that Vera Lynn song on the wireless – We'll Meet Again – and I always think of you when I hear it. It can't be long now, surely.

Your loving wife,

Molly

Dear Daddy, I am missing you lots. Mummy has that lovely picture of you in your uniform and I like to look at it. I always say a prayer for you at night. Please come home soon.

Hugs and kisses,

Sarah xxxxxxx

Unlike her relations in Edinburgh, Molly did have personal experience of the effect of bombing, from her time in Shanghai. Although not directly affected, she had had herself driven out in a rickshaw to inspect the damage caused by the Japanese bombing of the city and had been appalled by the total destruction caused and the terrible slaughter in the poorer areas. She comforted herself with the thought that the more substantial buildings of London would provide better shelter especially as one thing that could be said about James was that he would be sensible. But she was not the first wife to give unnecessary advice.

As the months went on, Molly gradually became assured in her work at the Consulate. It was chiefly dealing with requests for help from Poles who had somehow made their way through war-torn Europe and reached Scotland without papers and were trying to re-establish themselves. Molly was enthralled with the stories they told of the hardships they had suffered, although she was often overwhelmed with their tales of lost relatives and the terrible fate of the Jewish people herded into the Warsaw Ghetto and then marched out again by the Nazis to who knows where. Their stories made her feel part of a wider world beyond Edinburgh, even more so than she had felt in Shanghai.

Added to her enjoyment of her work was the fact that the other members of staff, mostly from Polish backgrounds, made her feel welcome and often invited her to their homes. Her immediate boss was Mickey, who was tolerant of her initial mistakes and then, as she grew into her job, began to rely on her more and more. As she wrote in her letter to James, he was a big man with a little moustache who rarely raised his voice and was punctiliously polite to all the staff. What Molly liked, in particular, was that he was friendly to her but never for one second flirtatious, so that she felt totally at ease with him. Her previous experience with men, both in her prior existence in Edinburgh and in her life in Shanghai, was that she had always been aware of a frisson between her and them. That could be attractive, but not restful, and she welcomed the difference with Mickey.

One beautiful late summer's morning Mickey stopped at her desk. 'It's too nice a day to spend all of it indoors. How about taking packed lunches and going for a picnic? I've got the consular car and we can drive into the country and find a nice spot.'

Molly jumped at the chance to get out of the city, which she had not left since James had gone to London. They drove into the country and found a good spot in a clearing leading down to a stream where Mickey spread out his greatcoat for them to sit on. Mickey also produced food for the picnic which was not available to Molly because of rationing and he insisted she should share it and also a bottle of wine which he brought out of his bag. They talked quietly together. She told him about her time in Shanghai and he spoke about his family back in Poland and his worries about them.

Mickey laughed when she told him the difficulty she had with Polish names. 'What about Scottish names?' he said. 'Although to be fair I like some of them. Like Crianlarich, and Killiecrankie and Pittenweem. I like the sound of Pittenweem. And pronunciation? Why Milguy and not Milngavie?' He pronounced it phonetically, lying back and mouthing the two words, until she could tell from his breathing that he had fallen asleep.

Molly remained sitting with her arms round her bent knees. There was a slight breeze and she started to enjoy the way it blew under her dress and against her thighs, bare above her stocking-tops. Keeping an eye on Mickey, in case he woke, she gradually pulled out her dress from under her so that, although her legs remained completely covered, they were free to feel the rough cloth of the greatcoat against them through her knickers, a sensation which she strengthened by straightening her legs so that they were completely extended against the cloth.

After a bit, she turned to lie in her stomach, with her head on her arms, and turned to watch Mickey, who was still dozing. She wondered what it would be like to kiss that mouth with its moustache. James had once tried to grow a moustache but had had to give up the attempt. Molly had to chase away the thought of that moustache on other parts of her body, but she still allowed her mind to wander. She had thought that, lying flat on her back, she was open to attack but now that she lay on her front she felt that she was totally exposed and making herself available, and she let herself luxuriate in that feeling – although she knew that, in reality, if Mickey made a move towards her she would repulse him forcibly.

Although James seemed totally unaware of it, Molly had prominent and very sensitive nipples and, at the thought of that moustached mouth on them, she rubbed her breasts against the greatcoat until she almost gasped out loud. She longed to rub herself between her legs but was afraid that Mickey might notice. Instead she contented herself with rubbing her damp groin against the coat, all the time thinking of those big hands on her. She imagined him leaning over and gently tugging her skirt up above her waist and then slipping her knickers down to leave her bottom bare. She mentally raised her bottom slightly so that it was more exposed to his gaze and actually mouthed, 'Yes, please, spank me,' as if in reality he had asked her. She gasped as his imaginary hand then slipped up between her legs and grasped her. She felt totally at his mercy as she ground down on that strong hand and rubbed and rubbed. And rubbed again on that hand and the fingers which were probing her more and more deeply. She felt her whole body diffused with blood and then she almost screamed as all thoughts were overwhelmed by an explosion of sensation. When she recovered, she frantically looked round at Mickey, but he was still sleeping, snoring slightly, and she let herself subside into a relaxation of a type she had never previously enjoyed. Later, when Mickey stirred, he and Molly gathered together the remains of the picnic. As she stood up Molly was relieved to find that the wetness she could feel between her legs was not showing through onto her dress, although she found herself a little unsteady on her feet.

'You often find that when you've been sitting down too long,' said the unknowing cause of her dizziness as they made their way back to the car. 'I enjoyed our picnic. I'm sorry I fell asleep.'

The reason Molly had such a clear memory of that picnic was because she found out later that just about the time she was rubbing herself against Mickey's coat, James was ending his service for King and Country by stepping absentmindedly in front of a double-decker bus while eating a Spam sandwich.

5

Pat McLaughlin was also with the Army in London and, as he was known as James' closest friend, he was one of the first to be told about James' death. Rather than having Molly learn of the tragedy by telegram, he volunteered to travel up to Edinburgh to tell her personally. When he arrived, he first called at her parents' house and enlisted the help of Annie in breaking the news.

When Molly opened the door, her first reaction was one of pleasure to see them, but this was immediately replaced by fear as she read their faces, and then by horror as Pat told her that James had been killed in a road accident. Molly, with tears streaming down her face, asked Pat about what had happened. When she heard the accident had taken place the previous day, she gazed at him in even greater horror. Still standing on the doorstep she pressed him for more details, and he was able to tell her that it had happened just after lunchtime, about two o'clock. Molly knew it was right at the time when she was lying next to Mickey at the picnic and she howled in anguish before Annie and Pat managed to help her into the flat to sit down. Luckily, the flat was empty – Pat was able to get from Molly through her tears that Sarah was still at school.

Molly had no doubt about the connection between James' death and her picnic writhings on Mickey' greatcoat. God had punished her in disgust at what she had done. She, who had become so sure of herself, was almost paralysed by what had happened, so that arrangements for bringing James' body home and for his funeral had to be taken over by her family. They were shocked by her extreme grief and even scandalised by its so public expression, unaware that it was not grief that smothered Molly, but horror, horror at what she had done. She excoriated herself, hating her pride, '*Maureen* was it? No. *Molly* is right. I'm just a common slut.'

Annie, typically, took over. 'I don't think Molly is capable of looking after Sarah,' she told the rest of the family. 'I don't think she knows what she's doing. I'm going to move into Molly's flat. I can look after both Sarah and Molly there.'

On the night before the funeral, as was the Catholic custom, the coffin containing the body of the deceased James was brought into the church to lie there overnight and a short service of reception was held, at the end of which an opportunity was given,

to those who wished, to go to confession. Molly was in torment.
She would have found it impossible in any event to say out loud to
the priest what she had done but that was not the problem. In her
tortured mind, she did not want forgiveness, she wanted
punishment. The priest who was an old man, recognising her
distress and thinking to give comfort told her to forget any sins she
might have committed, gently speaking over her tears of a loving
God who forgave everything and would bring her peace. Molly did
not believe that, nor did she want to believe it.

The funeral next day took its normal course and was followed
by the usual purvey in a local hotel. There people were able to get
together, relieved that the strain of the funeral Mass and the
internment had passed, and have something to eat and drink, while
reminiscing about James and other family members who had died
before. Molly, a shrunken figure dressed in ill-fitting black clothes
which one of her sisters had obtained for her, was able to get
through the Mass with her head bowed down. After Mass was
over, she managed to face one or two people who approached her
to offer condolences, but she recoiled in horror when she saw
Mickey and other staff from the Consulate approaching. She rushed
from the church into the waiting car.

Also, by custom, only male relatives and friends accompanied
the coffin to the graveyard for the final internment; the women
went direct to the hotel to await their return. Molly did not appear

at the purvey, much to the disgust of many of her female relatives who felt that her failure to appear was just another instance of Molly not doing what was expected of her.

The other members of the family agreed in thinking that her grief was excessive. As her younger sister, Betty put it, 'It's part and parcel of the way she's behaved since she came back from Shanghai. She became just a bit uppity. It's not as if she was besotted with James. He was a nice enough fellow, but I thought she married him because he was there, and he had a good job. And she didn't seem to care much when he was away in London, especially when she got that job in the Polish Consulate she used to brag about.'

The male relatives did not give such thought to the matter but applied themselves enthusiastically to the food and drink provided, which, in the view of Uncle Tom, made a funeral much more enjoyable than a wedding – at a funeral there was only your own family involved.

As she waited for people to disperse, Molly sat alone in a separate room, too ashamed to come out to meet the gaze of any of her relatives or friends, until finally Annie came in to take her home.

6

Sarah was nearly five and a half when her father died. Although she was aged just over two when they'd left Shanghai she retained a vivid memory of a road accident there, when a rickshaw in which she and her father were travelling lost a wheel, throwing them both on to the road. She was taken to hospital, found not seriously injured, but she remembered being in James' arms when the doctor was examining her. And it was being in his arms which was her abiding memory of her father because, although her mother cared for her, she always had the impression, even as a very young child, that Molly was being strict with her, not driving her, but pushing her on to do more and more things. Her father, on the other hand was just delighted to have this unlooked-for gift of a daughter.

The gentle nature, which precluded any advancement in James' career, led him to relish the time he spent with Sarah as the highlight of his life. He loved to take her walking in the park, sometimes with her perched proudly on his shoulders; he loved to have her sitting on his knee as he patiently listened to her doing her reading; it was he who most often tucked her up in bed and read her, her bed-time story; it was to him that she first turned, if a fall or a disappointment had marred her day.

When her father was away in London Sarah kept the picture of him in uniform beside her bed and kissed it every night. She took great delight in adding her bit to her mother's letters, taking great care, with the help of her tongue between her lips, to form her letters properly.

She knew something terrible had happened that evening when she came home from school to find her Uncle Pat and Auntie Annie there and her mother stretched prostrate on a settee. Molly pressed Sarah in her arms but, sobbing, she was unable to speak and it was Annie who tried to tell Sarah that her father was dead.

Annie, herself, was so distraught she was almost incapable of saying anything. She managed to extricate Sarah from her mother's arms and led the frightened child to her bedroom. There, she merely lifted Sarah on to her knee and sobbed into her hair. It was Sarah who moved first and kissed her cheek and said, 'It's all right, Auntie Annie.'

Annie managed to control herself and said, 'Daddy's been in a terrible road accident and...'

'Like the rickshaw in Shanghai?' asked Sarah.

'What? No, there has been a terrible accident and Daddy has been killed. Oh! I'm so sorry, dearie, but Daddy has been killed. He's gone to be with Jesus and the angels.'

'When will he be coming back?'

'He willnae be coming back. You must be a brave girl, dearie. Say a prayer for your daddy, but you won't be able to see him again. He cannae come back. You be good now and look after your mother.'

Sarah frowned. 'Can I write to him?'

'Oh! God, no, hen. Being dead means he has gone to heaven. But he'll still be thinking of you and looking after you. You just have to remember him in your prayers.'

Sarah cried then but it was merely because Auntie Annie was crying. She still didn't understand what had happened. She associated her father not being there, with his absence in London, and for some time she linked being in London with death. It was only gradually she realised he would never be coming home again; that he would never hold her and comfort her; that she would never be able to kiss his cheek and feel safe in his arms. It was then she cried properly, lying frightened in the dark.

The apparent lack of sympathy shown by the family reflected the way that Molly had drifted away from them because of her absence abroad but they were still sufficiently concerned to hope that over time she would learn to live with her grief. In the meantime, it was agreed that Annie, who had no family of her own, would stay with Molly and Sarah until things got back to normal and even thereafter should do what she could to shield Sarah from what the family regarded as the worst excesses of Molly's grief.

And that is what happened. Annie stayed about three weeks, during which she tried, without success, to get Molly to talk about things. Eventually she decided that Molly was sufficiently recovered to look after herself – and, in particular, Sarah – and she went back to her own house.

Annie had wanted Molly to talk through her grief, but it was still not grief that was tearing at Molly. It was guilt. And guilt that had to be punished. She could not talk about that to Annie. She could not talk about it to anyone – depression is essentially a self-centred condition, and a lonely one. Molly was glad when Annie left, and she was free to think on her own. As her mind twisted, she suddenly came to the conclusion that her only remedy was suicide. She had been taught in church that suicide was the worst sin because it was against the Fifth Commandment and a rejection of the hope of God's love; a mortal sin which would lead to eternal punishment. And it was eternal punishment which she craved.

One thing held her back from the abyss: the thought of Sarah. In the weeks after her father's death, Sarah, in the way of children, sensed her mother's woe and played quietly with her toys, keeping her demands on Molly to the minimum. Indeed, it was her attempt to help with the housework one night, by clearing the table after their tea that first brought a little warmth back into Molly's frozen heart. She smoothed Sarah's hair and, for the first time since James' death sat in the easy chair with Sarah in her arms. And after that things got better. It was like when an ocean liner docks, the sailors on board, first throw out a thin line for the harbour man to grab, and as he pulls it in a heavier line is attached and then an even heavier one until eventually the hawser, which is strong enough to tether the ship, is reached and attached to the bollard.

So, it was Sarah who brought Molly to a harbour of sorts. Molly remained a virtual recluse in a house which was dark and not welcoming to callers, but she had found a reason for living in Sarah and she devoted to her the stunted and twisted love which was all she had left. It was not a consistent love. There were periods when Molly virtually ignored Sarah as she again fell prey to the guilt still buried deep in her tortured mind, and it was as if Sarah was not there. On other occasions, when the pangs of guilt seemed less real, Molly smothered her with attention. Through time, indeed as she grew older, Sarah came to realise that the episodes of rejection were not caused, as she at first thought, by her behaviour, but were a

40

result of the grief from which her mother continued to suffer. In this she was helped by her Auntie Annie who took it on herself to call regularly at the flat to chat to Sarah and to take her out to see her cousins. In this way, without meaning to, she supplied the continuing love which she intuitively felt was missing.

Sometimes Molly did not take kindly to Annie's interventions. She would be irritated by her presence and just wanted to be left alone. At the worst times, she made offensive comments.

'Why are you always here, Annie? You're not wanted. Why can't you mind your own business? Just leave us alone, for pity's sake. Just because you have no life of your own, there's no reason why you should impose yourself on us. Everyone says you're just a big lump.'

Molly knew she was being cruel, but she couldn't help herself. There was a viciousness in the attacks, as if she was stabbing Annie with a knife. Then it would all be over, and she would fall into Annie's arms in a flood of tears. Annie would hold her tight while making a pretend kiss over her shoulder to Sarah, who played on the floor with her dolls as if unconscious of what was happening. Inside, though, she was torn by this fight between her mother and her much loved aunt.

Although Annie was hurt by the remarks, she bore them, and Molly's subsequent apologies, with apparent equanimity. But she wasn't a saint, she couldn't just discount the attacks on the basis of

Molly's grief. The worst insults are those which contain a grain of truth and Annie, when she was alone, would sometimes ask herself, 'What use am I? Molly is right. I have no life of my own.'

And she would cry a little in the dark before drifting off into a sleep which seemed to wash away her doubts.

7

One day, Sarah got lost. It was shortly after James' funeral and although it was a bright sunny day her mother had taken to her bed with the bedroom curtains tightly drawn, leaving Sarah to play with the few toys she had. After a while, the child became bored and, as she looked out at the sun, decided she would slip outside and play. She still thought that her Daddy would come back someday from this London place and she wandered a little from their tenement, half hoping that, as she turned a corner into another street, she would meet him coming towards her. As she skipped along, she played in her mind with the things she would say to him. Then she came across a small terrier, which jumped up on her and wanted her to chase him, which she did through a few more streets until it suddenly disappeared, and she decided that she should go home. But which way to go? She turned down one street which looked familiar, but streets lined with tenements all look much the same and Sarah had to turn back and try another one and then another one.

'Where are you going to, young lady?' said a voice, finally. It came from a large policeman who, unbeknownst to Sarah, had been watching her walk up and down.

'I'm just going home,' she said.

'And where might that be?'

Sarah hesitated. She felt herself very confident but realised that she did not know her address. 'I think I may be lost,' she eventually said.

'Oh, no you're not,' said the policeman. 'You are just round the corner from the police station and if you give me your hand we'll go there now and get things sorted out.

On the way, Sarah chattered away, telling the policeman all about her Daddy who was in London and had not come back for ages. At the police station she was made a fuss off by the staff. They gave her a desk to sit at and some pencils and paper and she was quite happy drawing and sipping the tea and eating the biscuit they brought her. All she could tell them was her name, and the desk sergeant decided the best thing was to leave her be and eventually someone would turn up looking for her; they could tell from her clothes she was not a waif.

In fact, she had not been there long when a voice said, 'Hello Sarah. What are you doing here?'

She immediately recognised the speaker as a policeman who lived up the same close as she did. Sarah could tell that he was important as all the other policemen addressed him as 'Sir'. The policeman who had brought her to the station explained what had happened and how she had chattered away about looking out for her Daddy who was away in London.

'I'm afraid her father isn't in London,' said the Inspector. 'I think she believes he is, but he was killed there two or three weeks ago, and she maybe doesn't know what that means. Puir wee lassie. I'll take her home. Her mother is in a terrible state and maybe hasn't noticed she is missing. He turned to the little girl. 'Let's get you home, Sarah.'

And Sarah cheerfully went off home, hand-in-hand with him. When they got there, before he knocked the door, thinking to spare Molly further stress, he whispered to Sarah, 'Let's play a little game with your mother. We'll pretend that you saw me from the window and came out to say hello, letting the door close behind you.' Sarah was delighted to go along with this game and when, after some delay, Molly came to the door she played her part in the little innocent deception, even with her eyes, sharing with the policeman her acceptance of the reprimand for having gone out of the door.

Thereafter, Sarah was known to all the local policemen as Inspector MacMurdo's wee girl and they always gave her a big smile whenever they met her. Until she started to go to the secondary school, she visited the police station on a regular basis to chat to whoever was on duty there.

Although Sarah was a bright girl her personality was inevitably cowed by the atmosphere in which she lived. Not that she was aware of it. Just as children played happily in the remains of blitzed houses because that was all they knew, so Sarah accepted her life as normal. This involved, for example, frequent attendance at Church Services. On Sundays, it was morning Mass, with afternoon Sunday School and early evening Devotions. For the rest of the week, there was daily morning Mass with evening Devotions on a Tuesday and a Thursday, and in Lent and Advent there were additional Services. She wasn't permitted out to play with the few children who lived nearby and at the convent primary school she attended, other children mostly shared a similar church- centred existence.

Things were different when Sarah moved to the secondary school, which was run by the same Notre Dame nuns as the primary school. There she had been quite a pet with the nuns, partly because they knew of her background and partly because she was a very gifted artist who astonished her friends and the nuns with beautifully drawn sketches of birds and flowers, and elegant ladies' gowns. She even tried her hand at caricatures, but these were not shown to the nuns as they often portrayed them in less flattering poses. But the secondary school nuns were impervious to her drawing skills. What they saw was that she used her left hand and they compelled her to change to her right for writing. It caused Sarah terrible anguish because it made her so much slower than her classmates, and her work, using a steel nib dipped in an inkwell, was messy and splodgy, attracting constant criticism from her teachers.

She also found herself an outsider because, while other girls could exchange home visits, she was unable, because of her mother's reclusive state, to invite them to her house. This led to her to be bullied, not physically, but by exclusion, when plans were made ignoring her. At first, she was a little favoured because she was part of a small group whom the nuns held up for special attention because their fathers had been killed in the war. But then, one day, one girl, Mary O'Callaghan, who for some reason had taken a dislike to Sarah, shouted at her in the playground,

'You shouldnae be part o' the dead heroes' group. Your father wisnae killed in the war. He was knocked down by a bus!'

And she got her cronies to mock Sarah as a stuck-up fraud.

As a young teenager, Sarah was not sure enough of herself to realise that Mary's dislike of her arose from Sarah being different from most of the other girls: better spoken, less physically aggressive, and, despite her mother's poverty, better turned out. It was just a form of jealousy, but, even from the mouths of fools, criticisms hurt. And Sarah was hurt, but the disparaging reference to her father gave her strength because the memory of his kindness and love was a rock on which she could depend – possibly even more so because of her mother's continuing absorption in her own loss. Sarah did not tell her mother of her unhappiness. Children don't.

8

One aspect of Sarah's comparative isolation was that she was thrown back on her own resources. She had always been a voracious reader and eventually was borrowing six books a week from the local library. She started off with simple children's books then moved on to Enid Blyton, whose stories she loved because they always involved groups of children working together. She became absorbed in them as a substitute for the lack of playmates in her real life and revelled in stories of life at boarding schools – including books for boys after she had exhausted the library's stock of girls' ones. She read and re-read Treasure Island and stories by another Scottish author, R. M. Ballantyne and from there, just because he was Scottish and came from her own town, she moved on to Walter Scott, although at first, she had problems with the more adult complexity of the writing. Because she always identified with one character in a book, she lived her life through that character and rarely felt lonely. The only drawback to this inner life was that she was not used to communicating with other children who, in turn, thought of her awkwardness as being stand-offish.

Sarah also had lots of solitary time to think about her life and the world around her. Her initial blanket admiration of the nuns – she imagined they went around with roller skates under their habits so smoothly did they move – was replaced by a more critical appraisal; they didn't seem quite so holy. Sister Mary Joseph was a snob and treated girls from poorer families with disdain, and Sister Gertrude had quite obvious favourites who were always given the most attractive roles. Sister Margaret hadn't spoken to Sister Anne Consuella for years and the two swept past each other in the corridor with heads averted. Sarah was sure they were all good women, but they didn't seem to have goodness in them.

Sarah, at one time, had herself thought of becoming a nun, but now she was not sure. When she read the Gospels, she was overwhelmed by the concept of love taught there but it didn't seem to apply in practice where the emphasis seemed to be on rituals of observance. She shared in the nuns' excitement at the forthcoming visit of the bishop and attended diligently to all the preparations, but he proved to be a disappointment. In Sarah's mind a bishop should be tall and spare with a firm but gentle manner – almost as she remembered her father – but when the actual bishop arrived he proved to be small (which was not his fault) and rotund and smug; basking in the attention bestowed upon him by the nuns. He spoke with a slight lisp and when he walked down the aisle with the holy water, he did so almost with a slight sway of his hips, flicking out the holy water on either side with an insouciant wave of his wrist. He was not the prince of the church Sarah had expected. She said nothing to her mother, but she spoke to her father about her doubts just as she shared with him in her prayers the everyday worries she couldn't share with her mother.

The bright spots in Sarah's life were the visits of Uncle Pat McLaughlin. Because of the friendship he had developed with James during their army training, Pat felt he had a duty to keep an eye on his widow and he made a point, on his visits to Edinburgh, of calling in to see how she was faring. In truth there was little pleasure in his visits because Molly's continued low spirits made conversation awkward and the visits difficult for both parties. But he persisted and, as Sarah grew a little older, things became easier as she became involved in the conversations. Many of Pat's Edinburgh visits involved business at the Court of Session and, after taking her along once, it became part of the ritual that she would accompany him and watch quietly as he went about his business.

'I love being in Parliament House,' she told him. 'I love when we're in that huge Parliament Hall and I can watch the advocates in their gowns and wigs walking up and down with solicitors like you and your clients discussing their cases.'

Sometimes Pat would let her be present when he discussed a case with an advocate and occasionally, she went with him into one of the courtrooms and listened enthralled as a case unfolded before her.

One day she asked him, 'Do you enjoy being a lawyer, Uncle Pat? I shouldn't say this, but you always seem so stressed whenever I see you and I think I'm just another nuisance to you. But I do love it so much.'

Pat smiled. 'Oh, Sarah. Don't mind my face. When you spend your life reading and concentrating your face tends to fall naturally into a sort of frown, but it is just because you are thinking so deeply.' He went on, 'I love being a lawyer. I think it's the best job in the world and I wouldn't do anything else. I'll tell you what. I'll send you a quote by the man who became the second President of the United States, James Adams, writing to a friend. You may find it a bit high-flown but, in those days, they were a bit more formal than we are now. What it does do, is set out a vision of what a noble calling the practise of law can be.'

A few days later Sarah received the promised quote from her Uncle Pat. In his letter he wrote:

My Dear Sarah,

This is taken from a letter by James Adams to his friend Jonathan Sewell on his desire to become a lawyer.

"Now to what higher object, to what greater character, can any mortal aspire than to be possessed of all this knowledge, well digested and ready to command, to assist the feeble and friendless, to discountenance the haughty and lawless, to procure redress to wrongs, the advancement of right, to assert and maintain liberty and virtue, to discourage and abolish tyranny and vice."

It sets out an ideal, Sarah. Now, few of us achieve the ideal. A number don't have that high feeling for their vocation and behave disgracefully and those are the ones who receive publicity. Quite honestly, cynics would say that none of us achieve the ideal. And most of the time we are engaged in humdrum affairs which seem far removed from these lofty ideals. But this should be the base rock on which we build.

It was lovely to see you and your mother on Wednesday. I think her spirits were higher.

I will let you know when I am next coming through to Edinburgh.

Your affectionate Uncle,

Pat McLaughlin.

That night Sarah told her Daddy, 'I'm going to become a lawyer.'

9

As Sarah grew older her time at school became easier. Her less academically minded and more boisterous classmates left school to take up working life, leaving a rump of those who were hoping to go on to higher education of some sort. In that environment, Sarah stood out as she was the outstanding student in her year although her pre-eminence did not make her any more popular with the nuns, who disliked her constant questioning of ideas and practices with which they were comfortable and did not want their placid acceptance to be disturbed.

One day, Sarah asked Sister Anne Consuella, 'How is the Holy Family held up as an example of the true Christian family when the only child was not the child of the ostensible father, St Joseph, and when, apparently, the parents did not have sexual relations throughout the course of the marriage as The Blessed Virgin remained just that, a virgin.'

The good nun gazed at her pupil in horror before giving a shriek, covering her ears, and marching Sarah to the lavatories where she made Sarah wash her mouth out with soap.

The cleansing did not, of course, wash out the ideas from her mind. The ceremonies which played such a big part of the convent worship seemed to Sarah to obscure the real meaning of Christianity and even when Christianity was being taught from the pulpit it seemed to be a litany of don'ts. Once a year each class in the school had a day-long retreat when complete silence was observed, and spiritual contemplation was enjoyed. Sarah enjoyed this but it was ruined for her when the priest running the retreat gave homilies of which the chief subject was sin and damnation. In a curious contradiction, just at the time her mother continued to seek punishment for her sin, Sarah was looking for the love of God to bring redemption.

When it came to the expression of love Sarah was fortunate to have her Auntie Annie there to compensate for her mother's inability to do so. It was Auntie Annie who gave her the hugs and kisses which her mother failed to give. It was to her Auntie Annie that Sarah turned when she was bullied at school or a nun turned against her. When her cheap but much-loved little tricycle was stolen, Sarah cried in Annie's arms, 'How can anyone enjoy using something which doesn't belong to them?' Annie had no answer and could only cuddle her niece in her arms.

Despite this, Sarah was, however, becoming closer to her mother. A mother is just a mother. She exists in a world where no fault is laid at her door even though logically it should be. If Molly was silent for days, Sarah just accepted that this was how she was, and she didn't compare her behaviour adversely with the more obviously affectionate conduct of her aunt. And this unquestioning love gradually brought some warmth back into Molly's heart. Even when Sarah was at primary school she had started to help with shopping, coping naturally with the ration books which were a necessary part of it and, as she grew older, she took an increasing role. Her mother would write down a list of shopping, but Sarah prided herself on being able to remember what was required without reference to a list. She mentally divided the messages into groups of three of similar types and could repeat them without hesitation to the shopkeepers. Because of this she gained a reputation in her neighbourhood shops as a clever girl.

And the knowledge of her daughter's fame as it percolated back to Molly again helped to bring Molly back into the world. She permitted the purchase of a new wireless to replace the primitive one that exasperated Sarah because of its frequent breaking down and, eventually, after much cajoling, she agreed to accompany Sarah to the cinema. Molly found that she actually enjoyed it and looked forward to the change of programme halfway through the week.

Molly also recovered sufficiently to look rationally at her financial situation. She was in receipt of a War Widows Pension and a small pension from James' previous employers, but the payments were scarcely enough to cover basic food and rent, leaving little over for clothing and other essentials. She decided to look for employment but, still haunted by guilt over James' death, determined to seek a job at the lowest possible level, almost as a continuing punishment for what she had done. Much to her family's dismay she took a job as a part-time cleaner in a solicitors' office.

The problem was that Molly, being Molly, could not help but do the job in the most efficient way possible. Every room was cleaned to perfection; all necessary materials were obtained in time and stored neatly; waste bins were emptied and the waste disposed of; when the staff arrived for work in the morning they were greeted by clear, spanking fresh rooms; the whole office was organised in a way it had never been done before.

Her employers became quickly aware that in Molly they had found someone of real value, especially when she demonstrated her high typing skills. They persuaded her to extend her hours beyond those required of a cleaner, giving her administrative tasks, which eventually resulted in her being appointed as a full-time assistant to the office cashier. She managed to put behind her the notion that her job should be punishment and relished her new position, being able, as an unconscious part of her recovery, to smile at the thought of how James would have reacted to her new role; he had had no high opinion of her arithmetical abilities.

10

Sarah, too, was changing; from a little girl to a teenager and finally to a young woman on the threshold of life, although she remained, because of her upbringing, quiet and restrained. She was rarely in company and, when she was, the company tended to be her immediate relatives; even then she found difficulty in joining in the noise and chat of her cousins. She was never in company with boys of her own age because her school was for girls only and, away from school her free time was spent mostly with her mother or on her own. When she came to study 'The Tempest' late in her school career she identified herself with Miranda and romanticised her lack of contact with these strange other creatures.

Sarah grew to be just above medium height, with – to her red-headed mother's disappointment – thick dark brown hair over a high forehead, like a Quaker. Her eyes were deep black emphasised by the pallor of a face composed and serene, in Pat McLaughlin's mind, like a Madonna. He thought Sarah's serenity was remarkable given the early loss of her father and the years of living with her mother's depressive behaviour. But Pat was mistaken in his assessment. Just as the calm surface of water can conceal swirling undercurrents, so Sarah's public face gave no hint of the insecurity and need for affection deep within her. Unaware of this, when he saw her growing up, Pat thought she was becoming a lovely-looking young girl.

'She's turning out just as beautiful as her mother,' Pat to Molly said more than once.'

'That's just nonsense, Pat,' Molly would respond but she was pleased by the compliment. She also took delight in telling Pat how Sarah was different from her cousins. 'They're good people but Sarah just has a finer personality.'

'Not only that' replied Pat. 'But she's also far brighter. She's a clever girl. You should be very proud of her.'

In her mid-teens, Sarah rarely attended much to her appearance. She took little exercise and, as a result, was not fat, but certainly plump. She was much too engrossed in whatever book she was reading to bother about her clothes, wearing whatever was closest to hand. To be fair, wartime clothes' rationing, and also the family's finances, imposed limits on what she could do, but others in a similar predicament made better use of what was available.

Money was tight but her Uncle Pat McLaughlin helped out in two ways. Firstly, he made sure his birthday gifts to Sarah were more than generous, and secondly, he secretly passed funds to her Auntie Annie. These enabled Annie to purchase presents of clothes well in excess of what she could otherwise have afforded. Annie disliked being in the position of being thanked for a generosity not really hers, but she comforted herself with the determination that, in due course, she would tell Sarah the real truth.

For a long time, Molly took as little notice of what Sarah was wearing as she took of her own clothing. However, when she gained her new promotion, she had to consider more carefully what she wore and this, in turn, led her to pay more attention to Sarah. For the first time ever, she had the sort of discussions with Sarah that mothers normally have with their daughters. This brought about an improvement in Sarah's clothing – only slight as Sarah was not really interested – but did focus Sarah's mind on her weight and lack of exercise and this resulted, over a period of years in her becoming as slim as her mother was when she was young.

Sarah was also committed to the resolution, confided to her father years previously after her talks with Pat McLaughlin. She was going to become a lawyer. She had no idea what sort of lawyer she wanted to be and, indeed, if asked, would have been vague as to what various lawyers actually did; but she was determined. When she told her mother, Molly, who had been so engrossed in her own misery that she had taken almost no part in shaping her daughter's activities, could find nothing helpful to say to her.

'How would you get a job as a lawyer? In the lawyers' office where I work all the lawyers are men. There are no women apart from typists and clerkesses. You can do better than that. Would it not be safer to train as a teacher? There's lots of women teachers.'

Sarah listened but was not persuaded. In turn Molly decided that, while she might be proud to let it be known in the office that her daughter was to go to university, she would not disclose Sarah's intention to qualify as a lawyer. 'In my position it wouldn't look right to have a daughter with such an ambition,' Molly told herself.

The nuns in the convent echoed Molly's feelings that Sarah would be better off training to become a teacher. At one time, Sarah had been looked on and encouraged as a possible recruit to the Order but that time had long passed. In truth, although they enjoyed the reflected glory of her examination achievements, they were secretly pleased to be rid of a pupil who had become more and more of a problem with her questioning of long established matters of religion, and who, they thought, might infect others with her opinions.

Her family, too, looked askance at her decision. They, too, thought that, with her brains, she was destined to become a teacher. But a lawyer! Despite the fact that they lived in a city which was the seat of the Court of Session, the highest Scottish court, and which had a much greater proportion of lawyers than cities comparable in size, they operated in a society which had no contact with lawyers and if anything regarded them with suspicion rather than respect.

As usual it was Betty who voiced their disapproval. 'She's just the same as her mother. Just trying to be different. And we all know how that turned out.'

As might be expected, Annie was a supporter but only because she loved Sarah like a daughter even when, as here, she had little idea of what was involved.

Given this general opposition, Sarah was not too surprised at meeting the same response when she went up to the university to be interviewed by her adviser of studies. He thought that, with the high level of her examination results, she should be aiming to study for an honours Master of Arts degree, with a good chance of a First Class degree leading to a promising career in – she could see this coming – teaching. But Pat McLaughlin had advised her that, with legal qualification involving firstly, a Master of Arts degree followed by a degree of Bachelor of Laws, there was little point in her pursuing the narrow curriculum of an honours degree. Rather she should take the more general Ordinary degree which, as well as giving her a wider education, would give her the opportunity of taking part in University life in general, which Pat thought would be of more use to her later. She could then go on to the legal degree.

Her adviser pointed out that there would be a further difficulty in pursuing the law degree as the regulations laid down that, at the same time as taking the University course, the student had to serve an apprenticeship with a firm of solicitors. Legal firms, understandably, in the adviser's view, would be reluctant to take on a female apprentice. Sarah bridled at 'understandably' but merely insisted she was committed to the law training. The adviser of studies was not well pleased that his advice, the fruit of his years of experience, was being ignored by this slip of a girl, but he had to accept her decision and agreed with her the subjects she should take in her initial degree course.

11

University was a let-down for Sarah. When she went up to matriculate, she was bombarded with information from a large number of student clubs all wanting her to enrol with them. But she was not by nature a joiner and, although she ended up with a bag full of pamphlets, she managed to avoid committing herself to any of them. At least, she thought she had but, what with the noise and the bustle in the hall, she was not sure whether she might have unwittingly enrolled in the Gastropod Club. They had been the most persistent and she wondered what they did.

As a consequence of not involving herself in any of these student activities, Sarah found her day consisted of two or three lectures in the morning, after which she merely went off back home to eat her sandwiches by herself in the kitchen. At the lectures, the sexes were split, just like in a parish social, with the males at the back making more or less noise depending on their opinion of the lecturer and the small group of girls together at the front. The other girls smiled pleasantly at Sarah, but they mostly knew each other from school and had little to say to her. And, of course, she did not know any of the boys.

When she had moved from the primary school to the secondary school, she had found it difficult to adjust from being someone of importance to being a nonentity but at least she had her fellow classmates for company. Here she was a nonentity on her own. Her feeling of unease was heightened by what she regarded as the dull quality of the lecturers. In her first year, she was studying English, Maths and Latin and she felt that the lecturers, instead of being the inspiring teachers she had looked forward to hearing, were just covering ground she already knew.

She shared her misgivings with Auntie Annie who was agog to know how she had got on, and, in doing so, Sarah was able to find a humorous side to the whole experience.

'You know, Auntie.' She giggled. 'I think I've joined a club whose function appears to be something to do with snails.'

But, when Sarah told her about the antics of the male students, Annie didn't think that was at all funny because she had a high opinion of the learned scholars who studied at university.

'Every so often, Auntie, during the English lecture, one of the men makes a whistle like a descending bomb and the men all bang their desks as if it's exploding on impact.'

Annie shook her head when Sarah said it never failed to give them great satisfaction.

Matters did, however, gradually improve. Their joint studies gave her something to talk about with the girls – and even some of the men – in the classes and, through time, she spent less and less time at home, filling the periods between the lectures either studying or talking with the other students over coffee. For the first time Sarah enjoyed going parties, where she learnt to overcome her initial shyness and even began to sparkle a little and cope with the drunken attitudes of some of her fellow students.

Sarah herself did not drink. She had tried beer once but disliked the taste and, on the only occasion she tried spirits, she hated the feeling of not being in control of the composure she valued above all else; She told one of the other girls in her year, 'Never again. I don't like the feeling and I don't need it. But I love the way some of the men change from tongue-tied mice to loud singing party animals under the effects of the alcohol and next day they're back to being mice again.' And she avoided dances. Her mother had not taught her how and, in any event, she was not inclined to 'waste' money on suitable clothing.

She continued to find the course work uninspiring until, in her third year, she studied Logic, Political Economy, and Philosophy in smaller tutorial groups and, for the first time, felt her brain was being stretched into new areas.

One of the members of Sarah's tutorial group stood out from the others, initially because of his age. Whilst most of the students were just turning twenty, Mark Fitzgerald was aged thirty. In addition, most students came to university straight from school, but Mark Fitzgerald had already had an Army career. He had been drafted just before the end of the War, but it had ended before he saw any active service apart from a brief period in occupied Germany. He had, however, elected to stay in the army after the War and had fought in Malaya and Korea. With his education, he could have obtained a commission but had chosen to remain as an enlisted man and had ended up as a sergeant but not before some bumps on the way. Without giving details, he hinted that, despite his air of authority, he did not quite fit into the army ethos.

To the other students mostly coming from sheltered environments, Mark, with his flowing black hair and his vaguely Irish background, was an exotic figure, especially as he took a leading role in challenging the propositions which were put to them in the lectures and tutorials.

Mark was full of enthusiasms which he loved to share. One day it would be, 'You must look at these books I have on modern art.' A week later he was eagerly talking about the new American jazz musicians. 'You can hear them on 'The Voice of America Radio Station in Tangiers. They're mind-blowing.'

Sarah did try but decided that they were not for her and told him so.

His next big thing was Irish literature. 'Have you not tried Yeats? What about Joyce? Ulysses has changed the course of English literature. You must read him.'

Sarah did read Ulysses and stuck at it and doing so gave her the confidence to go back to Mark on a writer she had come across whom Mark had never heard of – Emily Dickinson. 'You must look at her poems,' she told him. 'There's a new edition of her collected work just published. I've found in her a kindred spirit. She led a hidden life restricted by circumstances and I emphasise with that. Some people seem to find Dickinson's poems obscure and awkward; I see in them a clear reflection of my own feelings.'

But Sarah could see that Mark was not convinced. The thought crossed her mind that it was possibly because Emily Dickinson was a female writer and thus could not merit the same attention

Mark's only drawback in her eyes was that, when he was drinking – a regular part   of student existence – the virtues which were the attractive part of his character became vices. His questioning became argumentative; the strength of his opinions became intolerance; the force of his character became belligerence. Normally, when she was in his company, Sarah felt totally protected and at ease as he seemed completely in control of himself and of the situation. When he had been drinking, however, he seemed to become a new person, on occasions becoming almost manically out of control. Once she was terrified when he started to throw beer glasses just missing other students as they smashed against the wall. The male students, seemingly cowed by his bulk, were unable to intervene and it was Sarah, despite her terror, who remonstrated with him and forced him to calm down. She was rather proud that it was she who had this influence on him.

The students in the tutorial spent much of their free time together and thought of themselves as 'The Radicals'. And mostly their discussions hinged on what they considered the higher levels of thought. They discussed endlessly (and fruitlessly) the existence of human beings and their relationship (if any) with a supreme being (if there was one). Mark's new passion was with French writers and he introduced the group to the writings of Camus and Sartre. But Sarah preferred Simone De Beauvoir and Simone Weill although, again, she could not persuade Mark to share her interest. 'Too feminine?' she wondered. But, as she had found a kindred spirit in the poetry of Emily Dickinson she now found a spiritual mentor in Simone Weil whose insistence on love and the love of those things that are outside Christianity chimed exactly with her own feelings.

Sarah now understood the reason for her Uncle Pat's advice not to take an Honour's Degree but to use the less concentrated Ordinary Degree course as a basis round which other interests could develop. She felt her whole attitude to life had expanded during the past year.

The Radicals continued as a group throughout the whole of Sarah's final year. In that time, Sarah sensed that she herself was becoming a more dominant force in the group... No, not dominant, that was not consistent with her personality. Prominent was the more accurate word. While Mark continued, with the force of his personality, to lead, she became aware that he listened to and valued her opinions more than those of the others. She liked that and was content with it.

Then, one day, one of the other girls in the group said to Sarah, 'I think Mark fancies you.'

Sarah frowned. 'How to you mean?'

'It's just the way he looks at you sometimes. I think he fancies you.'

'That's just nonsense, said Sarah. 'And quite annoying'. But, despite herself, she, who tried to emulate her heroine, Simone Weil, by dressing as inconspicuously as possible, could not help but take a bit more time in doing her hair in the morning and in arranging her dress more neatly. And her responses to him in discussion were subtly more feminine although neither she nor any of her companions were aware of it.

As spring came, the group decided that they must be more than bookworms and embarked on a regime of walks for which Edinburgh was ideally suited. However, fairly shortly, it became clear that most of the group were indeed bookworms and the number of walkers dwindled down to three consisting of Mark, Sarah (who loved walking) and one of the other girls, Mary Livingstone. Then the walkers were reduced to two when Mary twisted her ankle and was unable to walk for two months. This presented a dilemma to Mark and Sarah but he, with his usual energy, said he was going to continue, and Sarah said that she would too.

'We have a great time on our walks,' Sarah told her Auntie Annie, who took a greater interest in her stories from University than her mother did. 'Sometimes we walk for up to two hours; sometimes up Arthur's Seat to look at the view from the top. It's great. Some days we will talk the whole way; other times we will go for an hour without speaking. He'll help me over the rough bits but mostly it's easy walking or scrambling. It's a pity some of the others don't come because we are all such good friends.'

Annie nodded wisely and said nothing.

Sarah sailed through the final exams of her year, gaining distinctions in all three subjects exactly as she had in her previous years. She also learned she was to be given an interview by one of the top Edinburgh law firms and was virtually assured of an apprenticeship with them for the next three years. So, when her year group decided on a final party to celebrate the end of their studies, Sarah took much more time preparing for it than she did normally. She chose to wear the red dress which she intended to wear at her graduation and which she thought suited her colouring, with a light coat on top, and for the first time ever, she had her hair done in a hairdressing salon. She had never felt more secure in herself and there was a bounce in her step as, having given her mother a cheerful kiss, she set off for the party.

12

27 Coyltonbridge Crescent

Edinburgh

31 May 1956

Dear Pat,

I am sorry to trouble you, but I desperately need advice about Sarah, and I know you have always taken a keen interest in her welfare. She passed all her subjects with flying colours and she left here on Saturday to go to a year party to celebrate everyone having finished the course. She was in great spirits. I was in bed when she got back but I heard her come in and go to her room. She is always an early riser but next day she was still in her room at eleven o'clock, so I knocked on her door. She didn't answer at first then cried that she didn't want to be disturbed. By tea-time she had still not come out and I went to her door to see if she wanted anything to eat. She said no but came out about an hour later and made herself a cup of tea. She looked awful. Her hair was tangled, and her eyes were bloodshot, but she wouldn't say anything to me. And that has continued ever since. She just comes out every so often and makes herself a sandwich and then goes back to her room without saying anything. I reminded her that she had an interview with Weatherburn & Maxwell to arrange her apprenticeship, but she just shrugged her shoulders and didn't turn up. When I asked her about the arrangements for her graduation, she said she wasn't going. And I was so looking forward to it.

Annie thinks that it's all the result of a failed love affair. Sarah has never had a boyfriend, but Annie says that Sarah kept talking to her about a boy in her year called Mark, who I think who is much older. She wonders whether he being older didn't regard the relationship as being important whereas Sarah put her whole being into it.

I don't know. All I know is that she is intensely unhappy and seems to be intent on throwing away all that she has always worked for.

Please, Pat. What can I do? I shouldn't really impose this on you, but I have no-one else and you have always been so good to us since James' death. I'm sorry about this but I am at my wit's end.

Your affectionate friend,

Molly

SHAW MCLAUGHLIN & CO

Solicitors & Notaries

5 Waterloo Street

Glasgow

3 June 1956

My Dear Sarah,

I have heard from your mother and your Aunt Annie of the terrible time you are having. I am sorry that I can't be nearer to you to give some help. Even if I was, sometimes when you are really troubled the last thing you want is someone pushing in with offers of assistance which you don't really want.

I have however some thoughts which I want to pursue. I will look into one or two things and write to you again in a few days' time.

In the meantime, as you know Constance and I have no children of our own and I have always looked on you as a daughter, one whom I love and cherish.

With all my love,

Pat McLaughlin

SHAW MCLAUGHLIN & CO

Solicitors & Notaries

5 Waterloo Street

Glasgow

10 June 1956

Dear Sarah,

As promised, I have been thinking a lot about you and have been making some enquiries.

Firstly, I hope that you will pursue your wish to become a lawyer. I have long thought that you would make a great lawyer. You may remember that I sent you a quote from John Adams. I think that the image of the ideal lawyer which he sets out perfectly fits you.

If you have taken a scunner to Edinburgh, that's fine. We in the West would regard that as completely natural. If you make the necessary application, you can take your degree in absentia.

I have then spoken to friends at the University here and there is no reason, especially given your grades, that you can't take your LLB in Glasgow. And you can help me out with regard to your apprenticeship. My firm normally has two apprentices but there appears to be a current shortage and we have only been able to secure one so far. You would fill the gap perfectly.

You could also help me with regard to accommodation. Some time ago, Constance's cousin left her a tenement flat in Sauchiehall Street near Charing Cross. We have used it only occasionally and it would suit us to have it occupied. It is high up but if you don't mind living on your own it would be a good base for you.

You told me once that you still liked to talk to your Daddy. Talk to him about this. I think I know what he would say.

Whatever you decide please be assured of my love and my prayers.

Pat McLaughlin

13

Sarah, with all her worldly goods and chattels (which, once she had started to study Scots Law, she understood were correctly referred to as moveable property), was delivered to 510 Sauchiehall Street in Glasgow on 24 June 1956. Accompanied by her Auntie Annie and also by her nephew Billy, Jean's eldest son, who had been pressed into service to help in carrying the luggage, she travelled through from Edinburgh on the train and then took a taxi to the flat. This had all been arranged by Annie and Sarah was glad that she had done so because she was surprised at the amount of clothing which Annie thought necessary for her stay. To this was added the huge number of books which Sarah, if not Annie, decided was indispensable.

It was bad enough getting to the train and then from the train to the tenement in which the flat was situated but, unusually for

Glasgow the tenement had five floors and the flat was right at the top. Annie had problems just walking up the stairs without any burdens, but she managed it with some judicious pauses to regain her breath, leaving Sarah and young Billy to do the carrying.

The flat had two rooms overlooking Sauchiehall Street with a good-sized kitchen and a bathroom having windows at the back giving on to the back court. The furnishings were spare but perfectly adequate and Pat McLaughlin had obviously made a big effort to have the flat in good order for Sarah.

Annie wanted to help Sarah to unpack but Sarah insisted she would do it herself. 'You sit down, Auntie, and I'll make you and Billy a cup of tea.'

While she was preparing this, Annie wandered round the flat. 'It's so big' her aunt said. 'It's much bigger than I thought it would be. It's not much smaller than your mother's flat. I was going to scrub out all the cupboards, but your Uncle Pat has left the place spotless.'

When Annie had had her tea, Sarah helped her on with her coat and sent her on her way back to Edinburgh with a hug and an admonition to Billy to look after his aunt which both he and she snorted as being unnecessary.

As Sarah closed the door behind them, she felt a wonderful sense of peace. Although she was alone, she was not nervous. She had all this to herself with no-one to tell her what to do or when to do it. She knew the hackneyed expression that an Englishman's home is his castle and for the first time understood what it meant. She did not unpack right away but wandered round the flat touching the furniture, looking out of the windows, turning on taps. She thought that later she would go down to Sauchiehall Street to get a feel for the neighbourhood – but then had second thoughts. Sarah shared the popular Edinburgh belief that Glasgow was a semi-savage place where you ventured forth in daylight only after taking suitable precautions and at night, not at all. She would leave exploring until tomorrow and, meantime, had plenty to do unpacking her things and making sure that her books were correctly arranged on the bookshelves.

That night, for the first time in a month, Sarah slept soundly. The hurt was still there but she felt secure and certainly not lonely. She had apprehensions about her new job and how she would cope and thereafter with her University studies amongst students who would be known to each other. But she had faced a similar problem at Edinburgh University and–

No. With difficulty, she banished the thought of Edinburgh from her mind using the method she always adopted in times of stress. She thought of her dear father and talked to him just as the nuns taught her that prayer was merely talking to God. It was after following her Uncle Pat's suggestion to talk to her father that she had followed his advice and came to Glasgow. She fell asleep with the distant squeal of a tram's wheels in her ears as it rounded the corner at Charing Cross.

14

The next day Sarah woke early and took a few moments to adjust to her new surroundings. Pat McLaughlin had left a note at the flat saying he would call round later to take her out to lunch and to show her the neighbourhood. In the meantime, Sarah thought that she should go out to buy something for her breakfast. But she dithered; she went around the flat doing various unnecessary things merely to postpone going out. She realised she still had difficulty in meeting people and, in the street, avoided their gaze. She gave herself a shake both metaphorically and physically. No-one knew her in Glasgow. What had she to fear? She had gone back to wearing drab clothes again and, so dressed, made herself go down the tenement stairs and, with tension in her chest, out onto Sauchiehall Street. As would be expected she was ignored by the crowds of people on the pavement, the adults rushing to their offices and the schoolchildren moving more slowly to their schools. Gradually, realising no-one was looking at her, she raised her gaze from the pavement and with more confidence made her way to a nearby dairy where she bought milk and her first Glasgow rolls.

Promptly at 12.30 there was a knock at the door and Pat McLaughlin presented both himself, still puffing slightly from climbing five flights of stairs, and a bunch of flowers. He normally greeted Sarah with a hug and a kiss, but he sensed a reticence on her part and merely exchanged a handshake as he handed over the flowers, which she put to one side. When she had heard him at the door, she had quickly put on her long raincoat, so she was ready to leave as soon as he arrived.

In those days, there was not the plethora of restaurants in Glasgow as there is now but there was one about three hundred yards up Sauchiehall Street at the rear of Ross's Dairies and they headed there. On the way, Sarah was quiet, and Pat had the opportunity to think about her. She was much more subdued than when he had last seen her. She was also much paler. He was used to staff in his office looking pale, it usually meant they had not applied any make-up to establish the basis for taking the next day off on the grounds of sickness. But he did not think of that in the case of Sarah. She was also shabbily dressed. Even when she took her long raincoat off in the restaurant, what she was wearing underneath would have been suitable for an aged maiden aunt.

At lunch, though, Sarah seemed to relax. In the company of one other person Pat was a natural conversationalist; he talked quietly but yet engaged the attention of his listener, and his manner, without pressing, encouraged the other to respond. There might be gaps in the conversation but no awkward silences. As Sarah found, after a chat with Pat you might not remember much what had been said but you would remember how enjoyable it had been.

After lunch Pat became a tour guide taking Sarah round the area, with Sarah carrying her coat, which had never been necessary in the fine weather.

'You can just see that Cupola over there. That's the Mitchell library, which is a good place to study, and just behind it is St Andrew's Halls, where the Scottish National Orchestra give concerts. Do you fancy dancing? Maybe not, it's not really my thing either but Glasgow's full of dance halls starting with the Locarno right under your flat.' He took her up Garnethill past the Glasgow High School for Girls, the Jewish Synagogue, and Garnethill Convent.

'And that's The Glasgow School of Art, which is world famous (Sarah didn't quite grasp why at the time) and here's St Aloysius College where I was at school and next to it we can go into St Aloysius Church itself, which will be your local parish church.'

Sarah didn't have the heart to say it was long since she believed in what she thought of as 'that sort of thing' but she admired the imposing marble decoration of the massive church.

On their way, back the flat, they passed a number of cinemas including the Cosmo which Pat explained was good for foreign language films, public houses, billiard rooms and some more restaurants. The only thing Pat did not point out were the numerous high -class department stores for which Sauchiehall Street was famous. They were of little interest to him but would have been, in the normal way of things, of great interest to Sarah.

By the time they returned to the flat and Pat had to return to his office Sarah was quite exhausted by their tour. She thanked him for his thoughtfulness, agreeing that she could not be in a better place to enjoy Glasgow, and she gave him a big hug and a kiss to show her appreciation. As he set off up Sauchiehall Street Sarah shouted after him that she looked forward to seeing him on the following Monday when she was due to start work in the office. That was scarcely true, but she felt she had to say something. When she went back up the stairs to the flat, she retrieved the flowers and took a little time and some pleasure in arranging them in two vases.

PART TWO

15

It was also on 4 October 1936 that Frankie Gilligan was born. Or about the fourth of October anyway, because at the time his father, Boxy, was halfway through a bender and was vague as to the actual date of birth. Frankie's mother, Maria, was in a not dissimilar state and had lost the documents provided by the midwife.

Maria, although she had lived in Glasgow for twenty-five years, had been born in Barga in Italy, before her parents, Pietro and Larena Chiappa immigrated to Glasgow in1920. They had made final arrangements to come in 1915 but then The Great War had intervened. Pietro was called up and had fought high up in the mountains surviving the various Isonzo campaigns against the Austro-Hungarian forces before being finally invalided out after the Caporetto battle, badly affected by the enemy's use of poison gas. He never fully recovered his strength and the move to Scotland, determined when he was fully fit, was followed through when he was a shell of what he had been and wholly lacking in the drive necessary to settle the family in their new environment. With the help of relatives and friends already in Glasgow they found accommodation but Pietro was totally unable to cope with setting up a business and the family were reduced to relying on the wages that first Larena and then Maria earned working long hours in a café owned by another friend from Barga. Pietro never mentioned the War and indeed Larena was constantly surprised to find that few people in Glasgow even knew that Italy had fought in the War on the same side as Britain. Pietro whiled away his time playing Scopa and Briscola with his friends, but he never regained his health and finally died two years after they had come to Glasgow.

Larena and Maria were able to cope merely because the Italian community looked after its own. Clothes were donated on the basis that the original owner had grown out of them, and although there were few outright gifts of food, Larena and Maria were invited to join others for the family meals. The flat they lived in was owned by an Italian friend who declared that he was glad that they could occupy it rather than having it become dilapidated from being empty. In this way, they survived.

Maria was nine when she arrived in Glasgow and, unlike her mother, who was never at ease speaking this ugly foreign tongue, she quickly picked up English – or at least Glasgow English, from her playmates and at school. She was a quick student and her teachers were anxious that she stay on at school to take her Highers but, with the death of her father, it was not an option. She left school as soon as possible, when she was fourteen, to work in the café where she had already been working part-time in the evenings and at the weekends.

She was small and neat with black curly hair and wide-spaced eyes, which looked at the world not boldly but frankly and confidently. Her bubbly personality helped her to cope with the death of her father and the hard times which she and her mother had to endure. She had one other endearing characteristic: she was totally at ease with boys. Where most of her friends were always in a flutter either because a boy wouldn't leave them alone or because a boy wouldn't pay them any attention, Maria, as she grew up, treated them just as friends which, of course, had the effect of them wanting to be more than that with her. But Maria wasn't going to waste time with the boys around her. She wanted to climb out of the conditions in which she found herself. She didn't actively have a plan. It was just there in her subconscious.

Like most immigrants, the Glasgow Italians organised social gatherings within their community where they could exchange gossip and make deals and generally talk together in the language which for most of them was more natural. Likewise, they were anxious that their daughters marry within the community and, for this purpose ran dances for the young people, supervised under the watchful eyes of their elders. Maria loved these dances, which she was allowed to attend from the age of fourteen, being chaperoned by her cousin, Luigi, who was six years older. He, however, was not happy that his pursuit of his latest love object was being hindered by having this young cousin in tow.

For one of these dances, when Maria was sixteen, Luigi arrived to pick her up accompanied by another boy, not an Italian. 'This is a friend of mine called Tommy Gilligan. At least that's his proper name but everyone knows him as Boxy.' Boxy shrugged his shoulders as Luigi went on. 'I don't think even Boxy knows why he is called that. Boxy and I were at St Aloysius College together and with me been telling him how enjoyable these Italian dances were, he pestered me to bring him along to one.'

The three young people were in high spirits as they set off, in a car Luigi had managed to get hold of. Boxy sat in the front passenger seat. Maria liked that. Any Italian boy she knew would have insisted on sitting with her in the back and been a nuisance on the way to the dance. She also was intrigued that someone could have a nickname and not know why.

At the dance, as Boxy knew no-one, it was natural that he stayed with Luigi and Maria and later – Luigi absent in pursuit of his latest potential conquest – just with Maria. She did not mind at all that he was monopolising her, although some of her Italian boyfriends were not happy to see their beautiful one being taken over by an intruder. However, Boxy had a way with him. He had a good sense of humour and great charm and the Italian boys soon became more relaxed about his presence so that the group round Maria soon widened to include four or five other boys who were happy to exchange jokes with Boxy and take their turn in dancing with Maria. Boxy also had the sense to dance with Maria only once and, most importantly, not to have the last dance with her, although Maria tried to manoeuvre it that he would have to.

As they were sitting together Boxy gradually opened out about himself. 'I live with my parents in Langside. I was in same class at school as Luigi and we played in the same football teams on the way up the school. After school I started working in a surveyors' office taking part-time courses to get a professional qualification but I'm now working in my father's builder's business trying to establish a side-line in plant hire.'

What Boxy did not say, but Maria later learnt from Luigi was that Boxy was by far the best footballer in the school and would have been picked for Scotland as a schoolboy internationalist had he not left school after fifth year.

Another mark in his favour, in Maria's eyes was that he was not too tall, being just about medium height and slimly built, which suited her as she hated the feeling of being physically dominated by some of the over-tall or overweight boys who seemed to be particularly attracted to her just because she was petite (as she liked to call herself).

So, Maria decided that she liked Boxy. She and Boxy gradually began to see more and more of each other and soon he was accepted by their Italian contemporaries as Maria's boyfriend.

Her mother was not so sure and expressed her concerns to her cousin Barbara as they talked together in their familiar Barga dialect. Barbara was a good bit older than Larena and had never married but Larena looked upon her almost like a substitute for her own mother who had died when she was young. Barbara was someone to whom she had always turned for help when she was troubled with something as she grew up.

'She's too young. There's no problem with her being friendly with boys. I was at her age.'

Barbara nodded her agreement and the conversation went off at a tangent as, to the accompaniment of much laughter, they recounted Larena's experiences with various boys.

'Larena, do you remember big Sandro? Maybe the most chaotic dancer in the world. A dance wouldn't pass but Sandro would bring you crashing down.'

'And he was so keen. You could avoid his feet, but he couldn't avoid his own. I remember I used to hide when he was looking for a partner. You felt sorry for the girl he eventually took up. Still he was a nice big soul. No harm in him. What happened to big Sandro?'

'He was killed in the War at Caporetto'

Larena looked down. 'Poor Sandro and here's us laughing at him. God rest his soul.'

After a brief pause as they thought of Sandro and the many other boys who had been lost in the War, Larena returned to her concerns. 'Yes, I had boyfriends but, at that age, no boyfriend. You know what I mean. She's too young. And then he's not an Italian. I know that the young people say that we are all Scots people now but if you go outside of the community you don't know what you're getting.' She thought some more. 'And there's another thing. He's too nice. That sounds terrible but he just gets on with everybody. Maybe I'm too suspicious. It's like he is so… soft that he fits in with everyone but in a different way with each one. I'm putting this badly. My Pietro, God rest his soul, had backbone. He stood for certain things. And that meant that there were some people who didn't like him and some people he couldn't stand. Like Mario Conti. Do you remember him, Barbara? But that's a good thing. We're all different. As you know Pietro and I had some great barneys but that made us stronger because we knew where we stood. I don't know where I stand with that boy.'

Despite Larena's misgivings, Maria and Boxy continued to see each other regularly and eventually Boxy very courteously approached Larena and asked her permission to marry Maria. Larena could think of no reason to object. She herself had married at the age of seventeen, which would be Maria's age at the time of the wedding. Boxy seemed to be well off financially because of working in his father's firm and the couple had identified a flat nearby where they could start off married life together. There was nothing to hinder the match. But Larena knew, deep down, that her late husband would not have agreed, and she lamented his absence at a time when she needed him most.

The preparations for the wedding took in a headlong course Larena was unable to slow. She met Boxy's parents who seemed very pleasant, if a little too loud for Larena's taste. They insisted – despite her repeated protestations – she, as a widow, could not be expected to bear the cost of the wedding, but they would do so. Larena had her pride and would have persisted in arranging the wedding in a simple way she could afford. But she yielded to Maria who, like most brides, wanted her wedding to be as grand as possible.

The young couple were married in St Francis' Church in Cumberland Street and after a short honeymoon in London moved into their new flat round the corner from Larena.

16

Now that they were married the young couple were accepted totally into immigrant Italian social life which involved, every weekend, but chiefly on Sundays when the various cafes and fish and chip shops were closed, a party at somebody's house with singing and dancing. In this Boxy excelled. He had an outstanding singing voice and developed an extensive repertoire of Italian songs both folk and operatic. In addition, he was a gifted pianist, capable of playing by ear any of the popular songs of the day and able even to accompany someone singing a song he had not previously heard.

Maria also had a sweet voice and the pair were much in demand at parties. As well as individual songs, their particular party piece was 'Nora Malone' which they sang as a duet in close harmony.

It was generally agreed that they were a perfect couple and Maria could not have been happier with her new husband.

There was one thing about him which she did not know. Indeed, Boxy, himself, may not have been aware of it. Boxy was an alcoholic. Maria only slowly came to realise this and the sense it made of various aspects of Boxy's previous life. As well as his footballing skills, Boxy was extremely gifted academically but, to the frustration of his masters, he had to leave school prematurely because he failed to appear to sit the public exams. Like many alcoholics, Boxy could be very funny about some of the escapades caused by his drinking. He told a circle of school friends about the exam fiasco:

'I had used up for drink the money my mammy had given me at the start of the week, and, with the brain working overtime on the booze, decided to steal the family wireless set and take the tram into town to pawn it. The problem was that I had no money for the tram fare. But I managed to dodge the conductor for most of the journey until I saw him making straight for me. Quick as a flash I jumped off the tram and gave him a farewell V sign. But it was a disaster. While I was waving a V sign the conductor was waving back holding in his hand the family wireless set which I had left lying on the seat.'

On that day Boxy had then made his way up to the school, late for his exam, and managed to borrow from his friend, Pat

McLaughlin, half a crown to see him through the rest of the day. Pat did not expect the 'loan' to be repaid and it wasn't, although Boxy was always determined that it should.

As there was no possibility of Boxy gaining the qualifications for university entrance it was decided he should leave school and start work, training as a surveyor in a surveyors' office with which his father had connections. A similar pattern, however, emerged. Boxy was popular in the firm and showed great aptitude for the job, but, after a promising start, he became increasingly unreliable. He was smart enough never to arrive for work smelling of alcohol, but he was often late and the foreman under whom he worked complained that, although he liked him, he just couldn't trust Boxy to complete a task correctly. After eighteen months, Boxy had to leave.

His father then took him into his own business, helping establish a separate branch of the firm through hiring heavy plant to other contractors who did not want to take on the cost of buying equipment for only the one job. Much of the negotiating of these deals was done at lunchtime, with much consumption of alcohol, and Boxy's father correctly surmised that Boxy might do well in that area.

Both Boxy's parents hoped that his drinking was a temporary phase which he could come through and they saw the marriage to Maria as something to help that process. It did not occur to them that they were handing their problem to someone else – possibly because Boxy's father was, himself, a hardened drinker.

The problem did not go away although for some years the young couple's life did not seem to be affected. Their first child, Lucia, was born in 1929 and their first son, Remo, followed in 1930. Although they were given Italian Christian names, from an early period in their lives they were known as Sheila and Ray. The new parents doted on their children but continued with their party life. There are bad drunks and good drunks; bad drunks become bad-tempered and noisy and are generally regarded as a nuisance; good drunks become more friendly, tell good stories and often are the life and soul of any party. Boxy was a good drunk. His friends were aware of his drinking but, in Glasgow parlance, he was regarded merely as taking a good drink. It meant that soon, Maria, too, in a vicious corollary of them being a couple who did everything together, began to drink heavily.

Two events occurring closely together put their lives under increasing strain. Firstly, Maria's mother, on whom she depended not just in practical matters like baby-sitting but as a source of comfort and strength, died not long after the birth of Sheila. With Larena went that link to Maria's Italian background which had been like a backbone in her being. Shortly afterwards, Boxy's father had a heart attack and died after a short period. His death posed the more immediate practical problem: who was to run the business? It was a small building business, run by the late Mr Gilligan without much regard for paperwork and there was not anything by way of office staff who could have been helpful. Even if there had been, Boxy was temperamentally unsuited to running a business and had no training to assist him. He went to his old school friend, Pat McLaughlin, who was now a lawyer, to help in winding up his father's estate. Pat did so with the greatest difficulty because of the absence of paper records and, as might be expected, Mr Gilligan had not left a will. But, so far as the future was concerned, the only advice Pat could give was to seek out someone in the same line of business with whom Boxy could join and who could provide the background expertise required. Privately he did not hold out much hope because he knew his old friend too well, but he told Boxy that he would always be there if he needed help. The lawyer's immediate task was to make sure that Boxy's mother's position was safeguarded, something that might prove difficult because, without a will, the family house passed to Boxy leaving Mrs Gilligan only a life tenancy.

With the agreement of his mother, but with some reluctance on Maria's part, Boxy and family moved into the Gilligan family home. It is never easy for a daughter-in-law, used to running her own household, to move into her mother-in-law's home and adjust to the domestic routine which the other regards as normal. There were raised voices on occasion and sometimes silences, the atmosphere not being helped by the fact that both Boxy and Maria were seeking solace in the bottle and Mrs Gilligan, as it turned out, was also a heavy drinker. However, after about six months of joint living, Maria went to see why Mrs Gilligan had not come down for breakfast one morning and found that she had died in her sleep.

Maria had never been close to Mrs Gilligan and, although any death affects those who knew the deceased, she could not honestly say that she mourned for her mother-in-law. She was sad for Boxy in losing his mother, but he, strangely, did not seem very much moved. When her own mother had died, Maria had been almost crushed with a grief from which she had not yet recovered, Boxy, by contrast, was almost unconcerned. She did not understand it, and neither did she ever learn the reason for it.

With money available from his parents' estates Boxy and Maria had enough to live on without relying on income from the building business. And this was fortunate because, after a few months in charge, Boxy took little interest in the business, leaving the running of it to the man who had been his father's foreman. Inevitably the ex-foreman took advantage of Boxy's absence to divert incoming money into his own pocket and in time, as he realised that Boxy didn't seem to care, he ended up doing all the work directly in his own name and pocketing the proceeds.

Eventually, forced to check on the affairs of the firm when the ex-foreman left to set up his own business, Boxy was shocked to discover that not only was there no money in the bank but that several suppliers and some of the workers had not been paid. He got over the initial shock by recourse to the bottle but then managed to face the problems and, with the help of Pat McLaughlin, raised a mortgage on his house, which gave him cash to pay off the debts and quite a bit over.

There was too much left over, however, as it gave Boxy a false sense of security and he and Maria continued to lead their fine life with their available cash. Then it ran out. This time Boxy was too ashamed to seek further help from Pat McLaughlin and he, himself, arranged further loans on the security of the house. With the funds raised, Boxy and Maria were able to keep up pretences and were still regarded, perhaps a little cautiously now, as good people to know. But there was nothing spent on the house, which dilapidated both inside and out, became known to the local children as 'The Witch's House' because in its abandoned state it reminded them of the witch's house in Hansel and Gretel. When she was sufficiently sober Maria was horrified at the state of the house so unlike the way her mother had kept hers; unable to face her horror she then blanked it out with alcohol.

Inevitably, Boxy was unable to keep up the payments due on these loans, the house was repossessed and sold and Boxy was left with nothing. The family managed to find a flat to live in, in the Gorbals, not far from the Cumberland Street church where Boxy and Maria had married with such high hopes not all that long ago. The flat was on the top floor of a grey sandstone tenement which had three flats to a floor, with the two side ones having a room and kitchen and the middle one, known in Glasgow as a 'single end' containing one room. There was a communal toilet for all the three flats on the half landing below. It was into this single end – all they could afford – that Boxy moved Maria and the children. It was also into this home that Francesco Gilligan, always known as Frankie, was born round about 4 October 1936.

17

How Frankie had been conceived was a mystery to both his parents. They had long since given up normal marital relations and instead of being a couple they were two separate couples each with an individual relationship with their alcohol friend. Boxy's bender when Frankie was born had nothing on the one actually celebrating the birth. And thereafter, more and more he took to disappearing for days on end, seeking shebeen alcohol and reappeared bearing cuts and bruises where he had fallen in the course of his bevvying. In his absence, Maria would seek solace in whatever cheap alcohol was at hand; the reason she herself was hazy as to the details of Frankie's birth.

Although the birth of Frankie had no effect on Boxy, to some extent it brought Maria to her senses. She determined to stop drinking and, having spruced herself up, was able to get herself a job as a cleaner, which meant that there was at least some money coming into the house. In addition, the two elder children were now of an age when they were aware of the state of the house and could do their bit to keep it tidy. Seven-year-old Ray would often return from school with food and other things Maria knew must have been stolen but she never questioned him about where they had come from.

Thus, despite the poverty in which they were living, there was a period of comparative tranquillity in the Gilligan household. The children were able to go out to play and Maria got to know her neighbours, finding in them a warmth and friendliness she had not experienced in years. This lasted for about five years after Frankie's birth, during which Maria fought successfully to stay off the alcohol. Boxy's drinking habits did not change; he stayed at home for maybe five or six days becoming increasingly restive and then gave Maria one of his disarming smiles which she, despite everything, still found irresistible and say he had to go to see a man. He would then be gone for up to four days before coming home in a shattered state.

This particular time the four days extended into five and then six and Maria knew something was wrong. She went with Ray to the police station to make enquiries and after a few hours the police called at her door to tell her that Boxy had been found in the street, two days previously, over five miles away and had only now been identified. He was in the Western Infirmary in a critical condition.

When she heard, it was after midnight, and with no public transport available Maria set out to walk across the river to the hospital. Before she saw Boxy, she was warned by one of the nurses that he was in a poor way but, even then, she was shocked to see the thin pale figure, lying almost lifeless on the hospital bed with various tubes attached to him. The nurse explained he appeared to have suffered a heart attack and to have collapsed in the street, where he had left by his drinking companions who did not want to be involved.

Maria sat with him for some time, rocking with fatigue and actually falling asleep once or twice. The second time he was looking at her when she woke and gave her a crooked smile. She bent over him as he tried to speak but all that emerged was a rasping croak. She smoothed his hair back from his forehead which was bruised where he had fallen. She sat with him not saying anything but patting his hand from time to time to show that she was still there, as most of the time his eyes were closed whether in sleep or not, she didn't know. Eventually, he did stir and very slowly tried to speak. He became frustrated when he couldn't say what he wanted to say, or at least Maria couldn't understand the words. She tried repeating what she thought he had said but to no avail and then, after numerous attempts, she said 'Pat McLaughlin?' and he nodded his approval.

'You want me to speak to Pat McLaughlin?'

Boxy nodded.

Maria couldn't think what she was supposed to say to Pat McLaughlin, but she gave Boxy the thumbs up and that seemed to satisfy him. She made sure with the nurse who brought her a cup of tea that Boxy was in no immediate danger and then left the infirmary to walk the two miles back into town to the lawyer's office. By this time, it was light, and she reached the centre of town by eight o'clock. She thought that, if she could get access to the office, she could sit and wait until Pat appeared, but he was already hard at work when she arrived and gave her a warm welcome.

Maria was a little overwhelmed to be in Pat's room, its walls lined with books, and she was very conscious of her poor clothing as she sat in the leather chair on the opposite side of his desk. She started hesitantly, as she did not really know Pat well, but gradually gained confidence and burst out with her story amidst a flood of tears she could not hold back. As he saw her distress Pat came from his side of the desk and, sitting on the seat beside her, held her hand and patted her on the shoulder to comfort her.

When she had calmed down a little, he said, 'What is it that you want me to do?'

'I don't know,' Maria replied. 'It was just all that Boxy said. Just your name.'

'No problem,' said Pat. 'I have nothing on this morning. Let's go and see this terrible husband of yours.'

When they left the office, Pat hailed a cab with a piercing whistle totally out of character with his quiet demeanour and they set off to the infirmary, giving Maria her first experience of actually travelling in a taxi. As they went, Pat pressed Maria on why Boxy wanted to see him but she really had no idea. Normally when a dying man asks for a solicitor it is because he wants to make a will, but Maria confirmed what Pat had expected, that there was no point as there was no money to leave.

When they reached the bedside Pat was as shocked as Maria had been when he saw the state Boxy was in. He was asleep and Maria sat beside him while Pat spoke quietly to the nurse. As he feared, as soon as he saw Boxy, the medical staff were treating him merely to make him as comfortable as possible and death could not be far away. As he sat down, the chair made a scraping noise on the floor and this seemed to waken Boxy who gave what might pass for a grin when he saw Pat. He painfully said something which Maria did not understand but Pat knew.

'What did he say?' she asked.

'He said he still owes me half a crown. I'll explain about that later. It's a long story.'

He turned to Boxy. 'I intend to sue.'

Boxy made another big effort and said something which again Maria did not catch and even Pat affected not to understand. He did, however, nod, and spoke again to Boxy in the way one does to reassure someone who is desperate to be understood. Boxy relaxed then but did not speak again. Pat took Maria by the arm and drew her away from the bedside.

'Maria, you have to be strong. Boxy is dying. I think he has only a few hours to live. I don't suppose he has done much chapel business recently, but I can get the hospital authorities to get the hospital chaplain to give him the Last Rites. Would that be alright?'

Maria nodded; Pat was merely confirming what she knew in her heart was true and she was pleased Pat had suggested the Last Rites. Pat was correct in his assumption that neither she nor Boxy had bothered much about religion for many years but she had been brought up by her parents in a strong Catholic tradition and felt a sense of comfort that she was returning to the haven of the Church.

Pat left Maria at the bedside and sat in a waiting room for the short period until Boxy died. He was able to assist in the formalities after the death and then left with Maria, sending her home in the taxi after he had had been set down at his office. Thus, it was Pat who made the arrangements for the funeral and the little meal thereafter, and it was Pat who, over Maria's objections –

feeble as they were as she had no way of paying – met all the costs involved and made sure that everything was done properly.

In doing this he was merely following Boxy's croaked final words: 'Look after the family and things, Pat.'

18

As it happened, Maria did not seek any further help from Pat and after making a few attempts he did not press her further; he felt she resented what she saw as his interference. Although he had been so close to his old school friend, Boxy, Maria did not really know him and persisted in calling him 'Mr McLaughlin'. He tried to insist that she should call him 'Pat' but gave up when he saw that she was not comfortable with that.

The one thing he did, to salve his conscience, was to take the elder boy, Ray, to one side and impress upon him that he should contact Pat if ever the family was in difficulties. Ray was by this time over twelve and gave the impression that he was mature for his age.

Ray was indeed mature for his age but not in the way that Pat imagined. He was already deeply immersed in the gang culture which at that time dominated the slum tenements of the Gorbals. He hung around the outskirts of the Cumbie Boys, at first being tolerated as a helpful look-out and then, as years passed, becoming accepted as a full member, especially as he seemed totally fearless in the gang's activities and completely ruthless in fighting off attempted encroachments by rival gangs. He bore the marks of his hard life with a broken nose and a scar down the left side of his face. The gang was involved in a variety of illegal activities from breaking into shops to dealing in stolen goods, especially alcohol, which had become especially lucrative because of the war, and to providing 'muscle' when someone wanted a debt settled without recourse to the courts.

Maria knew that the goods and money that Ray brought into the house were obtained illegally but she turned a blind eye because it meant that the finances of the family were on a stable footing. Indeed, she found that her standing in the neighbourhood increased because she was recognised as the mother of someone who was known as a leader in the community. Inevitably, Ray was arrested, though, and found guilty of some burglary and sent to Larchgrove, the remand home, but although Maria was traumatised by the experience of seeing him arrested and appearing in court, she found that, if anything, his reputation was heightened by his time in Larchgrove which seemed to be regarded as the Gorbals equivalent of a finishing school.

When Ray came out of Larchgrove he immediately resumed his criminal activities and within two years moved with his current girlfriend into another flat in the area, although he made sure that the remaining family was kept supplied despite his absence. This meant that Maria and the remaining two children had more space although still living in cramped, barely habitable conditions. Despite this, Sheila especially, was always neatly turned out. Like her mother, she was small with dark curly hair and had a lively way with her. From the age of fourteen she had started going out in the evenings and as she grew older, she spread her wings and spent more and more time in the local dancehalls. These were widespread in Glasgow, especially as the war drew to an end and Glasgow became full of soldiers of all nationalities, especially the Americans, who were a big magnet for the local girls with their free-spending ways.

Young Frankie idolised his big brother, despite being physically totally unlike him. Where Ray was dark and almost squat, Frankie had fair hair and a clear complexion, and he grew until he was just under six feet tall. Maria could never understand how she and Boxy could have managed to produce this tall handsome son. One disadvantage of having fair hair in certain parts of Glasgow was that you were regarded as a pansy and from an early age Frankie had to show a number of people that he was no such thing. He also had a certain charm about him which some mistook – to their cost – as a weakness.

Meanwhile, Pat McLaughlin realised that, with Ray now embarked on a life of crime, the duty to help the family which he felt his old friend Boxy had placed on him would not be fulfilled through the elder son. However, at Boxy's funeral, one of Maria's Italian relatives, in fact the only one, who had attended, was Barbara Franchi who was a cousin of Maria's late mother.

Barbara Franchi and Pat McLaughlin went back a long way. Towards the end of his schooling at St Aloysius College, Pat decided to study to become a priest and he was chosen to study at the senior seminary, the Scots' College in Rome, attached to the Gregorian University. He studied philosophy there for two years before deciding that he was not suited to a priestly life. Whether the daily presence of beautiful Italian girls had anything to do with his decision cannot be said but, certainly, within a year of returning to Scotland he had become engaged to a lovely Scottish/Italian girl called Constance.

Pat had decided to become a lawyer, but to do so, he had to obtain an apprenticeship in an existing firm and that was a problem. In Glasgow at that time, especially in the legal profession, there was a strong prejudice against Catholics (or Roman Catholics which was the preferred establishment phrase). His very name was enough to disqualify him from most interviews. When he was given an interview his education at a Jesuit school was held against him, and, added to that, his two years studying in a seminary in Rome, meant his chances were nil even when there was no competition for the post.

It was then that Constance took a hand. She spoke to her distant cousin, the formidable Barbara Franchi, who asked to see Pat and, happy with what she saw, arranged for him to meet Mrs Maxwell, the old lady for whom she acted as housekeeper. The old lady was suitably impressed and still had sufficient influence amongst those who mattered to get Pat an apprenticeship in one of the leading city firms. Once Pat qualified, Barbara Franchi became his first client and they kept regularly in touch although mostly for non-legal matters.

Therefore, when Pat saw that he could not help the family through the agency of Ray, he thought to turn to Barbara to assist. They agreed that there was nothing to be done with Maria and Ray, and probably also Frankie, but Barbara was attracted to the thought that she might help with Sheila, who reminded Barbara so much of Sheila's mother and dear friend, the late Larena, and she undertook to take her under her wing.

19

From the age of three Frankie spent all his waking hours out of doors, returning to the flat only for a piece or for his tea at night, always untroubled by his mother's recurring stages of sobriety and drunkenness. However, Frankie's sister Sheila, as she grew up, was badly affected by her mother's conduct. She tried to keep the house as clean and tidy as possible but, although she was always personally well turned out (just like her mother in her youth) she was often, under a bright exterior, ground down by the home life she had to suffer. Frankie, himself, never made comparisons between his home life and that of his fellows and, while other boys, without thinking about it, were proud of their family life, Frankie, again without thinking about it, took his pride in his life on the street. It did not occur to him to question why he never asked friends back to his house.

It did not occur to Frankie that part of the reason for his standing in his group of friends was that he was always on the street. Other children had fathers and mothers and a home environment which was reasonably comfortable and Frankie was often made welcome there as a playmate and even took part in family meals where a mother was happy to deal with one more head around the table. But Frankie had no father and his mother moved between periods of drunkenness and sobriety in which she was helped, in a perverse way, by her elder son, Ray, who kept her supplied with money out of his criminal activities. When she was sober, she could hold down a small job as a cleaner but then a crisis, major or minor would occur, and she would slip back. She could, almost calmly, see it coming. She would sit, sober, and know, without having any control over it, that she was going to start drinking again.

Like Ray, Frankie was exposed at an early age to the gang culture into which he was first welcomed *because* of his brother. By the age of eight Frankie had an unconscious realisation that of his standing on the street depended on his actions and even in carrying out the petty thefts which were the staple for the young boys he stood out as a leader by reason of his attack. Not recklessness; he was never reckless. On the contrary, every action was carefully planned and controlled. Even among the real gangs he was known as a cool kid not just because of the connection with his brother.

The words 'stealing', and 'theft' were rarely if ever used. They carried a moral aspect which the street gangs subconsciously avoided. The words 'lifting' and 'doing' were preferred, as they carried no guilty overtones. And, of course, houses in the neighbourhood were exempt from attack, although local shops were fair game and especially vehicles, mostly horse drawn, delivering goods to the shops. Because of his fair good looks, Frankie was often used as the 'front man' distracting the shopkeeper while his pals were making off with the spoils. He and his friends originally started stealing out of a sense of devilment or because they were hungry, but, as they grew older, they found a ready market in stolen goods in their general community where no questions were asked if a bargain were to be available.

After he started primary school, activities were centred round the disused washhouses in the back courts of the tenements. These frequently flooded with scummy water – partly from rain and partly from tenement toilets becoming blocked and overflowing – were the chosen playground for the children and one of the washhouses became the den for Frankie's gang. They played at soldiers marching in ranks, following the orders of Frankie who, naturally, was the leader. Or being cowboys, slapping their buttocks as if they were on a horse; or engaging in sword fights using bits of wood left lying around.

Frankie was contemptuous of the girls, and mostly ignored them although he knew who they were. Also, out on the street at all hours they did not mix with the boys but played their own games like peever or skipping ropes or planey-clappy, side by side with the boys' games, sometimes getting in each other's way. There was, one girl, Sally Maitland, whom Frankie kept a look out for and liked to watch surreptitiously – without knowing why he was doing it. Like all the girls she was slim, but she stood out because she was slightly better dressed than the others. Whereas they either wore no stockings or grey stockings straggling at various lengths up to their knees, she always wore white ankle socks neatly folded over, and Frankie liked to watch her slim legs when she was running or skipping. And she ran lightly and delicately. He might collide with the other girls in the course of their conflicting games and push and shove them or exchange friendly insults with them but, for some reason, Sally never seemed to be near him. Maybe she was different because she lived in a slightly more affluent part of the neighbourhood. If he had come up against her, he would not have pushed her or insulted her as he did the other girls, but the opportunity never arose. He was just left with a lift of his spirits whenever she appeared on the street.

Although the girls and boys did not really mix there was an acceptance, even amongst the girls, that Frankie was the leader of the group. Frankie was disappointed that, in some subtle way, Sally did not seem involved in this acceptance. At the same time, he would have been disappointed if she had. Frankie didn't know that one of the reasons that Sally came to play with the other girls was the chance of seeing Frankie. But then Sally didn't realise that either.

They all got their ideas from the films they saw in the local cinema – officially called the Kinema but known locally as the Kinsh. Entrance to the cinema involved the pooling of the gang's available resources to enable two members to buy admittance. Once the lights dimmed, they would slip round to the emergency exit and open it to let in the remaining members of the gang waiting outside. Occasionally someone would be caught and marched to the police station but more regularly the victims suffered just a thump on the head from the manager.

They played rounders and games with bools (marbles) especially one called moshie, which involved moving the bools through pits dug in the ground, and created constant fights because of allegations of cheating called *sheneaving* which involved failure to keep the hand still when flicking the bool with the thumb. In this Frankie emerged as a leader for the first time because he took the lead in adjudicating in the frequent disputes and his word was accepted by the others.

But by far the most popular game was football, played in the street winter and summer, with a ball or anything which could be wrapped up in the shape of a ball. This also brought the boys up against the police because they were not supposed to play football in the streets and the police were the sworn enemy who chased them and, if they caught someone, delivered justice there and then with a slap across the head. Frankie was never caught and because of this the local policemen kept a special lookout to see if they could nab him. They were also especially keen because they knew him as the younger brother of Ray Gilligan, prominent member of the local street gang.

The gang's particular enemy was Samuel William McCulloch, who was a born policeman, or at least, he was born with an immoveable sense that he was right – invaluable in a policeman. He was dark-haired, just over six feet in height and had been strongly built, although now going to seed. He was never known to smile, regarding it as a sign of weakness. He was a committed Christian, attending the kirk on Sundays and spending the rest of that day reading improving literature. McCulloch much preferred the Old Testament to the New, regarding some passages in the New Testament, such as the Beatitudes, as sops for the weak. In his thirties, he had married a small neat woman who kept his house tidy and was completely in awe of him. It is pointless to speculate on their married life as it was impossible to imagine Samuel William McCulloch out of uniform and in pyjamas. He regarded it as right that Glasgow Rangers should top the Scottish First Division but never went to Ibrox himself as he disliked the uncertainty about the outcome of a match. He prided himself that he was always polite when, in the course of his job, he came into contact with Roman Catholic priests, but he never felt comfortable dealing with them. In any event they were mainly Irish and therefore devious and always trying to insinuate themselves into his favour. He disliked children. The boys, he thought were mostly involved in petty lawbreaking like playing football in the street, from which they would inevitably develop into the fully-fledged criminals with whom in due course he would have to deal. The girls he ignored.

The children responded in their own way. At the local swimming pool there was an area beside the pool which held a number of small baths a little bigger than footbaths and the boys congregated there because the baths had hot water. They often joined in various ribald songs:

'Cocaine Bill and Morphine Sue
Were walking down Fifth Avenue
Saying 'Honey have a sniff, have a sniff on me.
Honey have a sniff on me'.

They sang it lustily without having a clue what they were singing about. But their favourite was one which some urban poet had concocted to the tune of the March 'Blaze Away':

Fat Sam McCulloch
Has only one bollock
And that one very sma'
His poor little tadger
Isnae much larger
And not much use at a'
His puir little Missis
Says his little thing is
Only one inch tall
'Where's it gone
It's slipped oot o' ma haun
Oh, it's hidden behind his one ba'

This, too, was sung with great gusto and often in the street when the policeman was within earshot but out of grabbing range. The lyric was well known in the area not least by the other policemen, one of whom made the cardinal error of whistling the catchy melody within the hearing of McCulloch and only stopped when he saw McCulloch's steely glare.

McCulloch also detested all lawyers, whom he regarded as pimps and parasites, living off criminals and trying to help them escape the just punishments which their clear guilt merited, while the police pursued them with implacable diligence. He regarded any crimes on his patch as a personal insult and would go to any lengths to have the perpetrators hunted down and punished.

He was known locally, except by the more refined ladies, as 'that cunt McCulloch'.

20

One day in March 1944 when Frankie was about eight, he returned from school to find the house empty. This was not unusual, and he made himself a piece in jam before going out to play football. He stayed out long after it was dark, playing by the light of the streetlights until Sheila shouted down that she was going out and that he should come in. He passed her in the close and she told him that their mother was still not back which was not unusual but after waiting in the flat for over an hour there was still no sign of her. Maria was now later than she had ever been, and Frankie became increasingly worried.

Eventually he went outside and started down the road he expected her to be on, but still no sign. It had been dark for some time and the street-lighting was poor as the wartime restrictions were still in place, but he kept on looking and went further afield straying away from the neighbourhood he knew. He was not lost but he was away from the comfort of his own streets where he was known. A man approached and beckoned him to follow but Frankie managed to shake him off, and when a noisy group came close, he hid until they had passed. He began to take fright at every shadow and every noise. He thought someone was dogging his footsteps, but it was only the slight echo from his own boots. A dog, which he hadn't seen, sitting in a close, gave a sudden bark as he was passing, and Frankie almost leapt into the road. After that, he approached every close with such caution that he was hardly moving at all.

It was bitter cold with the wind funnelling between the tenement blocks. To keep his hands warm, Frankie crossed his arms and thrust his hands up into his armpits as he stumbled along. The wind swirled up the dirt and debris lying in the street and beat it against his legs, bare under his short trousers. His teeth were chittering through a mixture of cold and fear. Frankie, who had started out with all the assurance of an eight-year old looking to safeguard his mother was now a frightened child crying for his mammy. He could not prevent himself from starting to cry and the tears made lines down the dirt on his face. In his panic, he felt the dark tenements with their blacked-out windows crowding in as if to suffocate him, and he scuffled on without any sense of where he was going.

He turned yet another corner and suddenly he realised that he was back on his way home because he recognised a shop doorway he had passed earlier, which had some old rags piled in it. But as he came level with it, he let out a shriek of terror - the rags suddenly came to life. He cowered back, unable to run away, and then realised that the bunch of rags was in reality a woman, who was now standing holding on to the wall. And when he plucked up enough courage to look more closely, he recognised that it was his mother. He moved towards her but suddenly became aware of a dripping sound and he realised in horror that she was urinating as she stood; he could see the water puddling at her feet. He looked around but, although he thought he heard a scuffle, and he sensed there was someone there, he did not notice anyone near who might have seen her.

Frankie could not bear to approach Maria, but she began to move unsteadily towards home, and he shepherded her like a sheepdog, keeping his distance but making sure she was safe. At the same time, he gained comfort from her nearness, despite the state she was in. A couple of times when she stumbled, he moved towards her to help but she recovered herself and gave a quiet laugh as if her unsteadiness was a joke. He then realised that she was singing. He recognised the tune as an old Italian song which she used to sing to him as an infant, 'Bella Ragazza Dalle Trece Bionde'. As she reached the close and began climbing the stairs she was still crooning quietly to herself, 'Babbo non vuole mamma nemmemo', but when she got into the flat she collapsed onto an armchair and fell fast asleep.

Frankie made himself another piece in jam and then climbed into his bed. He could not sleep but lay listening to his mother snoring in her armchair. His mind was a confusion of things he remembered and things he did not want to remember. Even when he did fall asleep the sleep was disturbed by frightful dreams of being on the street surrounded by hordes of people who were laughing at him and singing Italian songs and when he ran to the solace of his mother's arms she turned, as he reached her, into a grey-haired witch in rags.

When he woke up next morning he was almost frightened to turn to look for his mother on the chair on which she had slumped the previous night but she was up and about and had his porridge ready for him when he had dressed for school.

But if she seemed unaffected by what had happened the previous night, Frankie was not. He spent his time at school in a sort of a daze and when he came home and went out to play his mind was still in turmoil, although he assumed his position, as usual, as leader of the group. After they had played football for a bit, it was decided that they would go and see what they could lift. They spotted a horse and cart making a delivery to a shop and when the driver was inside, they scrambled onto the cart and grabbed what they could find. When the driver reappeared, they immediately scattered but, to the astonishment of the others, Frankie was slow to react and was grabbed by the driver who marched him off to the nearby police station.

When the desk sergeant saw who the driver had brought in, he was surprised – not that Frankie had been stealing, but that he had been caught, because his reputation as a police dodger was well known. The driver explained that it was as if Frankie had wanted to be caught; he had made little attempt to escape. The desk sergeant was not concerned. He was delighted that they had their hands on their man, or rather their boy, at last.

Frankie was too young to be charged with the crime, but the desk sergeant thought he would make him remember his arrest and locked him in a cell while someone was sent round to tell his mother. It was Sheila who came for him and when he was released to her, the sergeant was surprised how Frankie was little affected by his position and what little notice he took of the scolding he was given both by the policeman and by his sister. Frankie listened to them without any show of emotion and he left with Sheila, not quietly and not defiantly, but with that same emotionless expression on his face.

21

It was appropriate that it was his sister, Sheila, who came to fetch him from the police station because it was she who filled in the gaps in care left by his mother's frequent lapses into drunkenness. Sheila was nearly eight years older than Frankie and after he was born, she treated him like her baby, almost like a doll she could play with. She made sure he was properly fed, talked to him and sang him to sleep. She took him out for walks in the pram their brother Ray had stolen. Just as a young mother is sometimes cut off from her friends because she is so involved with her first baby, so Sheila might have seen less of her friends but she did not grudge the time she had to spend with Frankie and, indeed, shared Frankie with them so that Frankie, deprived of a mother's care (although not her love) was cossetted with female care as if he was being brought up in a family with six sisters who vied with each other to play with him and care for him.

As Frankie grew up, Sheila's care changed into a big sister making sure he was properly turned out and in time for school, and scolding him when he got into trouble – although he was a difficult child to scold as he would excuse himself and make promises of repentance with the charm inherited from his father. Later, as he started to mature into the street fighter he was to become, their relationship again subtly changed, and Sheila found herself almost like a maidservant at the court of King Frankie. She didn't mind, although some accused her of being a doormat. With their brother, Ray, in constant trouble with the police and their mother moving in and out of periods of drunkenness, Frankie was a solid contact for her with normal life.

Sheila hated the squalor of the dingy flat they lived in; the lavatory, shared with the other families on their floor, situated on the half landing below, in the common stair. There were no facilities for a bath in the flat, indeed no hot water except what could be heated up on the range. Like Frankie, Sheila lived in a house to which she was ashamed to bring her friends. Like him, she spent as much time as possible away from the dirty cramped flat, because she knew there was a better life for her somewhere if she could only escape the tentacles of the family life which dragged her down. She could have stayed on at school, but she had to leave as soon as possible to take a job in her Auntie Barbara's shop – while seeing friends with less ability than she had, being able to continue with the education that was the passport to a better life.

Sheila was fortunate in one way because she had been able to keep in touch with one of her Italian relatives. Her mother had been cast away from all of them because of her drinking and was not welcome in any of their homes but her grandmother's cousin, Barbara, who lived alone, had come to Boxy's funeral and thereafter, at Pat McLaughlin's suggestion, encouraged Sheila to keep in touch. At the time she was growing up, Sheila went on a regular basis round to her house where she found a sanctuary away from her own home life. It was Auntie Barbara, rather than her mother, who guided her through puberty and, with her frankness, made her at ease in talking openly with her about the sexual and emotional matters concerned. Auntie Barbara never probed her about what was happening at home but was able to draw her own conclusions from the details which Sheila let slip. She talked to Sheila about her own home life back in Italy and even taught her a little Italian.

Barbara Franchi was tiny. She had the misfortune to have been born with one leg shorter than the other (or perhaps, one leg longer than the other; she was never sure which). For this reason, she always had to wear shoes specially made to compensate but this didn't totally solve the problem and all her life she walked with a slight limp which developed, as she got older, into an increasingly painful hip. Because of this, or possibly because she had a sharp tongue she had never married. She made her own purposeful way in life without relying on anyone else. When she first came to Scotland she worked, like so many immigrants, in a café but, early on, she was asked to act as a housekeeper for an elderly Italian who had lost his wife and thereafter she acted as a valued housekeeper for a number of people living on their own, latterly for twenty years with Mrs Maxwell, a rich widow who lived in a large house in Pollokshields for whom she became maid, confidante, reader, nurse and increasingly friend. Barbara bustled round the large house wearing the highly polished tiny buttoned-up boots which she wore every day under a long dress which came down to the top of those boots and covered her substantial bottom.

When she died, the old lady left Barbara, amongst other things, the life tenancy of a nice flat in the Shawlands area, together with the income from a trust fund which was sufficient to enable her to live comfortably if not luxuriously. When Sheila first visited Barbara there, she found it warm and inviting, so unlike her own house. It was perhaps over-stocked with furniture and every wall and every surface was covered with knick-knacks and little paintings and some sepia-coloured photographs of Barbara's parents and even one of Sheila's own grandfather and grandmother on their wedding day that Sheila had never seen.

One of the things which Barbara had inherited from Mrs Maxwell was a Singer sewing machine which was operated using a foot treadle and which, when not in use, folded down to make a highly polished table. She was highly skilled in using it and she passed on her knowledge to Sheila and also showed her hand-sewing and knitting and crochet. Sheila loved to spend an afternoon with her, both engrossed in their work and chatting away as the mood took them.

One day, Sheila said to her, 'Auntie, why did ye no' get married?'

Barbara paused in her knitting. 'Well, nobody asked me, and I never fancied anyone well enough to make him ask me.' After a further pause, 'I'll tell you another thing young Lucia (Barbara never used the name 'Sheila'; she couldn't understand why people would ignore a lovely Italian name), you're poor. And when you're poor, there are only two ways you can make your way in the world.' And she pointed, firstly to Sheila's head and then to her belly. 'You've had to leave school before your education is hardly begun, and so, that route is maybe closed to you. So, you are going to have to rely on the other way.'

Sheila pretended to be shocked. 'Auntie, y'er no wantin' me to be a wee hairie and walk the streets up at Blythswood Square, 'ur ye?'

'Don't get smart with me young lady. What I mean is, that you will have to marry your way out of poverty. You're a good-looking young girl, or at least good enough looking. (Auntie Barbara didn't believe in too much praise). Set your sights on getting someone higher up in the world who can raise you up to his level.'

'But what about love?'

'The love you have for your mother and your brothers is fine. That goes in a circle and comes back to you. That other sort of love, with a man, means you have to give a part of yourself away. And the poor have little enough without giving bits away unless you get a lot more back in return. Your passport out of the slum you have been brought up in, is the man you should marry. Don't throw it away on some worthless individual like the ones around here.'

'Auntie, ye're a shocker.'

'Lucia, your auntie wants the best for you because you deserve it. Think about what I've said.'

On another occasion, she was showing Sheila recipes she had brought from Italy which Sheila would be able to take back to her own house to share with the family.

'I cannie dae this, Auntie. It's ower gooey.'

Barbara took over and showed her where she had gone wrong. Then she turned to her. 'How do I talk?'

Sheila frowned. Her Auntie just talked.

'I mean, do I speak the way the other people around here talk?'

'No. A suppose you speak more posh.'

'I don't speak posh, as you call it, I speak properly, and I taught myself to speak properly so that I could make my way in the world. And that's what you will have to do if you are going to catch – yes 'catch' – the man you should. You'll never do that if you continue to speak the way you do now. All you will end up with is another Glasgow keelie.'

Sheila listened but did not say anything and concentrated on her cooking.

22

Some years later, when Barbara died, she left her beloved Lucia the wedding photograph of her grandparents and the Singer sewing machine which was, with difficulty, manhandled up the tenement close to Sheila's house on the top floor, where its polished beauty sat incongruously with the tattered remaining furniture.

When Barbara had been in Pat McLaughlin's office making her will she told him about the advice she had given Sheila.

'You're just an old romantic,' he teased her.

She jabbed a finger at him. 'It's all right for you, Pat McLaughlin. You had the benefit of education. That was your ticket out. She has to use what she has. And I've told her she's got to use it wisely. Men are not to be trusted.'

Pat started to protest on behalf of his sex, but she waved him away.

'They are all the same. Not to be trusted. But they have a weakness. They are so full of their own importance, that you can wrap them round your little finger. I remember when your Constance asked me about marrying you. I told her that she might as well, as you were the best of a bad lot.'

Pat smiled and was tempted to continue the argument, but he kept his peace. He had too much respect for what Barbara had achieved in making her way in a foreign land without any help from any man or indeed any woman. And he agreed that Barbara's advice to Sheila was sound.

And to be truthful, the most important legacy left by Barbara were the words of advice given over the years, which had gradually seeped into Sheila's consciousness. With a maturity no doubt developed because of the struggles of her family life, she took a careful look at herself when she had to leave school and decided that, although not a complete beauty, she was attractive (at least the boys around seemed to think so) and this would indeed be the passport for the better life she craved. She avoided the rough and tumble which was a major part of sexual activity at her age, gaining her a reputation as an untouchable Catholic Miss High and Mighty, although religion played no part whatever in shaping her behaviour. She did change her way of speaking although doing so, like many others, by adapting her speech to the company she was in. Despite coming from her dingy flat Sheila ensured that, when she left the flat, she was always as beautifully turned out as if she had come from the height of luxury. In this she was helped by the lessons in sewing she had received from her aunt. These enabled her to make most of her clothes from discarded remnants turned into dresses in the most up-to-date fashions.

Auntie Barbara would have been proud to see her Lucia plotting her course in life, as she had advised. She would not have been so happy had she known what little supervision Maria gave to her daughter's comings and goings. She had started going to dancehalls from the age of fourteen and at first Maria tried to impose a curfew on her to be home by midnight. But she because of her drinking Maria became increasingly lax and, by the time she was eighteen Sheila came and went as she pleased, often not returning home until the early hours of the morning.

Sheila loved dancing and, at that time, there must have been ten dancehalls within walking distance of where she lived. She quickly learned the ones to avoid, especially on Friday nights when young men had been paid and spent their wages in pubs on the way to the dancehall. Trouble could easily arise between rival gangs, and on one occasion, total warfare had broken out between rival factions, leaving Barbara trapped cowering in a corner as men with blades of various types fought around her. Then a voice said, 'Hey, you're Ray Gilligan's sister. Ye shouldnae be here.' And she was taken by the arm and escorted to safety.

At the end of the War Glasgow was full of soldiers from all over the world who were able to lord it over the local boys because of the glamour of their uniforms and their stories of their martial exploits (often invented). When Sheila came to the dance halls, she was always prettily turned out and, following her auntie's advice, she spoke with her newer 'posher' accent, so that the men who clamoured to dance with her would have had no idea of the background from which she came. What Cinderella Sheila did not appreciate was that her dancing partners were not real Prince Charmings, but ordinary boys temporarily elevated out of their often, pathetic lives by war, which had given them an unrealistic status. For a brief period, in the middle of drab post-war Glasgow, all could live out their fantasy lives.

It was inevitable Sheila should become close to one of the American soldiers, one who came from somewhere in the middle of the United States. He was called Steve and had a moustache Sheila thought made him look like Clark Gable. He also talked like Clark Gable or so it seemed to Sheila. Possibly because of the moustache, he appeared to be quite a bit older than she was and more worldly wise, which was part of his attraction. He was quieter than some of the younger boys and perhaps he became almost a father figure for Sheila who had lost her father at such an early stage. If she sometimes wondered whether her Auntie Barbara would have approved, she speedily put the thought behind her, as she spent her time at the dancing and afterwards almost exclusively with him.

By the time he was eleven, Frankie was the acknowledged leader of his small gang and he continued to have that recognition even when he moved into secondary school. The only threat to his standing came from a boy called Jaikie Houliston who lived a few streets away and was associated with a rival gang in his own area. Jaikie, at every stage, had been big for his age and he had used his size to bully those smaller. His hair was short and spiky over a narrow forehead which was always set in a frown over deep-set eyes. He spoke in a loud voice with frequent use of foul language, which was the more offensive when used in a confined space like a bus when he seemed to be defying other passengers to object. It was obvious from the beginning that there was going to be trouble between the two boys and their respective supporters. Like little Capulets and Montagues, the rivals provoked each other at every opportunity, but for some time this was confined to looks, insults and deliberate brushing against the others as they passed.

One advantage of his reputation was that the young girls in the neighbourhood wanted to be associated with the gang and especially with Frankie as the strongest figure. Frankie took advantage of this by feeling up the girls who were available and finally, guided by one of the more complacent girls who, though younger was more experienced, had his first full intercourse at the age of twelve standing in a tenement close, experiencing, for the first time, the knee trembler he had heard others boasting about. After this he had sex whenever he felt like it and had no difficulty finding willing partners. It did not occur to Frankie either then or at any time in the future that the girls might enjoy the sex or that he should do anything to make them enjoy it. They were there to be used whenever he felt like it.

Needless to say, Sally Maitland did not feature in any of these sexual fumblings. Frankie did not want her to. He did not even fantasise about it. But he could not fix in his mind what he did want with her. If he had thought it through properly, he would have realised that what he really wanted was for her to be his close friend to whom he could have talked in a natural way. Although Frankie, despite the hard man image he was trying to cultivate, was totally at ease in the company of girls (that was possibly part of his attraction for them), he just found it impossible to speak normally to Sally Maitland.

He was a clever boy and full of initiative, but he found school a waste of time and made no effort either to learn in class or to do the homework he was set. Most of the teachers were concerned merely to keep their pupils under control which they did, not by engaging their attention, but by physical punishments ranging from the use of the belt to outright brutal assaults. One teacher known as 'Big Beanie' took a particular dislike to Frankie and on a number of occasions dragged him into a room privately and punched and kicked him. He was determined to break Frankie but, no matter what he did, Frankie took everything he did to him without flinching – no matter how badly he was hurt.

A small number of teachers did recognise that in Frankie there was promising material but, although he responded to them with his usual charm, their efforts were frustrated because in Frankie's world, a world of thieving and breaking into shops and selling stolen liquor, what schooling tried to teach him was irrelevant. He did, however, absorb some knowledge almost by a process like osmosis and he could read and write, although his writing was far from copperplate and he never lost the habit of following the words he was reading with his finger and mouthing the words as he went along.

One teacher, in particular, went out of her way to interest Frankie in her subject. She was the young art teacher, Miss O'Donnell, who kept trying to involve her pupils despite their complete lack of interest in art. Frankie had warmed to the way in which, despite repeated setbacks, she had kept on trying different approaches, and he had used his influence in the group to make sure that at least there was order in the class if not attention. She was the only teacher who recognised that Frankie was naturally left-handed and encouraged him, despite his reluctance, to try his hand at some drawing. To his surprise, but concealed pleasure, he turned out to be quite successful although it was not an accomplishment which fitted into Frankie's vision of himself. He also sat patiently when, from time to time, she made quick sketches of him.

A possible school area in which Frankie might have become involved was football, because, having spent most of his childhood playing football in the street, he was a gifted footballer. This was spotted by the school janitor who ran the school team, but Frankie did not want to be involved. There was some talk among the boys that the jannie was too keen to hug the players and he spent a lot of time hanging around when the boys were changing. Frankie could have handled that, but of more importance was Frankie's image of himself. He saw himself as a hard man. And hard men don't play football. They are too busy doing more important things like acting as lookout for the bookmakers who, because of the laws against betting shops, had to ply their trade on the street, all the time under threat of arrest if the police caught them in action. Or indulging in petty thieving. Frankie did not himself get involved in any of the actual thefts. He saw his role as the organiser and the 'muscle' if things blew up with rival gangs, leaving the actual robberies to his gang members.

By the time he was entering secondary school he had also adopted what he saw as the hard man walk, imitating his brother and his brother's friends. This involved square shoulders, slightly rolling with each stride, with hands not in the pockets but free for immediate action, and a gait designed to give an impression of menace. And, of course, a hard stare. A casual onlooker might have seen this as a little ludicrous in someone so young and, in reality, the outward look which Frankie was seeking did not properly reflect the inner Frankie which had a well of kindness and charm which he was trying to conceal. In some ways, he was merely repeating the kind of play acting which, like all young boys, he indulged in when he was younger, by imagining, as he went along the street, that he was a cowboy or a musketeer or some other character he had seen on the screen.

Not all the local policemen were like Sergeant McCulloch. Some felt that the way to attack youth crime was to involve the youngsters in other activities. Risking McCulloch's anger, one constable succeeded in getting some boys engaged in athletics. Another thought that he could harness their naturally aggressive instincts through boxing and he was able to point to the example of Benny Lynch who had been born round the corner from Frankie's house and who had become champion of the world the year Frankie was born. But Frankie was not interested. You could be as good as you liked with your fists but that wouldn't help you against someone with a blade.

23

To a middle-class person, Frankie's life as he neared thirteen would have seemed chaotic: his father long since dead, his mother moving in and out of an alcoholic stupor, his brother a well-known hoodlum, and his home life such that he spent most of his time on the streets. Frankie, though, felt at ease, secure in the esteem in which he was held in the sub-world which he dominated.

He was whistling as he pushed open the flat door on his return from school one day, glad to get out of the cold February wind. There was a short hallway leading from the entrance door to the kitchen and the first thing he noticed was that a kitchen chair was lying overturned on the kitchen floor. Then, as he moved down the hall, he was met by the ghastly sight of a body hanging from one of the hooks that supported the clothes pulley. He stood there unable to move, just letting out a howl like a wild animal. The body was dressed in rags and the head was distorted by the rope encircling the throat. At first, Frankie thought it was his mother but when he had the courage to go nearer, he realised it was his sister, and he again howled and sank to the floor.

He had left the door open when he entered the flat and the woman across the landing heard the noise and rushed out.

'Christ almighty. Oh fuck, fuck. Willie come quickly.' She called for her husband who was on the night shift and just getting ready to go to work.

Willie Robertson, used to his wife's dramas, ambled slowly out, still chewing on the remains of his dinner. At first, he didn't take in what he what he was seeing. Then, 'Fucking hell. Oh shite. Jeannie, you get the boy. I'll get help.' He ran down the close, knocking on doors as he went and gathered as many men as possible to come back up with him to see what they could do with Sheila's hanging body. He brought a knife from his house and they succeeded in cutting the rope and carefully lifting her down and laying her on a bed. There was no sign of life. One of the wives had had the sense to run down to the police station and all they could do was cluster round the bed waiting for a doctor and the police to arrive.

Jeannie Robertson took charge. 'Right. All of you out. This isnae a peepshow. Where's wee Frankie? God, he's still here in the lobby. Come on, son. You come with me.'

Frankie lay on the floor, curled up in a ball. He had said nothing since those initial roars of pain. At first, he wouldn't move and, as babies sometimes do, tensed up his body so that she couldn't shift him. She knelt beside him, whispering to him, cuddling him and stroking his back. Eventually he got up and supported, half carried almost, by Jeannie, he allowed himself to be taken through the crowds of people milling in the close and into the Robertson's flat where she laid him down on a bed and sat with him, stroking his forehead and murmuring to him, not words, nor even a song, just noises which came from the heart of her being. She told her husband later that he never cried, merely laid there with his eyes staring at nothing until at last falling into some sort of slumber.

Sheila's suicide was the talk of the steamie. Those who had seen the body were much in demand to tell what they had seen. There were other 'eyewitnesses' who had not seen the body but within half an hour had persuaded themselves that they had and told the graphic tale as they imagined it. Some said the body was naked ('the shame of it'), others that she had still been kicking and struggling as she hung from the rope; some even imagined last words.

Someone had got the news to Ray Gilligan and he reached the flat at the same time as the police. For a short while their mutual enmity was put to one side as they discussed what should be done, and it was agreed that Sheila's body should be taken to the police mortuary while forensic experts went over the flat. There was no suicide note and, as Ray told the police, the last time he had seen his sister the previous week she was in high spirits and he could think of no reason why she should take her own life.

Ray decided that he must contact Pat McLaughlin, their old helper in times of trouble. First of all, having checked that Frankie was safe with Mrs Robertson, he left the flat to try to intercept his mother before, on her way home, she ran into the crowd of spectators waiting at the entrance to the close. Luckily, he had a shrewd idea of where she would be coming from at that time of the day and what state she would be in. Sure enough, there she was weaving her way somewhat unsteadily along the street. She was delighted to see her big boy and was happy to fall in with his suggestion that she should come home with him and spend the night with him and his current girlfriend. Meantime, Willie Robertson had abandoned all ideas of going to his work and later that evening he was sitting with his wife over a much-needed whisky discussing what had happened. Although they strongly disapproved of Maria and her drinking, they had been fond of Sheila and admired the way she presented herself each day, from what was a tattered house, clean as a new pin.

Jeannie said, 'What I cannie get is what she had on. It was that lovely blue dress which she ran up from bits of material on her sewing machine. She was so proud of it. And yet, when you lifted her down, you could see it was all cut to ribbons and muddied. And she must have done it herself because her scissors were lying on the kitchen table.'

24

When Pat McLaughlin reached home that night, he was so visibly upset that his wife, Constance, hugged him and held him until he managed to gasp out the terrible news about Sheila's suicide. They sat together on the settee holding hands as Pat told her in dribs and drabs what he had been told by Ray. The mere telling of the story made it seem all the more real.

'I feel so guilty,' said Pat, with his head in his hands.

Constance was more practical. 'What could you have done? You told me that Maria just wouldn't allow you to help. You did what you could getting Auntie Barbara involved. And you told me that she was so good for Sheila.'

'I know. But I promised Boxy I would look after things and I feel that I've let him down.'

Constance could have said that, if it was anyone's fault it was Boxy's and Maria's, but she had the good sense to leave that thought for another day as she knew that, right now, saying anything would make matters worse.

They were in sombre mood for the rest of the evening and, at their night prayers, made special mention of Sheila and the remaining members of the family. Pat repeated these prayers the next morning when, as he often did, he went to Mass at St. Aloysius Church before going down the hill to his office. He knew it was not theologically correct, but he couldn't help getting consolation from the thought of Sheila being free from whatever demons had driven her to take her own life and being once more under the care of her Auntie Barbara.

When Pat reached his office, Ray was already there waiting for him. Pat had been thinking that there were practical matters to be dealt with, the most pressing being where Maria and Frankie were to live as they couldn't return to the horrors of the suicide flat. He found that Ray had also thought of that and had already moved their pathetic little collection of belongings to another flat which he had just round the corner. Pat couldn't help raising an internal eyebrow as to how Ray, with no visible means of support, could have such an alternative readily available, but this was not the time to raise a query.

Ray had been helped by the neighbour, Mrs Robertson, in whose house Frankie had spent the night. She told Ray that Frankie had said nothing since she had brought him into her flat and he continued to be tight-lipped as Ray was taking him round to the new house, merely following mutely what he was asked to do.

Ray had told his mother, when she had awakened, that Sheila had been involved in an accident and that she was dead. She would learn soon enough the details of the tragedy. Ray told Pat that she had seemed to shrink into herself at the news but was composed and had turned down the offer of a drink.

'I've asked my mates to ask around and see if they can find out why she did it. And the state she was in. You didnae see her, Mr McLaughlin. She was dressed in a blue dress which Mrs Robertson said was a favourite of hers but it was smeared in dirt which she must have got from the range because her hands were all covered in coal dust. And the dress was cut to ribbons and she must have done that herself because her scissors were lying on the kitchen table.' Ray paused. 'Why did she no' come to me? I could've sorted out any problems she had. Could she no' have come round. I know Mammy has her problems, but I was here. She just had to ask. Ah would have wanted her to ask. When I think of her all alone like that, it fair breaks ma heart.'

And big tough hard man Ray Gilligan bent over opposite Pat McLaughlin, sobbing, with the tears running down his cheeks, clenching and unclenching his fists in his agitation.

Pat McLaughlin, himself, was almost in tears. He said nothing. There was nothing to be said. He sat with Ray in the silence of the office with just the noise of traffic in the background.

Eventually Ray gave a great sigh and straightened up. 'Sorry about that, Mr McLaughlin. It's hard to bear. Right I'll be off and see what I can find out. You'll deal with the police? Better you than me. And you'll sort out about the funeral?' Ray shook Pat's hand strongly and then let Pat show him out.

Pat busied himself just to occupy his mind, just to make himself feel he was being of some use. He went down to Cumberland Street to speak to one of the priests there and was assured that, although suicide was a grave sin, there was now a presumption of grace and there would be no problem in giving Sheila a Christian funeral. Next, he spoke to the undertakers and arranged for them to deal with the burial once the police had released the body, and then he went to the police station to check the procedure there. He spoke to Detective Sergeant McCulloch who made clear his irritation at being distracted from more important work but who deigned to confirm that a routine post-mortem was being carried out that day and that the body would be released thereafter.

After Pat had left, McCulloch turned to one of his colleagues. 'Typical the fuss about that girl. Just another Papist slut who has made a balls of her life and leaves us to clear up the mess. Now they'll no doubt make her one of their saints.'

He would normally only have spoken to his colleague so frankly in the environs of the Lodge of which they were members, but there was no-one else in the room apart from the cleaner, Mary, who was washing the linoleum with her mop and pail and was like part of the furniture. She didn't count.

When Pat got back to his office, he found Ray waiting for him to report that Sheila had apparently been seen at the dancing, to the annoyance of the local boys, in the constant company of an American serviceman, and that he had recently been sent back to the States.

Pat shook his head, but he agreed with Ray that it was unlikely that this would have driven Sheila to take her own life. Her reasons would remain a mystery.

At the funeral Pat was shocked by how thin and old Maria looked but she was sober, and Ray confirmed that she had not drunk since she had learned of Sheila's death. The funeral Mass was held at the local St Francis' Church at nine o'clock in the morning being merely an extension of the normal parish Mass held at that time. There was accordingly a sizeable congregation, mostly women. Afterwards, as was the custom, only the men were to go the cemetery and so Pat, Ray and Frankie accompanied the hearse in Pat's car. Constance stayed behind with Maria, although she told Pat of her unease because she felt she stood out as the toffee-nosed wife of the lawyer McLaughlin with nothing in common with the other mourners.

At the cemetery Pat approached Frankie to put his arm round his shoulders but there was no responsive movement towards him, and Frankie remained taciturn throughout. As always seems to be the case at a burial, there was a cold wind gusting across the graveyard where Sheila was laid to rest, in the lair in which her father was buried, already marked with a headstone bearing his name. When the coffin had been lowered into the grave and the last prayers had been said, the final act was for mourners to throw symbolic handfuls of earth onto the coffin below. Pat and Ray did this, but Frankie shook his head when it was his turn.

As he stood at the graveside there came back to Pat the final words of a poem about a young girl who had committed suicide, which Pat had loved as a youth:

Cross her hands humbly
As if praying dumbly
Over her breast.
Owning her weakness,
Her evil behaviour,

And leaving, with meekness,
Her sins to her Saviour.

Pat, Ray and Frankie, each lost in his own thoughts, returned to St Francis where they met up with Constance and Maria. Some further brief words of sorrow were exchanged before Ray left with Maria and Frankie. As they waved goodbye, Pat became aware that Constance was exceptionally upset. She explained to Pat through her tears, 'I decided to take Maria to that cafe along the road run by the Catanis. There were lots of other women there and I heard some whispering. I then found out what was going on. That Detective Sergeant, McCulloch, had let people know the result of the post-mortem. It's terrible. Sheila was two months pregnant when she hanged herself. The poor, poor girl. God have mercy on her soul.'

Pat managed to console her on the way home, but he now knew why Sheila had committed suicide. She had thrown away her ticket, Auntie Barbara's passport to a better life. She had no other way out.

A few days after the funeral, a package arrived at Pat's office which turned out to be a crate of whisky as a present from Ray for Pat's help over the funeral. Pat had a shrewd suspicion that the whisky would not have been obtained in the normal manner but, in the circumstances, he could not reject it. He put it to one side but, in due course he gradually drank it.

25

The Monday after his sister's funeral, Frankie went back to school. His mother, still sober since the death, fussed about him, preparing his breakfast and setting out his clothes. Frankie allowed himself to be organised but, as he had since Sheila's death, remained taciturn, speaking only when spoken to and then with as few words as possible.

Though externally he showed nothing, internally he was in a constant state of fury. His rage was primarily directed towards his sister. When she was alive, he had given little thought to her, accepting her care of him without thinking of it. Now she was dead, and by her own hand, he was furious at the way she had abandoned him. The despair which had driven her to it was irrelevant to her rejection of him. And, while blaming her, he was in rage at the world which had deprived him of her.

When he reached school, he was conscious he was an object of curiosity, of wonder almost. The teachers were careful in the way they spoke to him, as if he had been away to some distant place where they had not been. His own friends nodded to him but said little as they instinctively knew that the abuse and ragging which was the normal fare was not appropriate and didn't know what to replace it with. This suited Frankie. He wanted to welter in his fury and felt that, once he started normal conversation, it would be dissipated. On that first day accordingly, he was left very much on his own except at the very end of the day when he felt a touch on his arm and turned to see Sally Maitland.

'I'm sorry about your sister,' she said.

'What's it to you?' he snarled and took a malicious satisfaction in seeing her face crumble before his glare.

She had summoned up all her courage to approach him and now turned away, already sobbing. Frankie also turned away and then half turned back as he was already regretting what he had done. But it was too late; she was gone.

On his way home, he was tortured by what he had done, and to the one person left in the world whom he admired and whom he wanted to think well of him. But then he told himself Sally was a chink in the armour he was putting round himself and that he would be stronger without that weakness.

Gradually, time at school returned to normality, with Frankie's friends being more relaxed with him although, because of what had happened, he, who had already been the acknowledged leader, seemed to have moved up to an even higher plane. Possibly because of this, Jaikie Houliston and his gang seemed more intent in creating trouble, being more aggressive in the school corridors and deliberately causing obstructions in the outside areas. Jaikie had grown much more quickly than Frankie and was itching for the opportunity to show who was the real hard man. A shoving match in the playground became suddenly more serious and Jaikie came at Frankie swinging punches and kicking out at him. They both exchanged insults before Jaikie yelled out, 'Is your fucking big sister still hanging about?'

Suddenly Frankie became totally impervious to the pain of the blows Jaikie was throwing at him. He threw himself on the bigger boy and hurtled him to the ground. Jaikie, despite his supposed superior strength, was unable to get back on his feet and then, as Frankie's punches grew more violent Jaikie became less and less able to defend himself. But Frankie did not stop. He held Jaikie by the throat with one hand and threw punch after punch with the other on Jaikie's defenceless face. The rival gangs stopped their individual battles to concentrate on the one between their leaders, and it was one of Frankie's own friends who realised that things had got out of hand. With the help of two others he managed to prise Frankie from Jaikie's inert body. Frankie still struggled with them as he stood but gradually stopped, panting heavily as he looked down on Jaikie's body, crumpled on the ground. Jaikie no longer had a face. There was just a shapeless mass in which it was hard to make out what remained of a nose or eyes. Everything was covered in blood, which dripped on to the playground tarmac where he lay.

The group looking down were suddenly broken by the arrival of one of the masters whom another of the boys had had the sense to call.

'Great God Almighty,' he said as he bent to check Jaikie's pulse, making sure he was still alive. He turned to the now frightened group of boys. 'Who did this?'

He received the customary silence until Frankie put his hand up and said it was him.

'Right. You lot get into the hall and wait there until I come for you. And not a bloody word from any of you. Jamie Forrest, you run round to the police station. Tell them we have a major crisis. Tell them to come right away. And bring an ambulance. We have a seriously injured casualty.

'You, Gilligan, go into my office and wait for me there. I'll have to stay with this boy until the doctor comes.'

Frankie sat and waited in the headmaster's office. Then he got up and wandered round the room, looking at the pictures on the walls, before hurriedly resuming his seat as he heard footsteps approaching. The headmaster came in, closely followed by Frankie's old enemy, Sergeant McCulloch.

'Och, it's those Gilligans again, McCulloch said to the Headmaster. I've done the brother for assault and the sister has just topped herself and now we've got this wee tyke. The mother's an alki and the father was one before he died. The whole family's just a waste of space.' He grabbed Frankie by the collar of his jacket and dragged him to his feet.

'Right, you ya wee shite. You're coming with me. From what the doctor says you're lucky not to be facing a charge of murder but you're in deep shit anyway.'

With that, Frankie was frogmarched out of the school, past groups of pupils, and half dragged along the road to the police station where, after his details were taken, he was tossed into one of the cells. All the time he stuck by his resolution to say nothing. This angered some of the policemen in the station and they decided to give him a doing. Fortunately for him, there was a young policeman there, Archie MacDonald, who was from the Highlands. He had had a soft spot for Frankie's sister, Sheila who'd always given him a friendly smile whenever they met in the street. He had hoped to get to know her better and, with that in mind, had tried to befriend Frankie. He now managed to distract the others from their purpose so that Frankie was left alone in the cell to await his fate the next day. It was the first time he had been alone since his sister's death. He lay gazing into the darkness and then an overpowering sense of loss came over him. He was no longer a hard man but merely a frightened, lonely, twelve-year-old child in despair and his whole body shook with his sobs as he collapsed in tears. Slowly he recovered and then gradually fell into a troubled sleep.

He was wakened next morning by the cell door being thrown open and a policeman came in with a bowl of porridge which he tossed carelessly on the bench that served as a sort of table. Frankie was told to eat it fast as he would be taken to the Police Court in twenty minutes. He gobbled down the food and, at the same time, set his face back into the dumb, uncooperative expression he had had before. He was so determined to keep to this attitude, that in blocking communication with others, he did not fully comprehend what was happening to him. It was only later, when he looked back, that he worked out he had first been taken into a large courtroom where his mother sat with Pat McLaughlin and from which Frankie was remanded for four days to Larchgrove. Subsequently he was back in the same courtroom where he was given forty days detention, again in Larchgrove.

All the time Pat McLaughlin was in the background, doing what he could to make things go smoothly and to give what assistance to Maria she would permit. After the second court appearance Pat went wearily back home, confessing to Constance that the duty which he felt he owed to his friend, the late Boxy, seemed to have no limit.

She hugged him and held him close. 'That's why I married you. Because you never shrink from what is right. And that's why you went into partnership with old Craigie. You're two of a kind. And thank God for it. Remember how you got involved and how long we discussed whether it was a good move for you. He was so severe-looking.'

The firm of Shaw McLaughlin & Co. was originally Shaw & Co., a one-man operation with William Craigie Shaw as the sole practitioner. A tall, austere man, he wore half-moon glasses and, until the day of his retirement, detachable wing collars. It was the job, once a week, of succeeding apprentices to take a box of the previous week's used collars for laundering to a firm in the town and pick up a box of freshly laundered ones in their place.

Craigie Shaw had originally studied to become a minister and he kept his attachment to the Church of Scotland all his life, being an elder for more than fifty years. He was always elegantly dressed but forbidding on first impression. In fact, when he presented his wife-to-be with a photograph of himself as a keepsake, she kept it hidden in a drawer, as she thought it almost sinister and her maid at the time when she saw it said, 'That would turn milk sour'.

He was courteous to all and this was a reflection of the real Craigie Shaw because, behind that severe exterior was a warm, caring nature. Also hidden was his impish sense of humour and a rebellious character, which made him ready to challenge conventions he thought were stupid. It was this which made him leave the leading legal firm in which he was a partner and set up on his own, free from the stifling restrictions upon which his former office was run. It was also this which led him to take Pat McLaughlin with him, originally as an assistant and shortly after as a partner.

This latter decision caused consternation amongst Craigie's friends and colleagues. At the Kirk Session, when his decision became known, a fellow elder questioned whether it was right that an elder should have such an association with a member of the Roman church. On a more practical level he was told that many of the clients who had followed him into his new firm would leave because they did not want to be involved in a firm with Roman Catholic connections. Craigie, although not his wife, was sanguine about all this. He declared himself well rid of such clients. What he did know was that in Pat McLaughlin, he was going into partnership with someone who had the same Christian values as he had, who was a first-class lawyer and, most importantly, was someone he could trust implicitly.

His decision was actually a reflection of Craigie's main weakness. He was a brilliant lawyer but a poor businessman. He lost many important clients because he was not prepared to do the things they regarded as essential to their businesses but of which he disapproved. On top of this, he took on work for clients just because it needed to be done. He would worry about payment when the job was done – and sometimes there was no payment forthcoming.

At his funeral, one of his poorest clients was to say, 'Mr Shaw was a real gentleman,' and Craigie would have settled for that.

At the time when Sarah Watson first came to the firm, Craigie was semi-retired and attended the office only occasionally. There were just four private rooms available and when Craigie visited, he was afforded his old office, with the other partners shuffling down leaving the junior partner with no office for the day. But his mind was still razor sharp and, if someone was searching for an authority on some point, Craigie could immediately tell him the exact location where he would find the relevant case. When he finished for the day, he would go off home in his bowler hat, clutching his briefcase, laden, not by this time with clients' papers, but with a bottle of sherry. He then spent the evening in his favourite way, sipping his sherry and reading Cicero or Virgil in the original Latin.

26

Frankie's time in Larchgrove was far removed from such elegant circumstances.

Larchgrove Detention Centre had been set up on the outskirts of Glasgow, in substantial walled grounds, to hold boys who were too young to go the main prison, Barlinnie, partly as a remand centre for those awaiting trial and partly as a detention centre where those sentenced served out their punishment.

After his initial court appearance Frankie was taken there in a closed van with other boys of much the same age. He tried not to show it, but he was terrified. Once there, they were marshalled into a washing area where they were stripped of their clothing, examined for obvious signs of disease, made to shower and then re-equipped with rough buff-coloured prison clothing (which, for some of the poorer boys, was better than the clothes they arrived in). They were then marched into a large room which Frankie came to learn was the Assembly room, where they learned the rules of the establishment before being allowed to join those already in custody and in having their dinner. Then they were allowed a short period of relaxation when Frankie was relieved to find that he recognised some boys he knew from his neighbourhood. Quickly thereafter, they were put to various tasks, which seem to consist mainly in scrubbing and cleaning the already shining floors of the establishment. All the time they were hustled from task to task, from activity to activity. Frankie tried hard to frame his body in what he saw as his hard man image, but it became impossible with the constant shouting of orders and the warders pushing and thumping them from place to place. He eventually gave up and allowed himself to be dragged abjectly along with the crowd of others in whatever direction and for whatever purpose the warders demanded.

On that first night he was given a bed in a small dormitory holding six boys, and he lay awake trying to make sense of the position he was in. He was exhausted by a combination of the events of the day and his treatment at the Centre but, although he was close to tears, he refused to break down – a decision made especially difficult because he could hear other boys in the room already sobbing. A couple of them were even boys he knew from outside and who were generally looked on as toughies. They all seemed totally cowed and were too subdued to speak when he tried to talk to them. As he lay there Frankie vowed that he would not give in but that did not stop him being terrified as he thought about what was to come. He lay a long time looking blankly into the darkness before, as dawn broke, he eventually drifted into a troubled sleep.

In the days that followed Frankie gradually got a hold of the place. Most of the inmates were boys from abject backgrounds who knew no way of life except petty crime at which they were pathetically inept. One boy was from Frankie's street. Frankie knew him as Jiffy, and he was generally regarded as being a bit simple. Because of this Frankie looked out for him, trying to shelter him from the treatment which someone like Jiffy naturally attracted from the more brutal members of staff. Because of this Jiffy followed Frankie round like a pet dog, which Frankie found irksome but put up with.

Another boy, Wee Limey, was badly crippled by rickets; another, Badger, had a skull which, possibly at birth, had become misshapen, leaving his face almost squashed to one side, with his mouth permanently agape disclosing his few rotten teeth in a sort of fixed grin. Boys like that were frequently mocked by some of the warders and, as boys will, the other boys joined in. It meant, at least, that they were safe from the attentions of the staff if only for a short period. At gym, one of the activities involved jumping over

172

a vaulting horse. For Frankie and most of the others, this was straightforward but for one boy, Fat John Ward, it was impossible, and the other boys would crow as Fat John could only hurl himself against the horse and then clamber over it with the assistance of numerous whacks from the warder.

Bobby Simpson, whom Frankie vaguely knew, had breathing problems, which twenty years later would have been recognised as asthma, but the other boys, like the warders, had little sympathy. He was generally regarded as being just unfit through his own lack of effort and he was mocked for his failure to keep up with rest. Until the day he suddenly collapsed. The warder stood over him, kicked him as he lay and ordered him to get up, before realising that there was something wrong and called for help to carry Bobby away. Among the boys it was rumoured he subsequently died but Frankie never found out for sure. He was not important enough to worry about.

During his time there, Frankie was treated in a way which later would be recognised as normal when men are put in unsupervised control of small boys. Some of the screws were helpful, recognising the backgrounds from which most of the boys came. Others exercised their authority more violently, slapping and punching boys who did not do what was wanted when it was wanted. Some took it further and Frankie was targeted because of his continued apparently sullen refusal to say anything but the minimum. On two or three occasions, he was taken to a separate room by one or even two of the officers and beaten up in an unsuccessful attempt to make him conform.

There was one officer, Mr Brown, who was friendly towards him. He took an interest in Frankie and appeared to recognise that Frankie was not just a thug but had a brain. Although Frankie persisted in his resolution to say the minimum to the warders, he would often engage him in conversation and tried to get him to speak about what he intended to do with his life. As Frankie's sole purpose in life was to be away from the Centre so that he could restart his activities in his gang, this was not a fruitful line of conversation but Frankie, despite himself, allowed himself to recognise the efforts the warder was making and relaxed a little with him. But he remained generally cautious and was therefore on his guard when one day he was told that he had a visitor and was left in a room on his own to wait.

27

'What a place to get to. I had to use the tram most of the way and it was those old-fashioned trams. None of your new Coronation specials. It was one of the old ones. You know, one of those ones where you feel that the forward movement is purely incidental to the shooggling about from side to side. They used to say that if a pregnant woman was late in her delivery all she had to do was get the tram from Dalmuir to Auchenshuggle and her problem was solved. Obviously – despite my shape - I am not pregnant but you get the idea. In my case it is more like a remedy for constipation. Of course, *you* wouldn't have the same problem with transport, getting here. You would have your luxury chauffeured service, courtesy of His Majesty's Government. And it doesn't seem too bad a place when you get here. Maybe you don't see it that way as you can't just walk out of the door. And maybe like a lot of the boys in here you shouldn't be here at all. It's just the way the system works. It's like the hair on a darkie's left leg; it's not fair and it's not right. But you just have to get on with. But it seems not too bad here. And for some of the boys here the big plus is that they get their three meals a day. And they won't be getting that back home. They would be scrambling for scraps from where they could find them. But why do they put these places so much out of the road? It's not as if it's Alcatraz. Did you see that film that just came out about Alcatraz? Hell of a place. The people here are short term. By the time they decide where to start their tunnel they're already away home. It's the same with that Lennox Castle place. You know, the place they put those they think are not the full shilling? It's the back of beyond. Put them there and forget about them. It's well called a looney bin. It's the place our betters discard the people amongst us who are an embarrassment and don't fit in. Out of sight, out of mind. And you know that a lot of them are perfectly fine. Sometimes they might look not quite right. Maybe people get frightened of them. Sometimes they might make noises when they shouldn't. But it is not a crime. What is a crime is shoving them off there? As I say, 'Out of sight, out of mind.' Do you know why they call it a looney bin? 'Looney' is short for 'Lunatic' which means relating to the moon. It used to be thought that some people went mad at the time of the full moon. Daft. But great for the movies. Did you see any of those with Bela

Lugosi or Boris Karloff? Great names for horror movie stars. Of course, you wouldn't be allowed in as you would be too young. Not that that would stop you lads. You wouldn't be getting in through the paying entrance anyway. Ah, I used to be the same when I was a boy. You'll have jaloused from my accent that I'm not from around here. I'm from Liverpool. You would like it. It's very like Glasgow. Lots of poor areas where the people stick together and look after their own. If a mother's maybe not doing her bit, there will be lots of other mothers who will step in. It's like Glasgow. A lot of people originally from Ireland or the kids or grandkids of people who came over from Ireland. You have to be tough to survive in Liverpool. Just like Glasgow. If you don't fight your corner, you get trampled on. Talking about fighting, what about your man Benny Lynch? You'll have heard of him. He was born just round the corner from you. What a fighter! He was the height of tuppence. Well, I suppose about my height, but he was scrawny. Not a scrap on him. But what a puncher! He had two great fights with a boy called Peter Kane who was from my bit. Lynch knocked Kane out in a fight in Glasgow and then the next year the two fought a draw at Anfield Stadium in Liverpool. What a fight. I was at that fight. I shouldn't have been, but you couldn't have stopped me. It was a crying shame what happened to Benny. Not all that long ago. It was the drink that got him. Just as it gets lots of folk in Glasgow and Liverpool. I don't have to tell you that, with your father, God rest his soul. And now with your mother, God help her. She hasn't had her troubles to seek. If you never took a drink in your life you would be doing yourself a big favour. I was a big drinker myself until I came to my senses. But I went through Hell till I got there, but I got there, thank God. And here's me talking away to you sixteen to the dozen and I haven't said a prayer. *Our Father, Who art in heaven, hallowed be Thy name, Thy kingdom come, Thy will be done on earth as it is in Heaven. Give us this day our daily bread and forgive us our trespasses as we forgive those who trespass against us and lead us not into temptation but deliver us from evil.* Father, look down on these two sinners who desperately need Thy help. Amen. And now I'd better go. I've enjoyed our chat together. I'll see you next week.'

28

'Who the fuck was that?' Frankie came from an environment where swearing was part of normal discourse but at some stage in his development, for whatever reason, possibly the influence of a forgotten schoolteacher, who knows, he had decided that, as part of his plan to stand out and be different, he would not swear. But this was different. 'Who was that wee round man?'

Because of his determination to have no truck with the warders, he couldn't ask them, even Mr Brown. The funny thing was that, although he was sure he had never seen his odd visitor before, there was something about him which triggered some memory deep in Frankie's mind. He tried to visualise the man in another context but he couldn't free himself from the memory of this wee man almost bobbing up and down, standing up, sitting down, going to look out of the window, then turning to scan a photograph of Glasgow Green, the sole decoration in the room. And all the time talking away in what Frankie supposed, from what he said, was a Liverpool accent one Frankie had great difficulty in understanding.

In any event he seemed unthreatening and Frankie began to look forward to his next visit – if it happened, and Frankie realised he would be desperately disappointed if the wee man did not come back. He tried to steel himself for the possibility, telling himself that he didn't care anyway. Despite this he was nervous on the morning of the proposed next visit and was totally crushed when he was told, at the last minute, that his visitor was not coming. The warder, who told him, could see from Frankie's expression how much the visit meant to him and took a malicious delight in telling him it was off.

What he didn't tell Frankie was that the mysterious little man was going to come the next day at the same time. 'Let the stubborn wee bastard suffer a bit more for all the snash he gives us,' he said to himself.

That was the cruellest blow Frankie suffered in his whole time in Larchgrove, far worse than any of the beatings he had taken. He reacted in the only way he knew by pushing back at a warder when he hustled him and kicking out, refusing to obey any instructions even though he knew that it would lead to beatings. He struggled with one warder who had grabbed hold of him and tried to put him in a headlock. Then another joined in. All three crashed to the ground with Frankie, who was by this time past all rational thought or feelings, being almost unconscious of the punches which rained down on him. He fought to get his hands and feet free so as to hit out at the warders who cursed as they fought with him. A third warder joined in and managed to yank Frankie's boots off. Then a fourth joined in and Frankie ended up spread-eagled on the ground with each of his arms and legs pinned down, unable to avoid the punches which still thudded into him. They eventually managed to subdue him, and he was frog-marched off, away from the other inmates, who had watched the melee in an almost awed silence. He was thrown into an unlit cell with a final kick from two of the warders and left alone with his bruises, and no food until the next morning.

The next morning, Frankie was brought before the Head of the Centre. Mr Salmond was a tall reserved man with neatly cut silver hair. He was known as Sally by everyone. His office was unlike any other room in Larchgrove Frankie had been in. It was carpeted and comfortably furnished with bookshelves and landscape prints on the walls. The guards thought he was soft in believing that the boys who came into their care could be turned into worthwhile members of society; to a man, they regarded the Centre as a staging post for boys en route to becoming fully fledged adult criminals of the unsuccessful sort, who merited the brutal treatment to which they were subjected.

Mr Salmond raised an eyebrow when he saw how painfully Frankie limped in and how badly his face was cut and swollen. He asked Frankie to explain his conduct, but the boy retained a sullen silence. He was also asked how he had come about the obvious cuts and bruises on his body. Again, he refused to speak.

The Governor sighed. 'I am disappointed in you, Gilligan. I thought you had the making of something more than just another Glasgow keelie, but I was wrong. Your conduct was savage and if it is repeated you will be taken back to the Court for further punishment. And certainly, all visiting rights should be taken away. However, in the hope that this was merely a temporary reversion, I will delay this sanction. Your visitor, Father O'Leary will be here at eleven o'clock. Let's hope he can knock some sense into that thick skull of yours. Take him away.'

O'Leary, thought Frankie. *Father O'Leary. I should have known when he did that prayer thing at the end. But he didn't seem to be wearing a dog collar. And what does a priest from Liverpool got to do with me? I don't know him, at least I don't think I do, but he seems to know all about me. And why didn't he turn up yesterday? As if I'm not important enough for him to bother about. I'll show him what I think of him and his daft chat.*

With these and other like thoughts Frankie waited for the priest to arrive, which he did by bouncing into the room as he had done the first time. But as soon as he saw Frankie he stopped.

'What in the name of the wee man have you done to yourself? What's happened to your face? You look as if you've just done twelve rounds with those two boys I was talking about last week, Benny Lynch and Peter Kane. No, sit down, boy (because Frankie had risen as the priest came into the room). Great God Almighty. The Governor said you had been involved in a fracas – there's a fine word for a beating – but nothing like this. And you know, and I know, there's nothing can be done about it. I was going to say you have to take it on the chin, but you obviously already have. He took a quick breath. 'I'm sorry I had to call off yesterday. But you would know about that because I called and left a message.'

Frankie shook his head dumbly.

'No? They're real bad bastards. Pardon my French. I stressed to them they must let you know because I've had rough times myself and I know what it's like to be promised something when you're locked up, and not be given it. No. You know Jimmy Robertson who lived across the landing from you? Big strapping man but he had a terrible heart attack last week and I was called to give him the Last Rites and that's what I was doing when I should have been here. Poor man, he slipped away later on, about two o'clock in the morning. But the whole family were there, and we were able to pray for him as he died. Lovely big man; his wife Jeannie will miss him terribly.

'You're still looking at me funny. Do you actually know who I am? I just presumed that you did. I'm Tony O'Leary and I'm a Franciscan from St Francis in Cumberland Street. I had the privilege of saying your poor sister Sheila's funeral Mass. God rest her soul.'

Frankie stared at him. He recognised the priest now he could visualise him in his Mass vestments, although at the time he was so crushed by the horror of his sister's death that the whole funeral procedure passed in the same nightmare as the suicide. He could remember very little of what went on.

Father O'Leary didn't say that it was at Pat McLaughlin's suggestion he had come to visit Frankie. He didn't know that Pat had initially thought of coming himself, before realising Frankie would have no empathy with someone of his age and background. Pat's next thought was of one of the Jesuits from St Aloysius, because he had been educated there and had retained a close connection. The Jesuits had shaken up elements of Presbyterian Glasgow who were accustomed to Catholic priests from what they regarded as an ill-educated Irish background. Now they were confronted with well-educated, urbane priests with Oxford degrees and high intellectual attainments who almost seemed to treat *them* as provincials. Pat had the highest regard for his former teachers but again, on consideration, he concluded there was no way Frankie would respond to such lofty priests, no matter how well-meaning their motives. And then, at Sheila's funeral service Pat had warmed to the way the celebrant, Father O'Leary, had coped with the terrible circumstances of the suicide, and he was delighted when the priest agreed to see Frankie. Pat's only stipulation was that Frankie shouldn't know of Pat's involvement.

The priest shook his head. 'It was a terrible thing. Your sister. We won't talk about that now. I suppose I'm not surprised you didn't know who I was. Your mother isn't much for going to church. Although your sister, God rest her... She used to come in from time to time. But you don't have to go to church to find God. He comes to you. You know the story in the Gospel that a sparrow doesn't fall without God knowing about it and caring about it.'

Frankie spoke for the first time. 'That's just keech, Father.'

'It may be keech, as you call it, son, but it's keech which keeps me going. Anyway, I'm running away with myself. They always told me at the seminary that I talked too much. And not much sense. You've got enough to deal with without me ramming religion down your throat. I'm a priest but I'm also a rough-head from Liverpool who has been through what you are going through and wants to help if he can. Can I come again next week? That's good. In the meantime, do me a favour. Can you try to keep out of those 'fracas'? The girls aren't going to love you if you've a bashed-in face. And we can spend the time talking about football if you prefer. God bless. See, there I go again. I can't help it. See you next week.'

And with that, the little round man bounded out of the room leaving Frankie once more on his own. He sat for a bit and when the warder came to take him back to join the other inmates, he found him shaking his head and in fits of laughter. He had just realised that over the two occasions that this nice wee priest had come to see him, his sole response had been, 'That's just keech.'

29

The wee priest did come the next week, and for the remaining weeks that Frankie was kept in Larchgrove, visits which Frankie came to relish. Father O'Leary kept to his promise not to talk religion, but he also had to keep apologising to Frankie because religion kept on drifting into his conversation. Franke didn't mind; he realised the priest talked so fast that most of the time he just said the first thing that came into his head, and Frankie supposed that that was religion. He talked a lot about how he saw his younger self in Frankie and what it was like to be a Scouser, which was how he referred to himself.

'The other priests at St Francis – they are so good at putting things across. When they give a sermon, it seems so logical and so clearly explained to the congregation. But when I do it, I always seem to be giving the parishioners my problems and difficulties and trying to get their co-operation in resolving them. Know what I mean, son?'

Frankie didn't know what he meant but he found himself more and more drawn into conversation with the priest about topics he had never previously considered: like the new Labour Government and the threat from the Soviet Union and the morality of the atom bomb and the death penalty (Frankie had strong views on the death penalty; he was very much of the eye-for-an eye school and was delighted when the priest, although not agreeing with it, told him that support for this was to be found in Holy Scripture).

But mostly they talked about football and especially the priest's beloved Liverpool Football Club. They had won the English League Title two years previously although, much to Father O'Leary's concern they were not currently doing so well. Their main player was a Scot, Billy Liddell, and Frankie had great pleasure in correcting the priest who pronounced his name by stressing the second syllable rather than the first one. Frankie was even more filled with glee when, in April, Scotland had one of their rare victories over England, beating them 3-1 at Wembley.

Father O'Leary paid his last visit a few days before Frankie was to be released. As he left, he asked if Frankie would like to come to see him once he was back in his own house and Frankie, delighted that he was being given the chance to keep seeing the priest, promised that he would come.

The gradual effect of all this talk was that Frankie almost forgot the air of sullen indifference he had decided to adopt towards the staff in the Centre. Because of his father's early death, not to mention his previous erratic drunken behaviour, Frankie had not been exposed to adult conversation at home. And the relationships he had with his teachers at school were grounded on survival (on both sides) rather than on an exchange of ideas. Frankie, himself, was not really conscious that he had changed, and the Centre staff generally were totally unaware of any difference. The exception was the warder, Mr Brown, who had previously shown an interest in Frankie, to which Frankie had very cautiously responded.

After Father O'Leary's second visit, he approached Frankie to say that they had something in common, as he too was a Catholic, and he used this as a way of gaining Frankie's confidence. He talked about St Francis in Cumberland Street which he knew well and about the Franciscan Order in general, for which he had great admiration. He disclosed to Frankie that he himself had gone to a seminary to study to be a priest but had realised quite soon that the priest's life was not for him. He asked Frankie to keep this information to himself as he felt that it would make life difficult for him if it became public knowledge.

189

Frankie almost felt more at home with Brown as, while he relished his time with Father O'Leary, Father O'Leary was still a priest and that kept an intangible but still sensible barrier between them. Whereas, with Brown, there was no such restriction, and, as time went on, Frankie felt able to exchange wisecracks and gossip. He discovered, for example, that Brown had a similar sense of humour to his own which showed when he discovered that, separately, they had given several of the other warders the same nicknames, like 'the Undertaker' for a tall cadaverous warder and 'Stinky' for one who was perceived, with some justification, to be less than careful with personal hygiene.

Another connection between the two was that Frankie was keen on exercise and Brown was in charge of what little indoor sports activity was available in the Remand Home, centred round a small gym with a little room off, which Brown used as his cubbyhole. It was officially out of bounds to the boys, but Brown encouraged Frankie to join him there, as Frankie demonstrated great dexterity in handling materials and helped him in repairing dilapidated items of gym equipment as they talked.

On the Friday afternoon before his discharge, Frankie went to Brown's cubbyhole, where he was half-way through repairing a broken gym bench. Brown noted he was limping, and Frankie explained he had hurt his leg playing football earlier.

The warder nodded 'Once you've finished that bench, I'll give that a wee massage with some oil I've got here. We don't want you going out of here looking as if we huvnae been looking after you.'

When Frankie had finished his job, Brown helped him to lie on his table and then he fetched the oil he was going to use for the massage. At first the rubbing was painful where Frankie's thigh had been stretched but the pain eased and Frankie became totally relaxed, almost falling off to sleep as he enjoyed the treatment. Then he realised that Brown's hands were slipping up further on his thigh, right under his shorts and then ultimately pushing up even further so that he was fondling Frankie's testicles. Frankie came fully awake with a jerk and as he turned towards Brown, he saw with horror that Brown had dropped his own shorts exposing his erect penis. Brown quickly grabbed Frankie's hand and pulled it on to his penis.

It lasted just a second, but remained in Frankie's mind's eye, frozen like when he was at the cinema and the projector had stuck. Then he shouted at Brown and pushed him away from him as he scrambled off the table. Brown tried to restrain him and would have succeeded, as he was a big man, but was impeded because his shorts were down round his knees and, as Frankie hit him, he staggered backwards and fell over the bench on which Frankie had been working, making it easier for Frankie to escape out through the gym.

There was no one about and Frankie made for the only place where he could be alone, a cubicle in the lavatories. As was normal, there was no lock on the cubicle door, but Frankie thought he would be safe there. He was in a state of shock and revulsion. He was almost sick, retching a number of times. He moaned out loud but then restrained himself, afraid he would be overheard. His mind was whirling. He tried to recall what had happened but at the same time his mind shied away from the memory. When he did think about having his hand placed on the man's penis he recoiled in disgust and slammed his hand against the back wall of the cubicle time and time again until blood was pouring down his arm. He sat there for some time, his body every so often racked with sobs. Eventually he recovered sufficiently to stand up and moved to a sink where he rubbed and rubbed his hands to remove from them the filth which he felt attached to them.

Luckily for Frankie, when he emerged, there were no warders who crossed his path because Frankie would have relished the chance to attack them no matter how many there were. As he sat down for his evening meal, he scowled at any of the other boys who attempted to speak to him, and they had the good sense to leave him alone. He felt physically ill and pushed away his plate of food without touching it (to the benefit of his neighbours at table who gobbled it up). Later, as he lay on his bed, he was unable to sleep long into the night. That frozen picture would just not leave his mind. Then, gradually, the feelings of horror were replaced with ones of anger. Anger at himself for allowing himself to drop his guard and so allow someone to hurt him. Never again. *You can trust no-one,* he thought bitterly. *And that applies to that wee priest. He would be the same. Making out that he is a friend in order to screw you at a later date when you're not expecting it.* Frankie Gilligan didn't need that and didn't want it. There was no way he was going to see O'Leary whenever he got out. And with that thought he did drop off into a troubled sleep.

30

There was none of what Father O'Leary called government chauffeur service when Frankie was discharged from the Centre. After having his breakfast, away from the other boys, as though he might infect them, he was put outside the door of the premises, which clanged shut behind him, and left to make his own arrangements for getting home in the late spring sunshine. He found waiting outside his brother, Ray, who showed his pleasure by giving Frankie a good punch on the shoulder and then a cuff on the back of the head - these being the Gorbals equivalent of an affectionate fraternal hug. Ray then led him to, wonder of wonders, a motor car acquired while Frankie was in the Centre, a twelve-year old Wolsey 14 with leather seats, and for Frankie it was the height of luxury.

They didn't talk much on the way home, but Ray did say that their mother, whom Ray had been looking out for when Frankie was in the Centre, was currently sober and had been since Sheila's death. This was the only mention of Sheila either of them made on the journey.

Home was the new tenement flat which Ray had arranged for Frankie and his mother. As they opened the door Maria rushed towards them and, throwing her arms around Frankie, covered his face in kisses, much to his embarrassment.

'Mamma mia, how you've grown. You're just a man now. And you are so like your father. Ray, don't you see your daddy in your brother's face? Round about the eyes?'

Ray made some vague noise which Maria interpreted as agreement, but which really meant, 'Who cares?'

Maria continued to hold on to Frankie, drawing him over to the table where she insisted he eat the breakfast she had prepared for him despite his protests that he had already eaten. While he was eating, Maria pestered him for information about the Centre and what he had done there, and while he was satisfying her curiosity, he had a chance to look at her properly.

The truth is that for most children, boys especially, a mother is just a vague person who is loved in an all-encompassing way as she goes about her job of looking after their needs, but is not really looked at in the manner that they would look at a normal person.

Her shape and her hair and her eyes and her nose are subsumed into the generic form of 'mother'. But Frankie, having been away, was looking at Maria as if for the first time. She seemed so old, far older than the late thirties which Frankie worked out she would be. She was paper thin, with streaks of grey in her hair and, never having been tall, now appeared almost shrunken. She looked as if just one more setback in her life would topple her completely. As she rambled on and complained that dragging information from him was like talking to a Trappist monk, Frankie wondered what was in store for them both. It did not occur to him that what was really concerning him was what would happen to him if she were not there.

When envisaging his release, he had imagined he would immediately go out into his neighbourhood and enjoy his freedom, just wandering around. In fact, he felt a strange reluctance to leave the house, spending the day vaguely listening to the wireless and footering with the various little bits of things he owned.

Even next day, when he was supposed to be getting ready to go back to school. Frankie felt that same almost timidity at the prospect of going back into his old world. He still felt that feeling of insecurity, so unlike his former cockiness, as he stepped out onto the street, but when he was greeted, within a few steps, by one of his old gang he quickly fell back into his old ways. When he got to the school, he became aware that there was a certain myth, not to say glamour, attached to having been at the Centre. With him were two or three boys who had been released just a few days before; he remembered them quite clearly as having been tearful for much of their time, and currying favour with members of staff, but here, at school, they were telling a totally different account of their time on remand, giving the impression that they had stood up to whatever the staff tried to make them do. But as well as describing their own bravado, they had already told of the time it had taken four members of staff to restrain Frankie and of the injuries he had suffered. As such, Frankie found himself treated as a hero by the other pupils and even regarded with some respect by teachers in the school. Reacting to this adulation, Frankie speedily forgot his previous misgivings and reverted to his previous confident self.

During his time in the Centre, Frankie had thought back on how he had rebuffed Susan Maitland when she had offered sympathy on his sister's death, and pledged that the first thing he was going to do when he was released was to apologise to her. From time to time he'd had a warm feeling as he fantasied how such an apology might lead to her treating him as a friend and how they would be able to talk to one another. But now, he couldn't find her when he went looking. Asking around, casually, he found out from one of Susan's friends that she had gone to another school called Charlotte Street. 'It was,' the friend said,' a selective school and was just Susan being her usual snooty self.' She also said that Susan was moving house, possibly that very day.

After school was over, Frankie rushed round to Susan's neighbourhood. He had no idea of her address, so he hung around until dark, hoping that she might appear. Eventually he approached an elderly woman who he thought might be a neighbour. She was initially suspicious of his motives for wanting to know, but she confirmed that the Maitlands, (a lovely family) had indeed moved away that morning, to live somewhere in Sandyhills. It might as well have been Outer Mongolia as far as Frankie was concerned. He was totally deflated as he made his way home and did his Trappist Monk impression when his mother pressed him for information as to his first day back in school. He was completely torn by the realisation that the dreams of Susan, which had sustained him in the Centre, were never going to be realised.

Another shock awaited him. Jaikie Houliston, his old adversary had transferred from Frankie's Catholic school to the non-denominational state school a mile away. Most of his old gang were still there, though, and they gravitated towards Frankie as a natural leader. But a leader of what? Frankie still had eight months to go before he could leave school in December and, despite his public face, his time in the Centre had made him reluctant to repeat the experience. In addition, he had a probation officer who was supposed to supervise him; in truth this placed little restriction on what he chose to do but it was still an irritation, nevertheless. He felt himself a marked man. He had now grown much taller and, with his fair hair stood out amongst his generally smaller, dark-haired contemporaries. For these reasons, but without making any conscious decisions, Frankie took less part in the illegal activities in the neighbourhood. He did, however, do look-out duties and other activities for his brother and his gang and this was sufficient to maintain his reputation as an up and coming hard man.

31

After the summer holidays, Frankie had just over four months left before he could finally leave school. He learnt nothing over that period. At a time when Sarah Watson, in Edinburgh, was starting to expand her education at the convent, Frankie was wasting his time, something which both he and his teachers both recognised. The weeks passed slowly and tediously but at least his home life was calmer; his mother was still sober and was even talking about looking for a job, although Frankie couldn't think of any work of which she was capable.

By the time that December came, Frankie had grown almost to his full height and had an athletic build – although the Gorbals, at that time did not 'do' athletics. On his last day at school, the art teacher, Miss O'Donnell, whom he liked and who had been especially nice to him, asked him to wait behind after everyone had gone as she had something for him. She took Frankie through part of the school new to him, reserved as it was for the teachers, and then led him into the staffroom, which was by this time deserted.

Having made Frankie sit down on a settee, she went and rummaged in her bag, one Frankie liked as it was unlike other teachers' bags, being much larger and roomier and fastened with unusual latches. Miss O'Donnell sat down beside him producing from the bag a package that she handed to him saying, 'This is for you.' He found it was a framed sketch of himself, one of those she had drawn when she asked him to sit for her. He made to hand it back to her, but she told him to keep it as it was a present. He, not being used to receiving presents, didn't know what to say and could only stammer out his thanks before turning to her and giving her a big hug.

As he was hugging her, her hand landed naturally on his thigh, and sitting side by side, she let it remain there. She turned to him, 'Do you find me attractive, Frankie? Now, if Frankie had been honest, to a boy of fifteen anyone of Miss O'Donnell's age of thirty-two is almost ancient, but he told her that he had always admired her. She turned more towards him and stroked his thigh as she looked at him. She slipped her hand further up to his penis, which was already almost bursting out of his trousers and then, as he placed his hands on her shoulders, she unbuttoned his trousers and pulled them and his underpants down. She fondled his penis and then gave a little sigh and bent to kiss it.

This was too much for Frankie to bear without exploding all over her. He pushed her back clumsily, pulled up her dress and tugged off her knickers, before jumping on top of her and thrusting into her. He was at first put off by finding that Miss O'Donnell, who had such clear fair skin, was so hairy between her legs, but that was a fleeting thought – almost as fleeting as his coming to a climax which was violent and prolonged. The teacher was overwhelmed by the vigour of his attack and pulled her skirt down after he had finished, almost fearful at what she had done.

After a short time, she made to get up from the settee but Frankie restrained her, once more climbing on her and entering her with the same ferocity, forcing her legs above her head as he climaxed into her. This time she clasped her arms round him and, with her hands on his lean buttocks, pulled him hard into her as he thrust.

When he had finished, she felt totally drained and lay beside him motionless. Frankie too seemed exhausted, but this time was the first to recover. He stood up and, despite her feeble protests, moved her around on the settee while he stripped all the clothes from her body and knelt beside her. He was astonished how small she was without the high heeled boots which she always wore. He had always thought Miss O'Donnell was sturdily built but he now saw it was an impression given by the layers of cloaks and scarfs in which she dressed. Without these she seemed fragile and vulnerable and Frankie, feeling oddly protective towards her, cradled her head in his arm at the same time as he gazed in wonder at her naked body. He had never seen a naked woman before. She tried to cover herself up with her arms, but Frankie gently moved them clear and then started to caress her body, starting at her neck. He cupped her little breasts then stroked her belly before fingering her navel and moving his hand over the little mound of pubic hair that had so surprised him earlier. Then slipping down to her legs, he let his fingers just brush her thighs and her ankles and her feet. Frankie was mesmerised by how soft and smooth she was. All feeling of control had ebbed from the teacher and she luxuriated in being helpless in his arms. She allowed him to turn her over and he caressed her back almost like a light massage. He patted her soft round bottom before stroking her legs and putting his hand up between them at which she gave a little sigh. He pulled her bottom up higher and entered her for a third time.

This time it seemed he was finished. They lay entangled together for a bit before Miss O'Donnell, shaken by what had happened, eventually sat up and reached for her clothes. Frankie, almost courteously, handed them to her one by one and assisted her with some awkward fastenings. She silently put them back on, relieved that nothing had been torn in the struggles, and then the pair headed through the dark corridors to get out of the school. During their whole sexual encounter, not a word had passed between them but now as they moved through the school the teacher was terrified by what she had done. She felt their whole roles had reversed; she was the child and he was the adult. She turned towards him nervously but with averted gaze. 'You won't tell what we've done, Frankie. Will you?'

Frankie shook his head. 'Oh no, Miss. I woudnae. I wouldnae do that. And thanks, thanks for the drawing.'

Outside they went their separate ways into the night without saying anything further.

32

While it is true to say that Frankie learnt nothing in his last months at school, his time was not totally wasted. He had no intention of getting a job in the normal sense, but he had to do something to get money for him and his mother to live on. His immediate contemporaries, most of whom rarely worked, got by with petty thieving and break-ins, both of houses and of shops. But the risk of being caught was high, especially as those involved were not very intelligent thieves, and they operated in poor areas, so that the returns tended to be small. Still, there were always some people who held quantities of ready cash; people such as pawnbrokers and publicans, and more particularly the backstreet bookmakers (betting was illegal, of course), spivs selling rationed goods on the black market, and thieves dealing in stolen goods. These activities were themselves illegal, meaning that the police afforded no protection, indeed hounded the perpetrators. Because they dealt in cash, they were vulnerable, and so Frankie determined to target them; not to steal from them but, in return for a regular payment, to offer protection against possible theft.

First, like anyone else starting out on a career, he had to serve his apprenticeship. He attached himself to his brother, Ray's, Cumbie gang where the cut-throat razor was becoming the weapon of choice. Frankie quickly established himself as totally fearless, especially in territorial fights with other gangs where the older gang members were in awe at the way he could get involved where both sides were armed with razors, knives, chains and hatchets, almost in a trance-like state, heedless of the near certainty of severe injury. He, himself, recognised the alteration in his personality which took place in such situations; he mentally thought of it as his 'maddies'. The first time he had been aware of it was when he was involved in the beating-up of Jaikie Houliston. His breathing became deeper, and what he heard seemed to come through a tunnel but at the same time was totally clear. Everything that was happening, was happening in slow motion so that blows aimed at him were mostly, easily avoided. He had no feeling of pain when he was struck; he had no feelings when he slashed or stabbed an opponent. He felt as if he was watching his own body from above.

And then, when the crisis was over, he came back to his normal self.

Frankie's chance to branch out on his own came in 1952, when Ray was arrested following a war with another gang. He came up in court before Lord Carment, who had made a public statement that he was waging war on razor crime and accordingly sentenced Ray to seven years in prison. For Frankie, such a fate was a fact of life but for his mother, Maria, it was just another blow crushing her down. She became more and more withdrawn but, possibly because Frankie was old enough and big enough to give her support, she didn't revert to her old standby, alcohol. And she went back to her old reliance on religion, becoming a daily communicant at Mass in St Francis, where she became close to Frankie's old friend, Father O'Leary – Frankie, himself, stayed well away from any contact though.

Along with Ray, a number of other members of his gang were sentenced to various long terms of imprisonment, and most of the others were content to give up the gang life. The improving economy in the country was opening up opportunities for other things, with the result that the gang started to break up.

Frankie was now ready to step into the breach. His reputation as the hardest of hard men was established and other boys still gravitated towards him as a leader. Up till now his prospective 'clients' had received de facto protection without paying because of the existence of the Cumbie gang, but with the disintegration of the gang that umbrella had now been removed and Frankie set about persuading his customers that he would provide even better cover – at a price. He was fortunate to come across one bookie's runner, just as a member of the Calton gang was threatening him for money. In a second Frankie had grabbed the attacker and had a knife at his throat. There was no doubt in anyone's mind that Frankie would use it and the villain muttered some sort of garbled apology before he was allowed to escape with the message that this was the new Cumbie gang's territory.

After a number of like encounters, Frankie established himself as controller of the area and people were glad to sign up to pay for his protection. But it was not enough for him. Frankie had developed the view that when a client had been threatened it was not sufficient for the threat to be removed. The client wanted to see the miscreant suffering because of his conduct. Frankie would therefore have the guilty one confronted in his own area and beaten up, making sure that the client knew what had happened. In this he was totally ruthless.

This policy brought him into conflict with rival gangs, whose territory Frankie was infringing, but Frankie was happy to deal with that, confident that in any gang warfare he would come out on top and thereby cement his position. The only prominent potential clients in his own area who held out were two brothers, Mick and Willie McGinty, who owned a pub called The Innishowen, known locally as the Showen. The brothers were big men who ruled their pub with a rod of iron; if any trouble broke out, they were over the counter in a flash, wielding baseball bats to deal with the offenders. So ferocious were they, after one particularly bad stramash, that as their erstwhile customers were taken off to hospital, the local police cautioned the brothers to go a bit easier otherwise they might have to be arrested for assault.

When Frankie approached them, they laughed at him.

'You go away and play with yer toys, son,' said Mick. 'Let the grown-ups look after themselves.'

Frankie's face showed no emotion, but he was barely able to control the fit that came over him; he could feel the fury building up inside. Mick was within an ace of having his face slashed wide open with the razor Frankie now always carried. But Frankie was able to control his maddies. He turned away. There would be another day.

Frankie had no male friends close to him. He had set himself up to be different, and he was. He was tall for that part of the world and had fair hair. He didn't smoke, he didn't drink, and he didn't swear. He affected to have no interest in football or in horseracing, the main topics of discussion for the male section of his neighbourhood. Other youths approached him because they felt they needed him. He didn't need them. The only person who was constantly in his company was Jiffy, whom he had got to know in the remand home.

Jiffy was not very tall and walked with a slightly tottering step as if he was on the point of falling. His lank hair fell over his forehead and his mouth was always open in what appeared to be a half smile. Winter or summer Jiffy always wore the same shabby clothing. On one occasion Frankie pressed on him a new coat about his size but he never wore it and Frankie suspected that it was carefully put away in the hovel Jiffy shared with his grandmother. She looked after him in the absence of his parents, who had long since disappeared, if indeed his father had made anything but that one brief intervention which had given him life. Jiffy was, what was called in those days, *simple*. He suffered from an almost paralysing stutter so much so that he confined himself to the one word he could say with confidence which was 'Jiffy', his equivalent of the naval, 'Aye, Aye, Sir'. He used it with an accompanying thumbs up, to acknowledge comments. On the rare occasions that someone asked about his welfare, he was able to get as far as to say, 'Just Jiffy', but that was the best he could manage, although his speech difficulties and his general appearance hid a mind much quicker than most suspected.

Jiffy was prey to cruel abuse from those who took advantage of him but not when Frankie was around and not at all after it became generally known that Jiffy was under Frankie's protection. Frankie did not know why he looked out for Jiffy and did not question his own motives. But he did, and he made sure that Jiffy and his grandmother had enough to get by on. For his part, Jiffy was devoted to Frankie and followed him around like a dog. Whenever Frankie came out of his house Jiffy was always there waiting for him, no matter what time of the day. Indeed, Jiffy seemed at will to materialise from, then disappear into, the shadows. He was never seen alone in the street except in the company of Frankie.

In complete contrast to the way he dealt with the men in the area, Frankie was totally at ease with the women. He knew all their names and the names of their children and was happy to take part in their general gossip, which most men found boring. Obviously, this, and his mounting reputation, made him attractive to girls of his own age, but, though he took easily what was on offer, he didn't establish any close relationships, and was content to move around his female friends, offering a sympathetic ear when required. So much so, that he found himself getting involved in domestic problems either about an errant husband or a child who had gone off the rails. One word from Frankie was generally sufficient to restore matters, at least for a time.

33

There remained the problem of the McGinty brothers. Not for one second had Frankie forgotten their insulting rejection of his original approach but they were popular in the neighbourhood and their pub was a much-favoured resort for the male population. He had to do something.

One morning, when the brothers opened up for the day, Mick called up from the cellar, 'Willie, come down and look at this.'

What 'this' consisted of was a heap of children's toys piled up with a bottle of paraffin beside it and a box of matches. On top of the pile was a note saying, 'I've finished playing around with toys. I mean business.'

Mick said, 'How did that get there? If someone had set a match to that lot the whole pub would have gone up in flames...

Wait a bit.' He went upstairs and checked all the windows and doors of the premises but there was no sign of forced entry.

The brothers discussed what to do but eventually decided to call Frankie's bluff.

About a week later, Willie McGinty was having a long lie on a Saturday morning, because he had been out late closing the pub and making sure that everything was tightly locked up, when he heard the noise of his children shouting. The two youngest burst into his bedroom and dragged him downstairs.

'It's like Christmas, look, Daddy, look.'

There on the living room floor was a heap of toys piled up, with a note on the top: 'I've finished playing with toys now.'

Willie's wife and his children badgered him with questions but all he could think to say was that it must be someone playing a joke, and he persuaded them to put the toys in a box and store them. Afterwards he went round the house but again there was no sign of a break-in.

Nothing happened after that, until one night, Mick McGinty had just locked up the pub and after bidding everyone goodnight was making his way to his car when he was suddenly aware of someone emerging from the shadows.

Frankie.

'What do you want, Gilligan?'

'I thought we should have another chat, Mick.'

'I've got nothing to say to you, ya bastard.'

'Tut, tut. Do you use that sort of language at 15 Dixon Avenue?'

Mick stiffened at the reference to his house address. 'How do you know where I live?'

'I know lots of things about you, Mick. And your three lovely wee girls. They're all at St Mary's, aren't they? Doing well, I'm told. Easy now, Mick. You haven't got your baseball bat with you now. And it would be nice if you could see all the family again.'

'You bastard, you wouldn't harm little kids.'

'Mick, I could. But I wouldn't. It's more a question of whether you will be around to see them.'

And that was the last Mick knew of that night. He was struck from behind by a heavy weapon and crashed to the pavement where Frankie kicked him two or three times in the ribs – a sort of argument enforcer. He then arranged for a member of his gang to contact the police to report that there was a body in the street, and an ambulance came and took Mick to hospital.

When Mick recovered consciousness, there was a policeman by his bed who asked him what happened and who had assaulted him. Mick said he didn't know; he was making his way to his car and was struck in the darkness from behind. He was unable to give any clue as to who had hit him. Against the advice of the doctors, he discharged himself that afternoon and made his painful way to the pub where he met up with Willie.

'Willie, this guy is totally mad. I will take on anyone in a straight fight, but I couldn't kill anyone. This guy could and will kill someone. And I don't want it to be me or you or any member of our families. It's just not worth it. The next time he comes in we'll do a deal with him. It won't be by us, but he'll get his comeuppance before long. And we can enjoy it then.'

And thus, the McGintys joined Frankie's 'stable'.

Over the next few years Frankie's hold on the criminal side of the area tightened. His activities were bringing in lots of cash and he started to be approached by people looking for short-term loans. The rate of interest on these loans was enormous but most of the people who asked were small time criminals, relying on their next job and confident they would be able to repay very quickly. When Frankie made it known he was prepared to make these loans, his business spread. The normal problem in such a business – ensuring repayment – did not apply to Frankie; not after an early defaulter was found near death in the street with injuries to his arms and his legs from which he never recovered.

As a business decision, Frankie did not lend to ordinary families. There was often much demand for this, when a husband lost his job or was sent to prison, but Frankie wanted to avoid the unpleasantness of trying to enforce repayment when the borrower was already totally impoverished. He preferred to help by supplying food or clothing obtained from some of his other criminal schemes; always on the understanding that no-one should know what he had done. Sometimes, too, when there was a problem over non-payment of rent Frankie would persuade the landlord that it might be in his best interests not to pursue the debt.

He also developed another activity: running shebeens – premises stocked with liquor obtained legitimately from licensed premises but sold outwith licensing hours. The difficulty with this business was that, as it expanded, Frankie was dealing with premises away from his area, which created friction with rival gangs whose territory he was infringing and led to frequent clashes. One of these resulted in a mass battle just off Crown Street, with about one hundred people involved, all heavily armed with knives, razors, bicycle chains, axes; any weapon which could injure or maim. The noise of clashes, and shouting and swearing, and the screams of injured battlers, could be heard several streets away. Frankie, armed with a large kitchen knife in one hand and a razor in the other, was like a man possessed in the centre of the most intense fighting. His whole being was absorbed in the battle, seemingly impervious to the blows from hammers and other weapons raining down upon him.

The next day, the fight was reported widely in the papers, because not only were gang members involved, but ordinary residents were drawn in. Editorials queried why gangs were allowed to roam the streets of Glasgow without the police apparently being able to do anything? Some stated that the savage Glasgow of 'No Mean City' had returned just as the Gorbals was being redeveloped, causing the destruction of many of the old tenements.

Frankie's name was mentioned extensively since previous newspaper articles had picked him out as the leader of a new gang culture. He revelled in that, just as he had welcomed the earlier publicity. It all went to cultivate the image of the Glasgow hard man he had 'trained' for, going through the process of learning just like someone pursuing a normal education. He had been through Remand and Detention Centres, Approved School, Borstal and finally Barlinnie, feeding off the knowledge of those who had preceded him and thus earning their respect.

And all the time he was pursued relentlessly by his old police enemy, Sam McCulloch, now Chief Superintendent Samuel McCulloch.

McCulloch took great delight in arresting Frankie for his part in this latest brawl but was furious when Frankie, with the help of his old mentor, Pat McLaughlin, received a sentence of only eighteen months imprisonment. While there were police witnesses, (strangely no non-police witnesses could be found) that told Frankie was involved, the prosecution was not able to produce any evidence that he had struck any blows or that he was in fact a ringleader, which McCulloch knew was the case.

When Frankie came out of prison McCulloch set up a campaign of harassment against him: constantly having him stopped and questioned; having him brought into the station when there was no reason; exposing him to being searched in as public a place as possible. Superintendent McCulloch's men knew he was out to get Frankie and that the one who nailed him would significantly further his police career.

About four months after Frankie came out of Barlinnie, there was a call to the police station of a break-in at the McGinty brothers' pub, with someone answering Frankie's description being seen in the vicinity. Superintendent McCulloch immediately sent a squad of officers round to Frankie's flat to bring him in for questioning. Frankie, by this time, was tired of the constant harassment and, when the policemen ignored his protest that he had been nowhere near the place, he refused to go with them voluntarily, making it necessary for them to manhandle him out of the flat door. When they reached the top of the stairs, one of the policemen surrounding Frankie tripped as he backed down the stairs and fell down the stone steps dragging Frankie with him. They both fell heavily but Frankie landed clear, although injuring both his arms. The policeman, who was a big man, crashed down much more awkwardly and collided headfirst with the stone wall of the stair landing. Frankie gingerly got to his feet, but the other policemen were more concerned about their colleague who lay motionless with his head at an unnatural angle, blood pouring from his mouth. Frankie went back up the stair to fetch a towel from the flat to help to stench the flow of blood. He then stood watching as the other officers bent over the stricken policeman. Someone had called for an ambulance and the officer was carried down the close in a stretcher with no sign of life. When one of the other policemen told Frankie that he had better come to the station with them, he had no hesitation in agreeing but it was a very subdued group who made their way there.

At the station Frankie waited at the front desk until the news came through that the injured policeman had died. He was speaking quietly about the tragedy to the desk sergeant when Chief Superintendent McCulloch came in. To Frankie's astonishment he came up to him and formally charged him with the murder of Police Constable James Murray while he was in the course of carrying out his duties. He formally cautioned Frankie and then ordered him to be taken down to the cells. Frankie protested that it was an accident, but McCulloch ignored him, and he was taken away.

Alone in his office a few minutes later McCulloch sat at his desk, then pounded it with his fist. 'Got him, got him, got him. And it's still a capital offence. He'll hang for this. Got the cocky bastard.'

PART THREE

34

As Sarah ate her breakfast on her first day of her new job, she idly flicked through The Glasgow Herald, a paper not much read in Edinburgh but one she thought she should take now that she was in Glasgow. She had lost the interest in current affairs she had developed in Edinburgh, where she had involved herself heavily in protests against the invasion of Suez and had taken to the streets in solidarity for the Hungarian up-rising. These no longer dominated the news although there were still repercussions dragging on. The main national news was about Harold MacMillan's endeavours to revive the Tory Party after Anthony Eden's resignation, something with which Sarah had little sympathy. She turned to local news, but the only item which caught her eye was of a notorious Glasgow gang leader called Frankie Gilligan, who had been found not guilty at the High Court of killing a Glasgow policeman in the course of a brawl. This was of no interest to her but obviously was important to the paper's readers as the paper devoted two whole pages to the trial and to recounting Gilligan's past criminal history. With nothing else newsworthy in the paper, she laid it to one side and set out for her new office.

Sarah's sad disillusionment with her new office hadn't dispersed, but as the morning wore on, she found herself a bit more relaxed. The secretarial staff went out of their way to get to know her – although they themselves were slightly ill at ease about how to treat her. For a start there was her Edinburgh accent, which sounded slightly 'toffee' to Glasgow ears (Sarah herself had difficulties with the girls' Glasgow accents, one girl, Rose, in particular being almost incomprehensible to her) but more importantly there was the difficulty of how to place her in the office social scale. Legal apprentices had always been, like Alastair Clarke, young males, and so easily placed in the hierarchy: someone to be socialised with on a special occasion like the Christmas night-out, but not someone who shared the domestic and family interests of the other members of staff. Would Sarah share these concerns? And there was the further consideration that she was known to regard the senior active partner in the office as her uncle. Would she perhaps be a spy in their midst, reporting back to Pat McLaughlin on their grievances and other matters which they would prefer to keep from their bosses' ears?

Luckily for Sarah there was something totally engrossing the whole office that morning. She speedily found out that the office had acted for this Frankie Gilligan she had read about in the paper, and all staff from the senior partner down to the young junior were agog with the news of his acquittal. For Sarah, the news was exciting. To be connected to something which had had such publicity in the papers! She had a feeling of great importance and being at the centre of things and could not wait to tell her Auntie Annie all about it.

She was puzzled, however, by the staff reaction. It was good for the office to have been instrumental in such a result but was this Frankie Gilligan not a vicious gang leader with the long list of convictions set out in the newspaper?

Eventually Janet, the head typist, explained. 'Frankie Gilligan, to us, is not a notorious criminal. He's someone who, whenever he comes into the office, always brings chocolates for us. He always makes a point of sitting down to have a cup of tea with us. He's even got his own mug. He chats away about our families and the latest love interests of the younger girls. He even makes a point of remembering the birthdays of the girls' children and sometimes brings presents for them. That's the Frankie Gilligan we know. And maybe we just ignore the bad things he does or is accused of doing.'

Pat McLaughlin confirmed that there was this strange contradiction in Frankie's nature, and he could only put it down to the nature of Boxy, Frankie's father. 'He was a boyhood friend of mine,' said Pat, 'and was one of the most charming men I've ever known. My involvement with Frankie Gilligan, had come about only because of my friendship with my old friend – and no, I've no idea why he was called 'Boxy'.' Pat shook his head. 'Apart from that,' he went on, 'the firm does little or no criminal work but concentrates rather on civil court practice, in particular reparation claims' (Pat saw Sarah's look of confusion and explained that was how damages cases were referred to) 'for workers in the big iron and steel works in Lanarkshire who are injured in the course of their employment.

'But I never want to go through again the strain of such a trial as Frankie's. To know that you hold someone's very life in your hands, dependant on your presenting his defence without mistake, feeling that if you make one error, or fail to follow up one piece of evidence, it might prove fatal, is a weight of responsibility which totally grinds you down. Never, never, again.'

After that, Pat told Sarah to go down to the Ordinary Court that morning with the Procurator (what did *he* do, she wondered?) who was called James Armstrong, but meantime she should talk to Alastair Clarke, her fellow apprentice.

Alistair had started his apprenticeship two months before Sarah came and with the advantage of two whole months experience and being a male, patiently explained for the benefit of Sarah's weaker female brain the complexities of the Court system she would have to learn leaving Sarah with a notebook bulging with new technical words.

Meantime, she was more concerned she had made a mistake on the timing of the Ordinary Court, which she was to attend with the – Procurator? She was sure it was due to start at eleven o'clock but here it was already ten minutes to eleven and there was no sign of him making a move. Sarah hung about in the corridor outside his room until eventually he rushed out, clad in what appeared to be morning clothes (pin-stripe trousers, black jacket and waistcoat) and, beckoning her to follow him, raced for the lift, leaving her to carry his brief case and his Sheriff Court gown. Once outside, he put both fingers in his mouth and produced the most piercing whistle, which made every taxi driver within a hundred yards leap to attention. The two of them jumped in the first car to respond and sped off the short distance to the Sheriff Court building on Ingram Street. A quick burst up the stairs and the Procurator had put on his gown and they were taking their seats in the Court just as the Court Usher announced the arrival of the Sheriff on the bench with a stentorian cry of 'Court'.

The proceedings lasted about an hour, during which Sarah had no idea what was going on. About twenty cases were dealt with, including one featuring James who rose to his feet when his case called, said that he had instructions to appear also for the Defendants in the case and asked the Court to allow a further three weeks for both parties to adjust their pleadings, to which the Sheriff consented. It intrigued Sarah that all the lawyers when addressing the Sheriff didn't use simple pronouns. It was always "Your Lordship" or "My Lord" or "His Lordship". She thought this sounded quite respectful and, she supposed, courtly.

When the proceedings were finished James took Sarah across the road to a small restaurant in what was a wholesale warehouse called 'Glens', where apparently the Court lawyers gathered before or after their court appearances, and where James treated her to a coffee and a scone. James introduced her to those who were there, all men, and who, she felt, regarded her with interest partly because it was unusual to have a female Law Apprentice, but partly also just because she was a woman whom the mostly young lawyers could not help but size up.

She picked up two further pieces of information when she was there. The word 'Procurator' in non-criminal matters merely meant a qualified solicitor who was not a partner in a legal firm but was employed by the firm to handle Court matters. And the gown which they wore in Court was not an academic gown but a specifically Sheriff Court Gown, without which the presiding Sheriff would not permit a solicitor to appear before him.

Sarah had just time for a quick lunch before returning to the office, where she was immediately sent back down to the Process Room in the Sheriff Court to lodge the bound papers called a Process relating one of the Firm's cases. This, Alistair told her later, was where much of the administration of the Ordinary Court took place and was presided over by what seemed to be a dragon of a middle-aged woman who did not appear to look at Sarah with much favour. When she returned to the office, she was immediately sent straight back to the Court House this time with a package for the Commissary Office – something to do with catering, Sarah imagined.

Back in the office once more, she was dispatched to the Faculty Library (faculty? she scribbled it down) with a letter of introduction as the new Apprentice for Shaw McLaughlin & Co, which gave her the facility to use the library for research and to borrow books on behalf of the firm. The Faculty Library was situated at a corner of St George's Place behind the Tron Church and was much more the type of establishment which Sarah had imagined would be her working environment. On the ground floor there was a grand meeting room with large windows looking on to the street. From the vestibule outside, there was a broad marble staircase leading on to an upstairs landing from which, by pushing open an impressively heavy door, Sarah found herself in another large rectangular room with a beautifully decorated plastered ceiling supported by what appeared to be marble pillars. There were large windows along one of the long sides and at each end, and the length of the room was split by bookcases filled with expensively bound books, which divided the sides of the room into a number of recesses with tables, chairs and reading lamps. Down the middle ran a large ornate table, lined with carved chairs, above which a number of chandeliers provided additional lighting.

'This is more like it,' Sarah murmured, but she was a bit unsure of herself as she entered the library, which was totally hushed although there were four or five people working at various tables. She stood a little diffidently before she was approached by a tall man with a slightly forbidding look, who appeared from some hidden door. She trembled a little as she handed him her letter of introduction from the firm but, having read it, he turned to her in a much friendlier manner than she expected from his appearance, explained that he was the chief librarian and welcomed her to the use of the library, saying that she should not hesitate to call on him if she ever had a problem with what books to consult. She was sufficiently put at her ease to smile at him and she handed him the list of books which she was to borrow on behalf of the firm. He went around the library with her showing where she should expect to find the books she wanted, which were all leather-bound collections of reported judgements in decided cases. He explained, with a smile, that although the collections were prepared on an annual basis, in older collections, just to confuse the public, they were often referred to by reference to the editor who had collected the judgments, following his year of collection, so that, for example a reference to 4 Rettie 206 meant the case report was to be found on Page 206 of the fourth year of Mr Rettie's collection for that year. More notes for Sarah's notebook!

The librarian entered up the books she was borrowing, and she loaded them into the large bag she had luckily brought with her, as they were both bulky and heavy. When she got back to the office, she was immediately told to look out an old file and Rose, the office junior, the girl whose accent Sarah had completely failed to penetrate, took her out of the office, down two flights, to a room at the back of the building where there were shelves of dusty files arranged in a manner which Sarah didn't understand but with which Rose was obviously familiar as she found the required file immediately. She told Sarah solemnly that it was of vital importance that the file was, in due course, replaced in the correct position and Sarah promised faithfully that she would do so as Rose clearly took pride in carrying out her filing responsibilities diligently.

Back upstairs, Sarah was captured by one of the typists who asked her to compare with her a five-page document which was a clean copy (an 'engrossment': another new word for the book) of an original draft which Sarah read out while the other girl checked the engrossment. Sarah was astonished, and thereafter never ceased to be astonished, how a skilled typist was able to produce typed foolscap page after page without a single mistake.

When that was done Sarah was called upon to assist in collecting the signed letters of the day which were to be posted, putting them in envelopes, (making sure that all relevant enclosures were inserted), stamping them with the correct stamp, which involved either licking the back of the stamps which was messy or using a little sort of wheel which was fiddly), and finally putting them in the postbag for Rose to take to the Post Office.

And then, at 5.45, Sarah's first day at the office was finished.

She walked up the hill and along Sauchiehall Street to her flat, where, having kicked off her shoes, she put on a kettle for a cup of tea. Unfortunately, while waiting for the kettle to boil, she sat down and promptly fell fast asleep in the chair. She woke up about two hours later and chided herself for not staying awake. She made some scrambled eggs and toast, then turned on the wireless to listen to the Nine O'Clock News. Before the end of it, however she found she could hardly keep her eyes open and she was fast asleep in bed by quarter to ten.

She slept soundly but at one stage had a dream in which rolls of papers tied with red tape chased her down some city lane shouting, 'Where's your Process?' until she ran into a gentleman in a frock coat and top hat who said his name was Rettie and asked her in which page in his fifth volume the case of Simpson - v - Ritchie's Trustees was to be found. Sarah was sure she ought to know and she was racking her brain when she was interrupted in her thoughts by the dragon from the Process Room approaching from a hidden close, yelling, 'You haven't lodged your Process yet!'

And then she woke up and it was morning.

35

Sarah's legal course at the University was not due to start until the beginning of October and she spent the four weeks up till then working full-time in the office. She was gradually getting the hang of what went on and understanding the strange words they used, although there seemed to be new ones every day. She now knew, for example that the Commissary Office had nothing to do with catering but was the office in the Court dealing with the supervision of the winding up of the estates of people who had died. And, no, not everyone who died had lived in a large house with extensive grounds and a gatehouse. 'Estate' merely meant the sum total of what the dead person had owned at date of death even though it might be as little as a few pounds.

She began to sprinkle these new words more confidently into her conversation, which gave her a sense of being part of an exclusive group, completely separate from the ordinary public. She even made her first Court appearance. As Alastair Clarke had explained to her, the Small Debt Court was routinely presided over, not by a Sheriff but by a Sheriff Clerk, and Law Apprentices were entitled to make appearances in formal proceedings.

The Court was a large room with an elevated bench where the Sheriff sat, if called upon, in front of which was a table and chairs for the Sheriff Clerk and his assistants, with the rest of the room filled with rows of benches. Apart from the first two rows reserved for legal representatives, the benches were normally occupied by those Defenders who had bothered to turn up and who, to Sarah's eye, were uniformly poor and downtrodden. The Court did not appear to have been decorated this century and the lighting was poor, apart from round the Sheriff Clerk's table. Added to that there appeared to be dust everywhere, swirling round the dim lights so that the whole atmosphere was totally depressing.

Sarah had only to say a few words but, as she sat there, waiting for her case to be called, her heart was beating in her breast, and she went over time and time again what she had to say. Eventually her case was called. She rose to her feet and said as confidently as she could, that she appeared for the Pursuers. She had been assured that the Defender would not turn up, but she had a sudden fear that he might and realised, in a panic, that she had no idea what to do if he did. Luckily, he didn't, and the Sheriff Clerk said, 'Decree' and moved on to the next case without even looking up.

As a first appearance it was not exactly a baptism of fire, but, in anticipation, she had worked herself up to such a pitch that it was only after a coffee and scone in Glen's that she completely calmed down. At least, she thought, she had hidden her nerves from the experienced lawyers around her.

Most mornings she spent in the Ordinary Court. When purely formal motions were to be made the firm often didn't bother to send the Procurator down but gave Sarah instructions to pass on to any of the lawyers who were present in the Court that day to appear on the firm's behalf. As a number of the lawyers had been apprentices with Shaw McLaughlin, that did not usually present any difficulty except on one occasion when one of the Sheriffs, notorious for his short temper, refused the request to continue Sarah's case for further adjustment although both parties were agreeable to it. Luckily the lawyer whom Sarah had asked to appear was the famously silken tongued Paddy O'Donnell who, without knowing anything whatsoever about the case, was able by elegantly-phrased generalities, to confuse the Sheriff so much that he allowed the motion.

Sarah was profuse in her thanks.

'No problem,' said Paddy. 'He's just had too much to drink last night. You can do the same for me sometime, Sarah.'

Sarah, marvelling at his fluency, wondered whether she would ever achieve that level of composure. She was delighted at the outcome but even more so at the fact that he remembered her name.

On one occasion, coming back from Court, Sarah was in the office lift, just about to go up, when there was a shout of 'Hold the lift' and a young man rushed in. Sarah felt there was an etiquette in lifts where there is an unusual situation of a small number of people who don't know each other crammed together in close proximity in a confined space. For her, this involved keeping her gaze down and she did this as the lift clanked its slow way upwards.

'How're you this morning, Mr Gilligan?' said the lift attendant and Sarah realised for the first time who it was who had rushed into the lift.

'Never better, Billy,' said Gilligan. 'Yourself?'

'Och, the old hip is still killing me, but at least I'm still this side of the sod.'

'That's all those midgie walls you jumped off as a wee boy. You should have stuck to peever.'

'You could be right. Still, never mind.'

'God, this must be the slowest lift on God's earth.'

'Right enough. But it's like me. It gets there in the end.'

While this conversation was going on Sarah was covertly examining Gilligan who was in front of her. He was smartly dressed in a suit with collar and tie and she noticed that his fair hair at the back was neatly cut. Under his arm there was a carefully folded copy of what looked like the Evening Times. When the lift eventually jolted to a halt on the top floor, he rushed out without looking at her and went through the door into the office without holding it open for her.

'Hmm,' Sarah said to herself. 'So much for the charming Mr Gilligan.'

Her work in the office kept Sarah fully occupied during the week and up till lunchtime on the Saturday. But how was she to fill her leisure time? Pat McLaughlin had made it clear that, while he and his wife would have been delighted to have her at their home, he thought it would be bad for office discipline and indeed for her position in the office if she was known to be socialising with the senior partner. Sarah, herself, felt that although it might seem to be snobbery (it was) it would be inappropriate for her to associate with the secretarial staff. The only other person was Alastair Clarke but, although she was coming to realise that he was not as unpleasant as some of his comments made him appear, just socially awkward, she did not think for a minute that they should do anything together outwith the office. There was really no-one.

But Sarah was not unhappy. She enjoyed being her own boss in her flat and, when she closed the door, she felt secure. One thing was certain – she had no intention of returning to Edinburgh, even for a short visit. But she did feel morally obligated to her mother, perhaps more than that, as the salary paid by Shaw

McLaughlin & Co was a paltry £3 per week which was in line with what other apprentices received but not enough to live on, so she relied on a further weekly allowance from her mother to make ends meet. Accordingly, one weekend she arranged for her mother and her Auntie Annie to come through to stay the Saturday night, as she knew they were desperate to see how she was faring and how she had her flat organised – even though it involved her in having to go to Mass on the Sunday so as not to scandalise them. If she was honest, although she enjoyed their visit, she was quite pleased to see them go.

Apart from that, the habit of reading, developed in childhood, stood her in good stead. In addition to her own books, she could use the nearby Mitchell Library, which although not a borrowing library had an enormous store of books she could access in the cavernous Reading Room. It was there she came across a biography of John Adams, the second President of the United States, which reminded her of the quotation Pat McLaughlin had sent her, which had inspired her greatly. In reading through it she came across a piece of advice Adams had given to his son. 'You will never be alone with a poet in your pocket.' This appealed to the bookish Sarah and thereafter she always carried with her a little leather-bound copy of Palgrave's Golden Treasury.

She also had the wireless to turn to; the combination of the Home Programme, the Light Programme and the Third

Programme covering all her interests. She never now turned to the Voice of America Radio station in Tangiers. Even the thought of it brought back hurtful memories.

Thus, Sarah was often alone but she was never lonely. She relished the anonymity which living in a big city brought her.

36

When the time came for Sarah to start her new degree, she
went up to the University with Alastair to matriculate in the Bute
Hall – this time resisting all attempts to enrol her by the various
student clubs whose stalls thronged the room. She felt she would
have enough to do with her time, as her course involved two hours
of lectures starting at eight o'clock in the morning with Roman Law
followed by Forensic Medicine, then back to the office to work
during the day, followed by two more hours of lectures starting at
four o'clock, with Scottish Legal System and rounding off the day
with an hour of Mercantile Law.

The Roman Law class was held, like most of the others in a
large lecture room. Rows of dark wooden bench seating rose in an
amphitheatre from the floor where the lecturers' table was situated,
with the back of the benches forming a working surface for the

benches behind. When she entered the room for the first time, she found herself amidst about forty students, only one other being female; and it was beside her that Sarah took her place. She wondered later whether, had the roles been reversed and it was two men in a class of women, the two men would have sat together. She decided that they would have but they wouldn't have sat in the front row as the two girls did.

She introduced herself to the other girl who was called Gwendoline Kinniburgh. She had a quiet demeanour, pale faced with a high forehead under straight fair hair. Sarah later found out that she was popularly believed to be a Quaker, purely on the basis of her looks and while the men, when addressing her, used her first name, when talking about her, she was always referred to as Miss Kinniburgh. Sarah was not given the same distinction.

In this first lecture, the lecturer, Dr Thomas, who had a high-pitched drawly English accent, explained something Sarah did not know, namely that Scots Law, unlike English Law, drew much of its fundamental principles from Roman Law– the reason why the study of Roman Law was such a prominent part of the curriculum. The only comparable jurisdiction was South Africa which had retained its Roman Law connection after the native Dutch Law from which it was derived was subsumed by the Napoleonic Code.

Sarah liked Latin, in which she had distinguished herself at school; she loved its conciseness and logicality. She had already come across numerous Latin phrases in her work in the office: 'Brevitatis causa', 'forum non conveniens', 'dies non' – more for her notebook, and so many little things separating lawyers from ordinary members of the public. It crossed her mind what a comparison there was between the elegant gentility of the educated learning she was imbibing, and the crude brutal world of which Frankie Gilligan was king.

After Dr Thomas finished there was a ten-minute break before the next lecturer came in. This was the famous (at least in his eyes) Professor Glaister. He was the author of a much-used textbook on Forensic Medicine and, to Sarah's relief after the somewhat dry Dr Thomas, he was a fascinating lecturer. Although, in her view, it was a subject about which it would have hard to be boring, as it seemed to combine gruesome images and violent crime with detective work to rival the best efforts of Agatha Christie.

Professor Glaister started, 'In my first lecture, I want to look at injuries caused by knives and like sharp weapons and how, from examination of the wound we can tell much about the type of weapon, whether the assailant was right or left-handed, and even the assailant's height. Many murderers leave their calling cards merely by reason of the weapons they use.'

Sarah was fascinated, her mind irresistibly drawn back to Frankie Gilligan, and the injuries he must have inflicted on those who opposed him – information she had derived chiefly from the local newspapers. (Sarah found it invigorating that, in contrast to her studies in Edinburgh, here she was learning about activities that formed part of her day-to-day life.) Since their encounter in the lift she had seen Frankie Gilligan in the office on about four or five occasions. She had no idea why he was there, but he always appeared impeccably dressed, with that day's edition of the Evening Times folded under his arm, which he left with Pat McLaughlin after his meeting. Sarah was frightened of Frankie, although he had given her no cause for that... No, she was not frightened, she corrected herself just ill-at-ease, restless. He seemed to her such a menacing figure. Whenever they met in the office corridor her only response was a short nod to which he would respond with a half-smile, as if he was not sure how to take her...

...And Frankie did not know how to take Sarah. He wanted to talk to her, but he didn't know how to start. She seemed stand-offish, but he felt instinctively that she was someone he could talk to and even someone who might appreciate talking to him. All he was certain about was that he liked it if their paths crossed when he came into the office. He wasn't so aware that he sometimes made an unnecessary trip to the office on the chance that he might meet her.

Frankie's office visits were mainly due to his concern about his mother. With his sister dead and his brother, Ray, in Barlinnie, he was having difficulty dealing with his mother's failing health, although one good thing was that her dependence on alcohol had been replaced with a reliance on religion. This, he did not share, but he had, however, gone back on his determination to have nothing further to do with the Father O'Leary who had visited him in the Remand Home. Frankie still had reservations about the rotund priest, but then he was wary about everyone; it was the way he survived in his environment. He was grateful (perhaps too strong a word, he wondered) to him; he appreciated the time the priest took in visiting his mother, and she certainly did, too.

The first thing Frankie had done when he was discharged from the Court in his murder trial was to go home and let his mother cook him an enormous breakfast. The second was to visit the flat of an old girlfriend, to spend the rest of the day luxuriating in the warmth and softness of her arms and her bed. After months of exclusively male, mostly rough, company he relished stroking the gentle smoothness of her skin. Although they made love numerous times during the day (the first time more like an explosion) most of the time he slept, as the strain of the last few months slowly eased out of his body.

The third thing Frankie did was to get back on the streets. When he emerged from his girlfriend's house there was Wee Jiffy, waiting to meet him as usual. Jiffy told him that, from the time of his arrest, one of the men on the street, Billy Morton, had presumed that Frankie would be facing a lengthy prison sentence and had taken steps to muscle in on Frankie's various interests. That had to be dealt with.

The first thing that Morton knew that Frankie was back was when his face was smashed against the sandstone wall of a tenement, breaking his nose. Frankie turned him round, pressing him back on the tenement wall, with a razor at his throat.

'I'm told that you've been looking after my business when I've been away. That's good of you, Billy. But now I'm back, I'll tell you what's going to happen. You are going to tell Wee Jiffy, here, where you keep your loot – you know, the money you've earned while I've been away, and you are going to give him all necessary keys for him to get his hands on it. While he is doing that, you and I are going to have a little chat somewhere quieter.'

It took Wee Jiffy about an hour to return with the money, to a neighbourhood square (hardly a 'square', just an open area where there were a few run-down shops), outside of which women gathered for a chat amongst themselves and with those leaning out of the tenement windows. Frankie soon appeared, dragging Morton with him. In addition to his broken nose, Morton was now limping badly and one of his arms hung loose where his shoulder had been dislocated.

'Hey, ladies,' said Frankie. 'Nice to be back home. Billy, here, has been very busy while I have been away, and he is now going for a holiday to recover. Somewhere very far from Glasgow. A long holiday. In fact, I would be disappointed if you saw him around for a long time. Now, a holiday is an expensive business. What have you got there, Jiffy? Good. That'll cover the cost of the holiday.'

There was a gasp from the women and a scream from Morton as Frankie turned to him and with a quick flick of a razor, cut a two-inch gash on his cheek out of which the blood oozed.

'That's just to remind you of us, Billy. And to warn you to stay out of the sun. Now get out of my sight and don't come back.'

As Morton limped away, the women were shocked by what they had seen, but they slowly gathered round Frankie to congratulate him on his acquittal. They felt pity for Morton but no sympathy because, in Frankie's absence, Morton had speedily become unpopular by reason of the brutal way he had operated in the district.

Frankie's involvement in the killing of a policeman had given him additional notoriety, a notoriety he did not relish. Although many of his associates hated all policemen as the enemy and had done so since they were boys on the street, Frankie did not share their views. He detested Superintendent McCulloch and with good cause, but he regarded policemen, on the whole, as just doing their job, which happened to be in conflict with what he chose to do. If they were brutal in carrying out their duties, it was merely a reflection of the sphere in which they operated. Most of what

Frankie did was illegal but was countenanced by the people he lived amongst. If Frankie was able to provide, say, whisky, at price below that charged by the normal providers, they didn't ask too many questions. Violence, although extreme at times, was directed mostly at others carrying on the same activities as he did. They expected it as he expected it in return. He was on amicable terms with most of the local police force and bitterly regretted the death of the policeman, whom he had known slightly. He was angered by the way in which the incident had been played up by the local press, anxious for a headline, but he was scarcely in a position to protest.

By virtue of Frankie's way of life, he had no friends apart from Wee Jiffy, and he didn't really regard Wee Jiffy as a friend. He was just someone who was always there, whom he looked after, and who repaid Frankie's care with a dogged devotion. And he wouldn't have said that Father O'Leary was a friend. He had never taken up the priest's invitation to visit him in the chapel house, but he talked to him if he happened to be at home whenever the priest came to visit his mother.

By this time Frankie had found a bigger flat for himself and his mother. It was still in the same area; his mother would not have dreamt of moving out of the parish and he needed to be close to the centre of his operations. It was on the ground floor of the tenement, which was easier for his mother, and had two bedrooms, a living room, a separate kitchen and, wonder of wonders, after

Frankie had made some alterations, a bathroom with a bath and hot running water. It was sparely but comfortably furnished, the main items being Sheila's sewing machine and one of the new television sets which Frankie had obtained for his mother through his connections.

But shortly after they moved house, Frankie suffered a grievous blow. His brother, Ray, had always been someone Frankie looked up to. To some extent Frankie had modelled himself on Ray as there was no other father figure in his life. Now Frankie learned that Ray, who, as a long-term prisoner, had been moved to Peterhead Prison, had been the victim of a fatal stabbing. It had been done in the usual prison way, in a corridor with two of the assailants in front and two behind. As soon as the blow was struck the knife was passed to one of those at the front who hid in it a safe place before the prison officers were even aware that the stabbing had taken place. No-one could be found who had seen it happen and the authorities were not too assiduous in trying to track down the murderer. If these thugs wanted to take each other out it was no real concern of the establishment, so long as no blame could be attached to any of the prison staff.

The reason for Ray's stabbing, no-one knew, and no-one seemed to care. Except for Frankie. He made enquiries through his connections and was reasonably certain that the killers were members of their rivals, the Calton Boys.

There was nothing to be done immediately but the time would come.

Frankie did not tell his mother about Ray's death. She had never visited Ray in prison and Frankie saw no good in distressing her by telling her of her elder son's death. She had had enough sorrows to deal with. At least she was now in a more comfortable place to be living in and for that reason Frankie was more often there when Father O'Leary came to call on his mother, which he did more often as, with deteriorating health that Frankie chose to ignore, Maria became less and less able to go out to her daily Mass, meaning that the priest had to come to the flat to give her Communion. Although the little round priest was there to see Frankie's mother, such was his unquenchable enthusiasm that Frankie could not help but get drawn into conversation with him about anything the priest's lively mind turned to, especially things like politics and books, things Frankie would never have discussed with anyone else in the area.

A book was something new to Frankie. Although both his parents were well-educated, by virtue of their alcoholism they had paid little regard to his schooling, while Frankie's attention at school was at best perfunctory. Despite this, almost by a form of osmosis, he did pick up enough learning to enable him to read reasonably well but, apart from schoolbooks, his reading was confined to the daily newspapers. He never consciously held a book in his hands.

When Frankie, in the course of a chat with Father O'Leary, mentioned this, quite matter-of-factly and without any show of reluctance, the priest was astonished. Frankie explained that, in his way of life, books were not a necessity, or indeed particularly desirable. Father O'Leary would not have described himself as a great reader, but the thought of a world lived without books was beyond his ken. Especially for someone like Frankie who, the priest recognised, had a fine intelligence despite his lack of schooling and the way he lived.

He decided to try to do something about this and the next time they met he handed Frankie a somewhat battered copy of 'The Citadel' a book by a writer called A J Cronin who, the priest explained, came from their part of the world and had latterly gone to school at St Aloysius College. He said to Frankie that he must have some free time when he wasn't 'aburgling', a Gilbert and Sullivan reference which the priest should have known was right over Frankie's head and which he rather resented anyway as that was not the way he operated. But he took the book anyway and promised to try it.

He did try it and, to his astonishment, became totally absorbed in it. So much so that, when he saw at the beginning of the book a list of the other books the man had written, he decided that he would try to get copies to read. By chance, when he was still full of the book, he was carrying with him, he was in Pat McLaughlin's office and he heard the secretaries discussing the latest Gregory Peck film. One of the girls said,

'But did you not see him in 'The Keys of the Kingdom? Wasn't he dishy in that black sort of gown they wear?'

While the girls were discussing the general dishy-ness of Gregory Peck, Frankie had a quick look at the booklist at the front of his book and, sure enough, there was 'The Keys of the Kingdom' listed as by A J Cronin. And then a dim memory came back to him of when he was about ten, sneaking into a film with Gregory Peck as a priest. It was very dark and quite violent, but he never found out what happened in the film as the cinema manager pounced on him and his friends and turfed them out long before the end.

When he went in to see Pat, he mentioned the coincidence to him. To his surprise Pat said, 'I remember him at school. He was much older than I was but, at one time he lived in Dumbarton, and my parents knew his mother, so that I knew what he looked like. He was also, like me, a big supporter of Dumbarton, the football club. I think he was in his final two years at school when I was in the primary. He was a great footballer. I remember that. I think three or four of his books were made into films. I've got some of his books in the house. I'll bring them in for you.'

They then went on to discuss the business which had brought Frankie in, but he was in a reflective mood when he left. To think that Pat knew someone who could write books, and books that were made into films. If things had worked out differently, he, Frankie, might have followed his father into St Aloysius College and might have met people who would write books. Might have written books himself. Instead of… Frankie shook off the thought. He would have to play with the cards he had been dealt. But the thought often returned whenever he encountered boys coming down the hill from St Aloysius after their school day had ended.

By chance, Sarah also was a big fan of A J Cronin. In the convent she had asked one of the more approachable nuns to recommend novels she should read. The nun expressed a lack of enthusiasm about novels in general, preferring the Lives of the Saints for recreational reading, but if Sarah had to read a novel, she could read a book by A J Cronin who was a Catholic author. When pressed, the nun expressed grave reservations about Evelyn Waugh, who was a sort of wishy-washy Catholic. As for Graham Greene, whom Sarah had never heard of, he was supposed to be a Catholic but was a disgrace. Helped by this advice, Sarah proceeded to read as many books by A J Cronin, Evelyn Waugh and Graham Greene as she could lay her hands on.

Sarah was thus able to ignore the nuns' advice on reading matter. What she was unable to disregard was the nuns making her use her right hand for writing instead of the left hand which came naturally to her. Through time, she adjusted to the change, but in some strange way it blocked off the drawing skills which she had shown as a primary pupil and she gradually lost the habit of drawing in her spare time.

Frankie was different. He, too, was left-handed but at school it was doubtful if any of the teachers noticed or, indeed, cared. The exception was the art teacher, Miss O'Donnell, who recognised that Frankie had some artistic talent and encouraged him to practise it. His most prized possession, not that he gathered many possessions, remained the sketch which the teacher had made of him and which she presented to him that memorable day he left school. Using that as a guide he began to make sketches of his own and found that he became totally immersed when he was concentrating on his drawing. He never showed the end results to anyone and, of course, would never have confessed to what he was doing.

37

Sarah was enjoying her first year at Glasgow University. Step by step she felt more comfortable in leaving her flat and mixing with other people and this was reflected in the change in her daily clothing. When she first came to Glasgow, and for some time thereafter, her outdoor clothing was always finished off with an all-encompassing almost ankle-length overcoat or, if it was wet – and being Glasgow it often was – an equally long trench coat, both unconsciously designed to conceal the feminine outlines of her figure. The girls in the office used to tease her a little about this but at University, where a certain eccentricity was almost expected, her clothing passed without comment.

Then gradually, perhaps mirroring the approach of spring, she began to adopt a less subdued lifestyle. And as the weather improved, instead of taking the tram up to Gilmorehill, she started to go on foot, walking along the grand sandstone terraces of Woodside Place and then through Kelvingrove Park up the hill to the University.

Coming back from University was a more collective affair. Apart from Miss Kinniburgh, who was doing her apprenticeship with a legal firm in Milngavie and who quietly departed there after the lectures, the students were all apprenticed to firms in the centre of Glasgow and descended en bloc, using the tram from its terminus outside the Men's Union. Originally, they congregated first for a coffee in the Refectory which was part of the University cloisters, then they started to use the Men's Union, which was more comfortable but at which Sarah had to be signed in as only male students could be members. The Union had the additional advantage that there they could meet up with such of their colleagues who had missed the last lecture either through bad timekeeping or (and there were regulars in this category) disinclination. Later, some of the students had the use of cars or had managed to purchase a second (or third or fourth) hand one, and they drove down to town in grossly overloaded vehicles, stopping on the way at a shop at Charing Cross that had an upstairs tearoom with a roaring fire, especially attractive in the winter months.

Because they shared so much, studying the same subjects, working in the same sort of environment, they were a close-knit group. Sarah had found it easier to fit in at first because of her fellow apprentice, Alastair Clarke, as it was natural for the two of them to travel back to town together. But soon she became accepted for herself whether or not Alastair was there.

They were a more mature group than her previous student colleagues in Edinburgh. Apart from herself, they were all MA graduates from Glasgow. At that time young men were required to do a two-year period of National Service. It was possible to delay this until after obtaining a degree, which the majority of the students had done, but some had elected to do their service after their MA but before embarking on their LLB and were thus that much older and much more worldly than their colleagues. One student had been a schoolteacher before deciding to study law. Another, Callum Fraser, Sarah found out later, had been at a seminary studying to become a priest, before, as he explained, his sins had found him out or he had found out about sin.

Like all students, they talked endlessly (or so thought their employers waiting for them to arrive at work) about their work, about books, and, most passionately, about politics. By chance that year one of their number was President of the University Conservative Club and one was President of the University Labour Club. There was even one who was heavily involved in Scottish Nationalism and who was an apprentice in the legal office of John MacCormick, a leading figure in the nascent campaign for Scottish

Independence. Possibly because they were that bit more intellectual or perhaps out of deference to Sarah's presence, there was little discussion about football which would have been the normal basis of conversation for young men of their age.

One topic on their lips, from the very beginning of the academic year, was the question of capital punishment for murder. There had been a campaign for some time for its abolition and this was now coming to a climax. To Sarah, capital punishment was clearly wrong, and she was surprised to discover that more than one third of her group was in favour of it – even Callum Fraser, whom Sarah had come to regard as the epitome of tolerance. The matter came up in graphic detail in the Forensic Medicine class where Professor Glaister, as was his wont, took ghoulish delight in describing the process of what Sarah regarded as judicial murder.

'What happens is that ¾ inch Italian hemp is used with a brass eyelet through which the rope is bent. The condemned man's head is covered with a hood over which the noose is placed with the knot under the left jaw which ensured that, when the prisoner falls through the opened trapdoor, his second and third vertebrae are snapped. And that's the cause of death rather than strangulation which most people imagine is the   cause. It's very efficient and much better than amateur attempts at suicide by hanging which, although usually ultimately successful, usually involve extended agony.

It was generally thought that the Professor's lectures had become more graphic since he had some young ladies in his class, but neither Sarah nor Miss Kinniburgh were much affected by the detail. On the other hand, Callum Fraser confessed to Sarah on one occasion that, after seeing so many slides of bodies roughly stitched up after a post mortem, he couldn't look at a young girl's throat without visualising a row of stitches running up it like a zip.

The capital punishment question was finally resolved, at least to Sarah's satisfaction, in the spring of the next year, when, with the passing of the Homicide Act 1957, capital punishment was abolished for all but a few categories. 'Thank goodness that is all over,' she said to herself. 'No more judicial murders.'

She did wonder whether, with the concentration on hanging, she herself was becoming too obsessed with murder and its consequences. By varying her walk to University only slightly she could walk past the houses in Sauchiehall Street and Berkeley Street where the serial killer Dr Edward Pritchard, the last man to be publicly hanged in Glasgow, had murdered his victims. By merely walking along Sauchiehall Street from her flat she passed 17 Sandyford Place where Jessie McLachlan was wrongly found guilty of murder, although the sentence was commuted. By deviating slightly on the other side of Sauchiehall Street, she could see 49 West Princes Street where Oscar Slater in 1908, in another miscarriage of justice which became a cause célèbre, was alleged to have murdered a rich widow in the course of a burglary. Again, the sentence was commuted, but he served nineteen years in prison before the verdict was overturned. After his release he, in fact, lived for a short time in a flat on Sauchiehall Street across from where Sarah now lived.

Then, if she went in the other direction, she would pass the handsome house in Blythswood Square in which the wealthy Madeleine Smith had allegedly murdered her lover. She was almost certainly guilty but was acquitted on a not proven verdict.

Sarah decided that she was being silly in taking these diversions because, although Forensic Medicine was a fascinating subject in its association with solving mysteries, criminal law was not something with which she would become involved, as the firm to which she was apprenticed handled almost no criminal cases. Their court practice was in civil matters.

And all at once she was asked to deal with one and she had a client.

Shaw McLaughlin & Co had connections with Trade Unions involved in heavy industry and because of this had a large practice acting for workers who had been involved in industrial accidents. As well as any compensation that could be obtained, the workers were also entitled to seek a Social Security Benefit for injury or disease arising out of employment. There was an element of set-off between the two sources, but the advantage of the Government scheme was that it did not depend on proving fault by the employer. The extent of disablement was assessed by a panel and the worker had a right of appeal if he did not agree with the panel's verdict. The disadvantage was that, although the worker was entitled to be legally represented at any appeal, Legal Aid was not available so that the few lawyers who were prepared to take on appeals did so on a *pro bono* basis, and human nature being what it is, this was low down in their list of priorities.

One morning, when Sarah arrived at the office from the University, the Procurator thrust a thin file of papers into her hands, explained he was rushing off to another case, and told her she was to appear in a Medical Appeal Tribunal for a man called Willie Thomson. The appeal was due to start in an hour's time.

In a fit of nervous anxiety, Sarah quickly scanned through the few papers there were, before going in to see the client. Willie Thomson, who was a gnarled middle-aged labourer, was not best pleased to find himself represented by a slip of a girl, but Sarah hoped that the outward face of calm she was putting on to conceal her inner doubts would reassure him. She wasn't convinced. Nor was he. On the way to the tribunal office he said nothing; and she was also silent because she was trying frantically to think how she was going to proceed.

The hearing took place, not in a courtroom as Sarah expected but in an ordinary room with the three tribunal members sitting at a table on the opposite side of which she and the client sat. This informality put Sarah more at her ease, but it made her very conscious that they must be aware of her fingers trembling as she sorted her papers.

The argument which had occurred to her on the way over was to emphasise the crucial role which her client's hands – it was his right hand which had been damaged – played in his working life. She ended:

'The original assessor, and you, gentlemen, and I myself, we all depend on our brains. Our brains are our tools of work. If our brains are damaged our ability to work is compromised. But my client, Mr Thomson, does not rely on his brain. His tools are his hands and there can be no doubt from the medical evidence, which you have seen that these tools are damaged beyond repair. For that reason, I ask the panel to reconsider the assessment.'

When she finished, the chairman of the panel asked her and her client to step outside while they considered what to do. After only a short delay they were asked to return, and, to Sarah's delight, the chairman announced that they had reconsidered the position in light of Miss Watson's most persuasive remarks, and Mr Thomson would be granted a disablement benefit commensurate with his injuries. He finished by asking Sarah to pass on his best wishes to her employer, Mr Shaw.

Outside, Willie Thomson was profuse in his thanks. 'You really showed them,' he said. 'Tha' was great. Am no sure that a liked being called a big thickie, but it was all in a good cause.'

He shook hands with her as they parted, and Sarah was sure she must be imagining that the crippled hands, the subject of the Appeal, seemed to have recovered much of their strength and elasticity. She couldn't wait to get back to the office to give news of her victory.

The Procurator was especially full of praise. 'I've never won one of those in three years of trying,' he told her.

38

One advantage in working in an office, from Sarah's point of view, was that although the University had the usual extended holidays at Christmas, Easter and during the summer, she had only two weeks holiday from the office, which gave her a ready excuse not to go home for any extended period. She knew this was unfair to her mother and her Auntie Annie, who cared so much for her in their different ways, but on the few occasions when she was on the train to Edinburgh she could feel the tension rising as she neared Waverley Station and, once home, she avoided going out as much as possible. So much so, she acquired a reputation amongst her relatives for being hoity-toity – just like her mother. Sarah was unconscious, or at least unmoved, by this, but she tried to make it up to her mother and her Auntie Annie by having them visit her in Glasgow as often as possible and to stay overnight, as she showed them the Glasgow she was getting to know well. Like most Edinburgh people, they regarded Glasgow as at the edge of civilisation and she delighted in showing them how wrong they were. Annie in particular was astonished by the fact that there were four dance halls packed out at the weekend, within a hundred yards of Sarah's flat – not that Sarah had ever been in one.

The reason that Sarah had difficulty in making time for her mother's visits was that, as her confidence came back, she allowed herself to become more and more involved with the social side of her legal classmates. This was fine when the activity was centred round the University area but all her classmates – apart from her – lived at home, at varying distances from the centre of Glasgow. It was awkward from a social point of view as it involved a lot of travelling to visit them, which could be difficult late at night. Sarah even took a taxi home on a couple of occasions, her first experience of travelling alone in a taxi, but it was not something she was happy with.

Then, as her second Christmas at University neared, she found herself tentatively suggesting that, if people wanted a place for a party, why shouldn't they use her flat, which was central for everyone. She instantly regretted having made the offer but before she could retract it, it was seized on with enthusiasm by the others and the die was cast. Her only out was explaining she must first obtain permission from the owner of the flat. But Pat McLaughlin

264

had no hesitation in agreeing. In fact, he was pleased that she asked. The reason he had organised her living in Glasgow was in response to her mother's expressed fears that for some reason, Sarah was becoming more and more withdrawn, in Edinburgh. But, having made the arrangements, he felt he and his wife could not entertain Sarah at their own home for fear of placing her in an awkward position as far as the other members of the office staff were concerned. So, socially, she was left to her own devices and Pat was pleased that the forthcoming party showed her coming out of her shell.

Sarah had never before organised a party and did not know where to begin. For a start she did not drink and so had no idea what people would want. Luckily, the matter was taken out of her hands by various girlfriends of her classmates. She was told to prepare fruit juice in as big a bowl as possible from which the girls could help themselves; the men would come fully laden with bottles of beer and wine and whatever else they fancied. Although it was December, there was no possibility of serving hot food, instead there would be a cold buffet with cold meats and various types of salad. Sarah insisted she would prepare the pudding as she was proud of her sherry trifle, following a recipe her Auntie Annie taught her. There was no question of her having to foot the bill for the party either. Callum Fraser had arranged for everyone to pay a fixed amount per head and Sarah found herself in the embarrassing position of having more money available to her than she needed.

On the night of the party Sarah waited nervously for the guests to appear. Nearly the whole class, with the exception of Miss Kinniburgh, was coming with assorted girlfriends. With the help of a few of the girls she had put up decorations, and even a Christmas tree, and she thought that the flat was looking absolutely at its best. The arrangement was for the men and the rest of the girlfriends to gather for drinks in a pub across the road, called Flannery's, and to appear about eight thirty.

Meantime, across the river, in the Gorbals, another gathering was taking place in another pub, The Innishowen. Trouble had been brewing for some time. Although Frankie Gilligan was looked up to as the main man in his area and although the young men collectively thought of themselves as The New Cumbie, there was not really a gang as such. They operated in their various criminal activities like separate small groups and were only bound together when required, in response to external threats. The basis of the collective was purely geographical: they all lived in a few streets in the Gorbals. Also, because the people who lived in those streets were mostly Catholics, the gang members were mostly Catholics, but that was incidental to the need to bind together when necessary. On these occasions, Frankie was looked on as the leader, but he was not, by nature, a group person, preferring to follow his individual course.

The main external threat was from the Calton Boys. Again, their origin was purely geographical, based on streets which bordered on the streets which Frankie looked on as his neighbourhood. But membership was also based on religious grounds which gave them more coherence and more organisation. No Catholics were allowed. Indeed, most of the membership were also members of the Orange Order and proudly strutted through the Glasgow streets on the appropriate days of celebration.

Like warring nations, most of the trouble between the gangs arose from border disputes where there were conflicts of control. Trouble was always bubbling below the surface like a dormant volcano, but matters came to a head out of a victory by Celtic over Rangers, with an unprecedented margin of 7-1 in the League Cup Final in October of that year, 1957. Rangers had been the dominant team for many years and their supporters had been taunted both at the game and in the weeks that followed, by the Celtic supporters revelling in their unexpected victory. There had been numerous scuffles all building up to an increase in tension, which would inevitably lead to a major confrontation. Wee Jiffy was Frankie's eyes and ears on the ground as no-one paid much attention to him and he confirmed, on that night, a large number of the Calton Boys, all armed to the teeth, had gathered and were looking for trouble.

As the news spread, those who regarded themselves as the New Cumbie gathered in The Innishowen. Just like a regular army, scouts were sent out and reported back on the increasing number of the Calton Boys and the fact that they were heavily armed with knives, hatchets, razors, clubs and bicycle chains. This was serious. Emissaries were sent out to gather together as many fighters as possible and to collect as many weapons as could be obtained from their normal hiding places.

As the boys in Flannery's drank as much as possible to get themselves ready to party, across the river the New Cumbie lads drank as much as possible to get themselves ready to fight.

The noise in The Innishowen grew louder and louder. Cursing and swearing became constant; drunkenness hid fear and quickened the need for action. Frankie had not been there earlier as he didn't drink but his arrival now signalled that the New Cumbie had to come out to meet the 'enemy'. They were aiming for a piece of waste land where an old tenement had been demolished as part of the regeneration of the Gorbals. Just like competing armies, outliers were sent and exchanged missiles from afar, mostly milk bottles and loose stones and bricks left after the demolition. One of the Calton boys was struck full on his head by a flying bottle and the gash sent blood streaming down his face. He staggered for a second, then moved on, seemingly oblivious to his injury.

Meantime, the students back in Flannery's were enjoying themselves. The bar was warm, and the craic became faster and, at least to those involved, wittier. The boys would have settled in for the night, but Callum Fraser reminded them that they had a party to go to and they would be in deep trouble if they dallied longer.

They headed across the road in high and noisy spirits and up the tenement close to Sarah's flat. Unfortunately, in the course of the horseplay, as they jostled their way up the stairs, two milk bottles which had been left out for the milkman were knocked over and smashed on the stone stairs; the boys put their fingers to their lips in a pantomime gesture of shoosh.

39

Across the city matters were coming to a head. Despite the weapons carried, it was almost regarded as cissy to wear any sort of protection – in the same way as it was only pansies who would wear an overcoat as protection from the rain or cold. The only exception to this was the leader of the Calton Boys, Frankie's old adversary, Jaikie Houliston. Outdoors, he always wore slung round his neck a leather satchel in which he kept his money. It earned him the nickname 'Bagman Houliston'. It was worn as a sort of bravado to show to the world how wealthy he was, although he now rarely carried much cash in it. He just liked the nickname. But it was also a protection against knife attacks aimed at him and its surface was scarred with many signs of its usefulness. It was positioned slightly to one side to free his right hand to attack.

When the mass of fighters came together the fighting resolved itself into numerous individual struggles, with each man grappling an opponent before he whirled round and found a new target. Blows from knives, razors and chains left faces gashed, and blood streaming. The noise was frantic; the yells of those attacking joining with the screams of those who had been most severely hit. Even in the poor illumination from the street lighting, Frankie stood out because of his height and his fair hair but his reputation as a fighter had gone before him, and there were few prepared to take him on. It was he who sought out men to attack, leaving them slashed and bruised.

In her flat in Sauchiehall Street, Sarah heard the noise of the men coming up the stairs and had the door open for their arrival. Before they came, the atmosphere in the flat was quiet, as the girls completed their preparation and then sat around sipping their drinks. What a change as the men entered, en masse, waving their bottles and hugging and kissing everyone within reach. As bottles were deemed unacceptable, glasses were found for the drinks, and some of the men, spotting the bowl of 'punch', thought they would make it more palatable by draining into it the remnants of their bottles of gin, vodka and whisky.

The noise level grew higher as everyone, arms about each other's shoulders, strained to make themselves heard above the din. When the cover was taken off the cold buffet table the men made a

271

beeline for it and the noise quietened a bit as people found seats or, for most, made themselves comfortable on the floor with their backs against a wall.

Over in the Gorbals Frankie had just sent one of the other side flying, when he stumbled across a body lying on the ground. It gave a cry and, in the half light, Frankie, to his utter horror, made out that it was Wee Jiffy. As the battle swirled around him Frankie knelt at his friend's side. It was as if he was in the calm centre of the storm which surrounded him.

'Jiffy, what are you doing here? You're not supposed to get involved in this stuff. In the name of God, what were you on about?' Frankie felt the warmth of Jiffy's blood as it pumped out of his body from a slash on his throat. 'Jiffy, Jiffy, are you all right.' He bent over to catch the muttered reply.

'Just jiffy, Frankie. Just jiffy.'

As he lay in Frankie's arms, Jiffy's body started shuddering. He gave a loud cry of pain, then his head fell to one side and Frankie knew he was dead.

Frankie looked up. 'Everyone knew Wee Jiffy. Who would do this to him?'

Someone said, 'It was Jaikie Houliston. When he razored him I heard him say, "That's another message to take to your boss".'

Frankie gently lay Jiffy down, then stood up. He moved through the struggling mob as if in a dream, a dream in which everything was in slow motion so that he had little difficulty in avoiding blows directed towards him. Even those that landed did not seem to hurt. Eventually, where the fighting was hardest, he found Jaikie Houliston, standing in an area where there was a pool of light.

Houliston sneered as he saw Frankie approach. 'Frankie Gilligan. You still around. I thought you were long gone. Yesterday's man. How's your wee friend, Jiffy, doing? Two of a kind. Two dummies together.' He made a stab at Frankie which Frankie easily avoided. He yelled further insults and obscenities at Frankie and got the result he wanted as Frankie lost control and threw himself at him

Jaikie made another great lunge at Frankie but in doing so fell slightly off balance making it easy for Frankie to get under his arm with his own left-handed stab to plunge his knife into his ribs up to the hilt. Jaikie staggered back with a bemused expression on his face and then, as another stab entered his stomach, fell to the ground. Frankie jumped on his prostrate body and stabbed him again and again, slicing through the straps of Jaikie's satchel, this time no protection against such frenzied blows, and throwing the blood covered satchel to one side.

While this was happening the two gangs almost unconsciously stopped their own fighting and, just like a playground brawl, gathered round Frankie and Jaikie's struggle. As Frankie, at length,

273

stood up over Jaikie's body, they separated to let him move away. The sudden silence was broken by the sound of numerous police sirens, which just as quickly scattered the throng. Then the police, led by Chief Superintendent McCulloch, ran along the street and stood over Jaikie's lifeless body.

McCulloch, as had become his practice since being appointed Chief Superintendent, was carrying his briefcase; his badge of office for those who did not know his rank. He put it on the ground as he knelt by Jaikie's body and checked for any obvious sign of life. 'Got you this time, Gilligan.' He muttered. 'Got you, got you, got you.'

Meanwhile, at Sarah's party, someone had brought records, including one of Scottish Country Dance music and as soon as the food was cleared away it was suggested they do the Eightsome Reel. In a party of fifty there are always two or three who can do the Eightsome Reel and who try to organise the others; some who have seen it done and are anxious to co-operate; one or two viewing the whole dance as an opportunity to whirl their partners around and release them to crash into the throng; and the majority just enjoying leaping up and down to the music uttering wild hoochs at appropriate moments. An Eightsome Reel in a confined space has many of the characteristics of all-in wrestling. Sarah had done some Scottish Country Dancing in Edinburgh, but it had never been like this. She was a little worried about the effect on the ceiling of the flat downstairs as the floor was bouncing up and down. At least she had told Mr MacTavish, the old man downstairs, that she was having a party, and he had told her that there was no problem as he was going to be away.

Actually, downstairs, old Mr MacTavish had completely forgotten his agreement with Sarah to spend the night of the party with his daughter in Dennistoun. As he lay on his bed, he could see his ceiling move and the central ceiling light swayed in rhythm to the music. He reached for his phone and called the police to make a complaint and soon had the satisfaction of hearing the police siren as it came along Sauchiehall Street… Until it kept on going and eventually faded in the distance. As it did so, the music upstairs became a little less loud and the partygoers started singing songs that Mr MacTavish recognised. Closing his eyes, he fell into a deep sleep, humming along to 'If You Were the Only Girl in the World'. When the police knocked on his door about two hours later, he was furious to be awakened from his slumber and denied ever having called them. To be on the safe side they listened at the upstairs door, but all seemed reasonably quiet.

Of course, the sirens Mr MacTavish had heard came from a police car on its way across the river to the Gorbals, where there were reports of a large-scale riot taking place. When it got there - along with what seemed to be every other police car in Glasgow - the mob scattered in all directions, leaving only a few groaning bodies on the ground, and Chief Superintendent McCulloch beside the motionless figure of Jaikie Houliston.

'Right, boys,' he said. 'Let's go. We know who's responsible for this.'

He led them the short distance to Frankie's house where, instead of knocking, he instructed his men to break down the door. McCulloch followed them as they burst into the flat where they found Frankie on his feet stunned by the crash as the door burst open. After the fight with Houliston he had walked slowly home with his mind still in a daze. His mother was in bed asleep when he got there and he had slumped down in a chair, his shirt still spattered with Houliston's blood, the knife he had used, left on the table beside him. His normal instinct for self-protection had deserted him.

'Right, Gilligan, you're done. We'll call it breach of the peace, meantime, but there's a lot more to come than that. Take the filthy thug away.'

As he was hustled to the door, Frankie struggled to turn round. 'Ma mother!'

'I'll deal with your mother. She's going to have to get out of here, as this will be sealed off as a crime scene until the CID have a chance to go over it. Sergeant, go across the landing to the other flat and get the people there to take the old scag in over-night.' He turned to see Frankie's mother peering round the half-opened bedroom door, with her shoulders covered by a shawl and a terrified expression on her face. 'You! You go with the sergeant here. Don't waste your time worrying about your thug of a son. You won't be seeing him for a long time.'

The sergeant was shocked by the brutal tone of his superior's voice and, taking Mrs Gilligan's arm gently, helped her as she shuffled in her slippers across the landing to the opposite flat.

Once everyone had left, McCulloch took his time walking slowly around the flat, looking contemptuously at the sparse furniture, pulling open a few drawers. Then he came out, put a constable on watch outside the shattered door and returned to the station.

At the same time, exhausted after the Reel, the partying students settled for some slower dancing. Then Sarah realised there was a problem. Her idea in making up the bowl of fruit juice was to provide something to drink for those who, like herself, didn't take alcohol. However, when she sipped from her first glass after the men had arrived, she realised that, with the additions they had poured in, it was no longer the thirst-quenching innocuous drink she had anticipated. She tried to warn the others and most heeded her advice, but one girl, Sally McHugh said she quite liked the taste. She very quickly became the life and soul of the party. Equally quickly she turned a little withdrawn and then, as Sarah watched her, she grew paler and paler. Trying not to attract attention, Sarah moved to her side and took her somewhat unsteadily to the edge of the room and then into the bathroom. In the quiet of the bathroom with the hubbub of the party surrounding them, Sarah held poor Sally, who suddenly gave a muffled scream and her stomach gave up the remains of the cold buffet and the punch which had been her downfall. After this she just wanted to lie down on the floor, but Sarah persuaded her to move into the bedroom. She managed to get Sally on to one of the beds which she had cleared of coats and, having covered her with a blanket, left her already sleeping, albeit somewhat noisily.

Sarah moved back to the centre of the party where people had started singing. Some had a song which was recognised as *their* song and no-one else would have dreamt of singing it, but mostly, they sang together whatever came into their heads. After the students had run through their repertoire, Callum Fraser organised some records to listen to. Traditional jazz was the popular music for students at that time, but he felt the party needed something more restful. He put on some Count Basie, then some Duke Ellington and these fitted the mood. He then put on a record of someone new to Sarah – Dizzy Gillespie. He played his trumpet in a way Sarah had never heard before and in the final piece he squeezed out notes which got higher and higher until he reached an absolutely impossible peak, almost like a scream, repeating that note over and over. Sarah felt it was like a stiletto piercing her being, again and again and again.

When he at last finished, Sarah felt emotionally drained, and the quiet in the room showed that others felt the same. The only noise was from outside where there was the sound of another police car, its siren blaring as it went up Sauchiehall Street, which Sarah later realised was probably on its way to the Gorbals. In the room people began stirring and there was a general movement to go. Some offered to stay behind to help with clearing up, but Sarah said it was already late enough; they had journeys to make to get home, and she would cope with the mess in the morning. The still sleeping Sally could stay the night and be of help next day.

After they had all left, Sarah shook her head at the mess which was revealed when the lights were all switched on. But it had been a great party. Quite a night in fact.

40

When Sarah woke up next morning, Sally was still asleep. Overnight there had been a fierce storm with thunder and lightning and heavy rain, but it had obviously not disturbed Sally. Sarah slipped quietly out of the bedroom, put on the immersion heater in case Sally wanted a bath, then started clearing up the flat. As usual, the clearing up took less time than at first appeared. Paper plates had been used for the food and once they had been put in a bin bag with the remnants of the food, all that was left was to wash up the glasses and put aside those which had been borrowed. Sarah was just finishing this, when the bedroom door cautiously opened, and Sally poked her head out.

'God, I feel awful. What happened last night? I feel so ashamed. I must have made a right fool of myself. God, my head is splitting. Did I do anything really stupid?'

Sarah hastened to reassure her that nothing had happened. People knew she wasn't a drinker and realised she had been caught out by the punch. She explained that, when she saw that Sally was becoming wobbly, she had got her out of the room before things got worse.

'And then I threw up in your toilet.'

'Yes,' said Sarah. 'But nobody knew about that and I told them you were resting. Your boyfriend – Jimmy, isn't it? – was concerned about you, but I told him you were better off where you were, and he agreed to come back for you this morning… And that will be him now.' She finished as the doorbell rang. 'You get into the bathroom and have a bath and a tidy up and you'll be fresh as paint when he sees you.'

Sarah let Jimmy in and gave him a cup of tea, while they went back over the events at the party. Sure enough, when Sally emerged some ten minutes later, she looked sparkling fresh, the only sign of the previous night being that she was still wearing her party clothes.

After greeting Jimmy, Sally turned to Sarah and said, 'I meant to say. I noticed when I got up first – someone left his boots after the party.'

And sure enough, there, sticking out from behind the settee, was a pair of boots. And on closer inspection it appeared there were feet inside the boots. The settee had been pushed back the previous night to allow more room for dancing, but its curved back against the wall provided a space someone had obviously decided to utilise.

Watched by the women, Jimmy approached the boots and tapped them somewhat tentatively, not knowing what to expect. There was a groan from behind the settee and when Jimmy pushed it back, there was revealed Sarah's fellow apprentice, Alastair Clarke, lying with his head on cushions from the settee. He blinked a little in the sudden light, sat up slowly, then explained that he was not much keen on singing (Sarah remembered that he was tone deaf) and when the others started he thought he would take a wee nap – which now seemed to have lasted longer than intended. After scrambling carefully to his feet and apologising to Sarah he left with the other two, leaving Sarah to sit down thankfully at last and have her breakfast.

Sarah was at first amused by the incident then, with a pang realised that, once again she had been left alone, unprotected (Sally didn't really count) against a drunken, potentially aggressive, bear of a man. She tried to put the thought out of her head as she prepared her meal.

After breakfast Sarah decided to finish reading a book she was enjoying but couldn't find it; she must have left it in the office the previous Friday. After hesitating, she looked outside to see that, after the overnight storm, it was a bright midwinter day and decided to take the few minutes' walk to retrieve it from the office. It would be closed, as it was a Sunday, but she had keys.

When she got there, she was surprised to find the office door already open and even more surprised to find Pat McLaughlin in his room. He was dressed as usual in his smart suit and tie, but his whole body looked somehow dishevelled. He looked old and worn. He didn't ask her why she was in the office on a Sunday and did not wait for her to ask him.

'It's Frankie Gilligan,' he said. 'I got a phone call in the middle of the night to say that he has been arrested. And it's major. There's a dead body. I don't know whether I can cope with this.' Pat slumped in his chair for a second. Then shook himself. Possibly the memory of his promise to his old friend Boxy came to his mind. 'Right. I'd better get on with this. Are you doing anything today? Maybe you could come with me. I might be better with a witness and it will at least be good experience for you.'

They drove in Pat's car to Gorbals police station and, after they had waited in a side room, Frankie was led in. He shook hands with Pat and gave a little smile of recognition when he saw Sarah. His face was heavily cut and bruised. When Pat asked if this was as a result of the fighting, Frankie twisted his face in a painful half smile.

'The police always like a wee bit of 'resisting arrest' when they pick you up.'

Frankie had spent a sleepless night listening to the thunder and lightning above him. He knew he had killed Jaikie Houliston and had no regrets about that. But what would be the consequences for him? He was thus uncharacteristically subdued now as he told his story. He explained how there had been trouble brewing with the Calton Boys for some time and it had come to a head the previous night down at a piece of cleared ground off Cumberland Street. In the course of this, he had been confronted by Jaikie Houliston. He had managed to avoid Houliston's initial attack and then, in avoiding further attacks, had stabbed back at him, leading to Houliston's death. After that he had gone back to his house but had been there under half an hour when the police broke down the entrance door, forced their way in, and arrested him. Frankie was more worried about his mother than himself. She had been fast asleep when the police broke in and lay cowering in bed as the police entered her house and took her son away.

Pat reassured him they would make sure that Maria was alright. Meantime, he would find out what charges were being pressed against Frankie and then come back as soon as he had further information.

After Frankie was taken away, Sarah whispered to Pat that surely it was a clear case of self-defence and that Frankie should be in the clear? Pat smiled gently at her and told her that what she had heard was Frankie's version of events. Others might tell a different story.

When they went into the front desk of the station, Pat was told that Frankie had been arrested on the basis of a breach of the peace, but this was merely a holding charge and other more serious ones were being prepared. They were also told that Frankie's flat was sealed off as a crime scene and that his mother, as far as they knew, had been taken in by the family across the landing. Pat decided to stay at the station to await further developments and Sarah agreed, at his request, to go and find out if Frankie's mother was all right.

This wasn't Sarah's first visit to the Gorbals. By chance, just the previous week she had gone with some University friends to the Citizens Theatre to see 'Clishmaclaver', this year's thirteen letter pantomime. But going to a theatre on the main street with a group of friends was very different from nervously walking in what she thought of as the depths of the Gorbals, with razor gangs waiting to attack her at every corner. Surprisingly, she thought, nothing untoward happened and the people she came across seemed peaceful enough, even smiling.

In Frankie's close, she climbed up the steps leading to the ground floor. His flat was obvious as it was blocked off, with a large policeman on duty on guard. Watched suspiciously by the officer, Sarah turned to the other side of the landing and knocked on the door. It was opened by a youngish woman who peered cautiously at her, but once Sarah had explained why she was there, she was welcomed into the house – at the same time as the woman cast indignant looks at the large policeman.

'I am Jessie Collins,' she told Sarah, and confirmed that she and her husband had been awakened in the middle of the night by the noise of Frankie's door being broken down and the other police activity. Then, when things seemed to have calmed down the police had knocked at their door and asked if they would take Mrs Gilligan in, as her flat was being closed off as a crime scene.

'A' thought they had a cheek, but when a' saw the state poor Mrs Gilligan was in, a didnae hesitate for a second,' Jessie said. 'We only have the two sma' bedrooms in oor hoose, but we moved the two bairns intae oor bed and settled Mrs Gilligan in theirs. They quite enjoyed it, but a'm not sure ma man enjoyed it quite as much. You know how bairns kick and move around when they're sleeping.'

Sarah, of course, had no idea what children did when they slept but she was overwhelmed by the kindness of people wakened in the middle of the night, who went to such trouble to care for an old woman whom they barely knew.

Jessie Collins, herself was a little in awe of this tall, well-dressed young lady who spoke with what Jessie thought was an English accent, but she seemed friendly enough. 'Mrs   Gilligan was in a terrible state of shock when we took her in, but she calmed down when a gave her a cup of tea and was able to fall off to sleep. A gave her some breakfast when she awoke and then a made her go straight back to bed. When a looked in on her just before you arrived, she was still fast sleep and a thoct a wid leave her to wake up in her own time.'

While Jessie talked, Sarah surreptitiously took in the apartment. The room they were in was sparsely furnished, with tattered curtains on the windows and the few old items of furniture showing signs of wear and tear. But the room was tidy, the windows were clean and the blazing fire in the grate meant that the room was comfortably warm. Sarah declined the offer of a cup of tea. She was later to castigate herself as to whether she genuinely was not thirsty or whether she could not face the prospect of tea served in a cup unacceptable to her refined tastes.

There was a brief silence broken only by the ticking of an old clock on the mantelpiece, then Mrs Collins spoke again. 'Ye ken, that Frankie Gilligan they show in the papers – the gang leader? That's no the Frankie Gilligan we know. Ye couldnae find a nicer bloke. Aye, polite and helpful. He always minds the bairns' birthdays and brings in toys for them.' She paused. 'He owns this hoose, ye ken. We just rent it from him. And ye know, a couple o' times Alec, ma man, was laid off by the shipyard when they ran oot o' work. Frankie telt us no tae worry aboot the rent till Alec was back in a job. Then when he got a fresh start, Frankie telt us no tae bother about the rent we owed.   He just liked us as good neighbours. Aye, he's a good man no matter what they say.'

Sarah said nothing, but she thought about what Jessie Collins had said and listened some more:

'A got a message the morn frae the RC Chapel. You an RC? Am a Kirk person maself. At least a don't actually go but that's where a should go. But the Kirk disnae seem to care aboot puir people like me. It's all aboot fancy clothes on a Sunday. The RCs seem to care more aboot puir folk. Maybe they've got more of them.   Anyway, they sent a message that they were arranging something for puir Mrs Gilligan and someone would come roon later on this morn to pick her up… There's the door. That'll be them noo.'

41

When Jessie Collins opened the door, there were two people standing there. One, Sarah was surprised to see, was Pat McLaughlin. The other was a little round man with a dog collar, obviously a priest. Pat said he had met him on his way and given him a lift. The priest seemed preoccupied, but Pat introduced both of them to Mrs Collins who didn't know what to do with these fresh visitors, especially as there were not enough seats for everyone. And the scene was completed by two more pairs of little eyes peering round the bedroom door at these strangers.

Pat whispered to Sarah that the priest, whose name was Father O'Leary, was quiet because he was carrying a Host to give to Mrs Gilligan – could Mrs Collins give them a little time alone to say some prayers? Jessie was happy to help and showed the priest to the bedroom. Before he went in, Father O'Leary turned to Sarah and asked if she would come in too, as he might need some help in moving Mrs Gilligan up on the bed.

Maria was still half asleep. Her eyes opened in fright when she saw people coming into the room, then, when she recognised the priest, her face relaxed into a smile. 'It's yourself, Father.'

'If it's not, me mother must have switched me at birth. What have you been doing, Maria? Bed hopping in the middle of the night. It must have been horrible for you. But we'll get it sorted out. Sarah, here, will help you to sit up a bit.'

While Sarah was doing what she could to get Mrs Gilligan's poor withered body into as comfortable position as possible, the priest opened the little briefcase he was carrying with him, bringing out a candle which he lit and placed on an orange box which served as a bedside table. Round his neck he placed a thin scarf which Sarah recognised as a stole, before turning to Mrs Gilligan who had clasped her hands in prayer.

'Right, Maria. I'll hear your confession, although God knows there's not a sin in you. I'll bend over, and you can whisper in my ear and Sarah won't hear a thing. That's just fine now.' He sat back and making the sign of the cross said, 'Ego te absolvo a peccatis tuis in nomine Patris et Filii et Spiritu Sancti. Amen.'

Sarah, who had rarely been near a church since she left the convent, involuntarily clasped her hands as the little ceremony was going on. She told herself that she still did not believe in all this, but, as she heard the words of absolution, which she had heard so often as a girl, there was a tug at her heart that she had to fight to ignore. She remembered that sensation of peace which would always come over her when she heard the priest say that her sins had been forgiven. 'Rubbish,' the adult Sarah told herself. But she did miss that old feeling.

The priest took from round his neck a purple cord, from which was suspended a golden circular container, just like a pocket watch. And just like a pocket watch it clicked open and disclosed the white round Host. He said a few prayers then, as Sarah supported Mrs Gilligan, Father O'Leary leant forward to place the Host in Mrs Gilligan's mouth.

Sarah, watching intently, was moved almost to tears by the quiet ceremony and by the calmness which had come over Mrs Gilligan's face as she lay back with her eyes closed in prayer. Sarah felt she had been privileged to have taken part in something special which she would never forget.

The priest let a few minutes pass, sitting with his eyes closed, then he rose, told Mrs Gilligan to rest a bit longer and that they would soon have her back to something like normal. He and Sarah then went back to the other room, where Father O'Leary gratefully accepted Mrs Collins' offer of a cup of tea which, to Sarah's private shame, was served up in a lovely clean mug. The priest turned to Jessie.

'Now, Mrs Collins… Ah, that's a bit formal. Can I call you Jessie? You call me Tony. That's the name my mother gave me, and we don't have to bother about the 'Father' business. You're not one of ours, Jessie, but I tell you: 'I was a stranger and you took me in. I was hungry and you fed me'. That's what the Lord taught us. And I am proud to meet someone who is a true Christian. There's many a one that goes to the Kirk or the Chapel on Sundays and makes sure that everyone sees them saying their prayers, would not have done half of what you did last night. The rotund priest nodded. 'And there's another thing. There were two other people who had to move their beds last night and who have been staring round the door at this funny wee man with the odd collar. Tommy and Jimmy, is it? If these two young gentlemen like to come forward, I've a bag of marshmallows here for them. That's not strictly true. I had brothers, and we would fight like tigers over things like the stump of an apple. So, I've brought two bags, one each. Here you are, boys. You deserve them. Did you hear the thunder and lightning last night? Well you can't hear lightning, but you know what I mean. The room I have in the chapel house is right on the top floor. They said I would be nearer to heaven. That's as maybe, but last night, with that storm, I felt that I might be called before I was really ready. There was one clap of thunder. Must have been right overhead. It was almost like a scream.'

Pat McLaughlin was about to speak but the priest was off again.

'I've arranged things at the chapel house. We've more rooms than we use because part of our mission is to give shelter to those who need it. And Maria Gilligan certainly needs it. Jessie, would you be kind enough to go over to the Gilligan house and collect any clothing which you think Maria will need. I think the CID have finished in there although there is still one of Glasgow's finest, stationed at the door. If you have any trouble with him let me know and I'll sort him out.'

After Jessie left, the priest turned to speak to Pat McLaughlin, leaving Sarah to smile to herself at the thought of the small round Father O'Leary 'sorting out' the large policeman guarding the Gilligan door. However, that was not necessary as Mrs Collins quickly returned with a suitcase full of Mrs Gilligan's clothes and other necessaries. She went into the bedroom and the two of them shortly emerged with Mrs Gilligan, fully dressed, still looking apprehensive, but better than she had been. They all prepared to leave, with repeated thanks to Mrs Collins for her kindness. Pat McLaughlin knew better than to offer Jessie any recompense, but he made a mental note that he would do something to reward the whole Collins family for what they had done.

Outside, they helped Mrs Gilligan into the car. As Father O'Leary said, she was so frail a puff of wind would have blown her away. They made the short journey to the chapel house where the housekeepers took over, leaving Pat and Sarah free to drive to Sauchiehall Street, where Sarah was to be dropped off. On the way Pat filled Sarah in on more detail of Maria's life, starting with her Italian immigrant family background; then her marriage to the charming Boxy; the descent of both into drunken penury; Boxy's premature death; Sheila hanging herself; Ray's criminal career ending in his murder in Barlinnie; and now this latest tragedy…

Sarah was totally overcome by the thought of what that little frail woman had had to bear. The wonder was that she had survived at all.

Sarah was in sombre mood as she climbed the stairs to her flat. How could poor Mrs Gilligan cope with her surviving son facing a charge of murder? How could Sarah help her? She consoled herself with the thought that at least Frankie's claim of self-defence should mitigate the offence.

42

On her way into the office next morning Sarah picked up a newspaper and, sure enough, the previous night's mass brawl was headline news. The emphasis was on the arrest of the notorious gang leader, Frankie Gilligan, including what were described as eye-witness accounts of what had taken place. Separately, there was an inset which narrated Gilligan's previous convictions and brushes with the law, including reference to the killing of the policeman for which 'Gilligan had managed to escape conviction'. Sarah said to herself that she was already adopting the standard defending solicitor's attitude as she considered what chance Frankie would have of a fair trial with jury members being already exposed to such influences. She also felt a real sense of importance that here was this huge public case and she, Sarah Watson, was playing a genuine part in it.

When she reached the office, she found that her fellow apprentice, Alastair, had taken the day off, but she went into the typing pool and told the secretarial staff what had happened the previous night. She did not go to see Pat McLaughlin, but he sought her out to say that Frankie was to make a formal appearance before a sheriff that morning. It would need Pat's involvement and Sarah should come with him for experience, even though it was a formality. Sarah was too young and inexperienced to realise that Pat was under great strain and that although she was of genuine use to him, he was also using her company to help to alleviate the stress

When she had come to the office in the summer of the previous year, Sarah had been immediately impressed by the shorthand and typing skills of the office secretaries. She enlisted in a night course in these skills and quickly found that she, too, was naturally suited to them. Her classmates were young girls with restricted educational backgrounds, who were training to become office staff, and most had difficulties grasping the concept of shorthand (in fact for many it proved impossible). Sarah, on the other hand, was immediately at ease with it and became the star pupil – much to the disgust of some of her classmates who were already resentful because of her 'posh' Edinburgh accent. And she quickly mastered the QWERTY keyboard, so much so that she had to disappoint her teachers who wanted to put her forward for some speed typing competitions. Sarah was merely happy that her speed increased and that her use of Tippex decreased.

She used her shorthand for taking notes at lectures, then typing them up. It was by chance that Pat found out about this, and thereafter she found herself in the role not just as a legal trainee (trainees being a necessary evil but of little practical use) but also as a secretary, who was of great value.

As they walked through Exchange Square to the Court, Pat explained that, Frankie was what was known as 'on Petition' and this first hearing was to establish that it was right he should continue to be held in custody. Before the hearing, they had a chance for a further brief meeting with Frankie, where Frankie repeated his story and Pat confirmed that the hearing was a formality. Frankie seemed not so much concerned about the case, more for news of his mother. Sarah told him what had happened the previous night (it was only later she realised that this was the first time she had actually spoken directly to Frankie). She said that his mother was in safe hands with Father O'Leary and that she, Sarah would visit her regularly in case she needed anything. She hadn't actually discussed this with Pat, but it was just something which had been in the back of her mind to do.

Frankie said, with a smile, 'Thanks…' For some reason he felt unable to use her first name when speaking to her. 'Wee Father O'Leary's a good man. It's good of you to take the trouble.'

Sarah didn't reply but felt strangely pleased by what he said.

Then Frankie added, 'But what about Wee Jiffy?'

Pat and Sarah were puzzled. 'Who is Wee Jiffy?' Pat asked.

'A wee guy, not quite the full shilling, who attached himself to me.' Frankie frowned. 'I don't know why, but I've always felt responsible for him. I'm almost sure that he was killed by Houliston during the riot on the Saturday night. If he is dead, what happens to his body? The only relative I knew of was his granny. He lived with her, but I think she died about three months ago. You've got a lot on your shoulders, Mr McLaughlin, and it's not fair to load on more but I'm stuck here and can do nothing. Could you or maybe…' He indicated Sarah, again unable to say her name '…find out? I wouldn't like to see him end up in a pauper's grave. You know, I don't even know his real name.'

Later, Pat and Sarah were the only people in the courtroom, apart from the clerk and the procurator fiscal who nodded pleasantly to them as they entered. Then there was a shout of 'Court' and the Court Officer came in followed by the Sheriff who bowed to them before taking his place on the bench. After a short delay Frankie appeared up some steps into the dock from a concealed entrance, flanked by two policemen, and with his wrists handcuffed. He nodded slightly to Pat and Sarah when he saw them. Sarah found that her hands were tightly clenched, and her mouth was totally dry.

The fiscal rose to his feet and, after dealing with some preliminary matters, requested the Court to remand the Panel (the technical name for the accused) to Barlinnie Prison to await trial on a charge of murder. Pat indicated that there would be no plea or declaration and the sheriff ordered Frankie to be placed on remand before leaving the bench. Again, Frankie nodded to them before he was led away.

They were in sombre mood when they left the Courthouse. Up till that moment they had been thinking about a serious assault which had resulted in a death. This was the first time the word 'murder' had been mentioned. And it had had a severe impact. After they left the Sheriff Court building, they would normally have gone across to Glens for a coffee, but Pat said he was not in the mood. He suggested that Sarah should go back to the office. He was going to walk down to the riverside to clear his mind.

As Sarah walked slowly back to the office, she thought that, although he told her the hearing was merely a formality, Pat had been badly affected by the whole process. That word 'murder'. She thought about Frankie. He had not reacted in the same way as they had. This was someone who, within the last forty-eight hours, had killed someone (no matter what you called it) but seemed more concerned for the welfare of his mother and the disposal of his friend's body. She also thought back to how excited she had been that morning to be involved in such a high-profile case. How infantile she had been. This was much more serious. Could she cope with it? The only small consolation was that with the passing of the Homicide Act the previous year which she had very much supported, the punishment for murder was, except in a few specific cases, no longer hanging, but life imprisonment.

When Pat returned to the office he apologised to Sarah for involving her in this terrible matter, but Sarah assured him that, although it was terrible, she had become involved and wanted to stay involved as long as she could do some good. As a first step she volunteered to go and see Frankie's mother and to see what the position was with regard to Wee Jiffy. These were things which she could handle and, at the same time, didn't require any input from Uncle Pat when he had more pressing things to deal with. Pat was glad to agree even though, as he explained, there was not much to do at this stage until the actual indictment was formally served on Frankie. The Procurator Fiscal, now that Frankie was officially remanded in custody, would spend the time interviewing witnesses, obtaining post-mortem and forensic reports, and establishing what productions would be required at the trial. Only then would he frame the indictment on which Frankie would stand trial and that would specify the alleged offence (which might not necessarily be the one specified at the initial hearing) and list the information which the prosecution would present to the Court. Based on the terms of the indictment the defence team would decide on their pleas and the basis of the defence.

Sarah, as she returned to her room, was reassured by the possibility that the offence to be tried might not turn out to be that dreaded word 'murder'. She also chided herself for doing the very thing Professor Glaister had, time after time, warned his students against she was getting involved with the client and thereby losing objectivity. But she couldn't help herself.

After she finished the formal business in the Ordinary Court that morning, she walked down to Clydeside and across the Suspension Bridge into the Gorbals. This time she didn't feel threatened as she made her way to St Francis Church in Cumberland Street. Father O'Leary was not there, but the housekeeper took her into see Mrs Gilligan in her bedroom. She seemed even more shrunken than Sarah remembered, dwarfed by the armchair in which she was sitting. She nodded to Sarah but had clearly no idea who she was.

When Sarah asked her how she was, she said, 'I'm frightened.'

'What are you frightened of,' Sarah said gently.

'I don't know,' she replied.

Sarah glanced round at the housekeeper, who shook her head and whispered that she had been like this since Father O'Leary brought her to the house. Sarah tried some general topics, but Mrs Gilligan remained unresponsive, looking blankly at her and then away, her eyes reflecting some inner torment. Eventually, Sarah realised there was nothing to be done and she pressed Mrs Gilligan's withered hand before leaving, her spirits totally downcast.

Determined to make some use of her visit to the Gorbals she went to the police station to enquire about Wee Jiffy. Her approach was viewed with suspicion, even when she explained the reason for her visit. The only information she was able to draw from them was that Wee Jiffy's real name was William Finlayson. For anything further, she was told she would have to speak to the Procurator Fiscal's office. Sarah felt eyes following her as she left the station and didn't feel totally comfortable until she re-crossed the Suspension Bridge back to the North Side.

Back at the office, Pat McLaughlin confirmed that now they had a name for Wee Jiffy they could pursue their interest. Because he had been killed in the course of the riot, the authorities would not release the body until they had completed their enquiries to see whether anyone should be charged in connection with his death. All that Sarah should do meantime was to prepare a formal letter to the Procurator Fiscal, confirming that the firm of Shaw McLaughlin & Co had received instructions to handle the disposal of the remains in due course.

43

After that nothing much happened. Sarah remembered reading that, after the declaration of war with Germany in 1939, there was a period that became known as the Phony War before the expected hostilities started. It was the same with Frankie's case. Until the Prosecution had gathered all their evidence and presented it to the Defence there was nothing for the Defence to work on. As Pat explained to Sarah, no matter how many people had been in the vicinity, it was unlikely that any of them would prove to be willing witnesses. The Defence would just have to wait to see how successful the police had been.

Pat gave a wry smile when Sarah suggested that this was good news for Frankie. He explained that the main convicting evidence would be forensic, and they had no idea what form that would take. In the meantime, all that had to be done was the appointment of senior and junior counsel to represent Frankie. Pat was confident that, with his connections, he had obtained the best possible team in James Galloway QC, with Robert Simpson as his Junior. Rather than some high achieving Edinburgh men who had no feel for the realities of Glasgow criminal life, both originated from the West of Scotland and Frankie would be more comfortable with them.

A few days after Frankie had been remanded, Pat took Sarah with him when he went to see Frankie in Barlinnie, really just to see if he needed anything. Barlinnie Prison lies on the north east side of Glasgow on the outskirts of what seemed to Sarah to be quite a nice tidy area of housing. The prison itself was approached from the main road by a long driveway. *No,* thought Sarah, *not a driveway. Just a flat road with some featureless ground on either side.* At the end of the road the enormous grey stone-walled prison loomed almost like a medieval castle, except that this was a castle with its back turned to the world. As they left Pat's car, Sarah suddenly felt cold, as if the building was casting a chill on its surroundings; the small barred windows seemed to glare at her. Her anxieties increased as she and Pat were examined through a spy hatch then allowed to enter a heavy metalled door into a courtyard, open to the sky but into which no sun intruded, and then into the prison itself. Here Sarah's main impression was of the echoing din of metal clashing on metal. Pat sensed Sarah's unease and whispered to her that she would soon become accustomed to these frightening surroundings, but her initial terror stayed with her for many days and recurred in her dreams for years to come.

They were shown into a freezing cold room, by a guard who seemed to Sarah, in her sensitive state, to be eyeing them with great suspicion. The room had whitewashed walls and no windows; light being provided by a single central bulb. A metal table separated the room into two halves, and the metal chairs on each side screeched on the stone floor when they were moved. There was also a door on each side giving separate access, and in each door a window, through which the warders could check what was going on inside. Pat and Sarah were admitted on one side and shortly afterwards Frankie was brought in and left on the other side of the table. The warder banged the door shut as he left the room, locking the door behind him.

Frankie seemed delighted to see them and stretched across to shake hands with them but was unable to do so because of the width of the table. Then, like a perfect host, he made sure they were seated before he, himself, sat down. To Sarah's surprise he was dressed in his normal clothing, not the prison uniform that Sarah had expected from her viewing of Hollywood movies. Pat, however, was prepared for this. He told Frankie to prepare a bundle of clothes for them to remove for washing on their next visit, which Pat would replace with items picked up from Frankie's flat. The whole exchange was so matter-of-fact. Not at all what Sarah had expected from her first meeting face to face in prison with a man facing trial on a charge of murder.

Frankie seemed quite relaxed. He *was* delighted to see them, just to talk, as, because of the gravity of the charge against him, he was being kept in a cell on his own and had contact with the other inmates only at mealtimes and exercise times. He was, he said, being treated reasonably by the warders, much better than he had been in previous prison stays when general rough treatment had been the norm. He grinned: they obviously wanted the scars, which he bore from the police 'care' of him at his arrest, to have disappeared by the time he came to trial. What about his mother?

Pat, sensing that Sarah was still cowed by her first experience in a prison environment, took it on himself to report on what she done. Frankie's mother was comfortable in the Chapel House, although she seemed to have withdrawn into a world of her own. Frankie nodded when Pat said that Sarah had had no reaction from Mrs Gilligan when she spoke Frankie's name. And Sarah had not mentioned that he was in prison.

Then Sarah did speak, although a little diffidently. 'I found out that Wee Jiffy's real name was William Finlayson. They won't do anything about his body until they have finished their investigations into his…' Sarah was going to say 'killing', then Frankie's own position crossed her mind and with a little hesitation she came up with 'death'. 'We've told them that we have been instructed to deal with the funeral arrangements and they will contact us in due course.'

'Thanks…' Frankie again had that difficulty in using her first name. 'Thanks a lot. I appreciate it,' he said. He shook his head, 'William Finlayson eh? I never knew that. I don't suppose anyone did. A big name for such a wee guy. He was from our street but the first time I came across him was when I was in the Remand Home at the same time as he was. He was a poor soul. A wee bit slow but not daft. He was small and when he walked, he almost tottered forward on his toes as if he was on the point of falling. He had difficulty speaking. That's how he got his nickname. For some reason one of the few words he could say was 'Jiffy'. He would use it like a sailor saying, 'Aye, Aye Sir'. Or, if you asked him how he was, he would always say 'Just Jiffy'.' Frankie paused, thinking back. 'You know what it's like in a remand home? Survival of the fittest. Anyone who can't stand up for himself becomes a target. And Wee Jiffy was a target. As I say, he was unsteady on his feet and they would barge into him and knock him over. Sometimes they would blindfold him and spin him round and hit him and then ask him to say who had hit him. And they would call him names. Like 'Dopey' and 'Thicko' and 'Looney' and 'Spas'.

Pat and Sarah sat quietly, understanding that Frankie needed to talk about his old friend. 'You know the saying 'sticks and stones may break my bones, but names will never hurt me'? Well, the names they used *did* hurt Wee Jiffy. And I could see that. So, I stepped in. I don't know why.' Frankie shrugged. 'I made it known that Wee Jiffy was a friend of mine. I banged a few heads. As you know, Mr McLaughlin, I had a bit of a reputation even then. So, they left him alone.

'Then, when I came out of detention there was Wee Jiffy waiting for me. He just attached himself to me and I hadn't the heart to put him away. When I came out of a morning, there he would be, waiting for me. Even when I'd been away, like the time I was up for killing that policeman, when I opened the door the first morning, I was freed, there he was on the doorstep. I suppose he was handy for me in some ways. He could get into places others couldn't – when there was no way in. God knows who his parents were. I don't suppose mine were ideal, but they were there. Wee Jiffy lived with his granny in a bit of a hovel, I think. I made a point of making sure they were all right.'

'And he was killed by Jaikie Houliston?' Pat asked quietly.

'That's right. How could he do a thing like that? To get at me? Sorry, but I don't want to talk about that right now.' Frankie sat staring into the distance.

Pat said nothing.

At length he said he and Sarah would have to go and for Frankie not to forget the washing. He knocked on the door, which was opened by a warder who then took Frankie away while another warder escorted Pat and Sarah out of the prison.

Outside, and during their journey back to the office, both Pat and Sarah were silent. Sarah's main thought was that she felt as if she, herself, had been released from the prison. But there remained a heavy weight in her breast.

44

At their next visit to the prison Sarah was still overawed but not quite as terrified as she had been. On this occasion Pat picked up the dirty washing which Frankie needed cleaned, and he got Frankie to sign a Power of Attorney in Pat's favour so that Pat had access to funds to pay for the various items Frankie needed. Pat did not reveal to Sarah the extent of Frankie's wealth, but he hinted that the criminal business was obviously the one to be in.

It was during this visit that Frankie made his first complaint about the position he was in. It was not, as Sarah had expected, about the terrible charge hanging over him. He was, he said, bored!

'I'm mostly kept apart from the other prisoners so that the only people within the prison I can talk to are the warders, and many of them don't want to talk to someone they think of as a dangerous criminal. You know my family background, Mr

McLaughlin.' He looked straight at Pat. 'But despite everything we were a close family. But now there's only me and my mammy left. It never fussed me. I prided myself that I could stand on my own two feet. Girls were for use rather than for friendship. He had the grace to colour slightly at this admission in front of Sarah. Men were there to carry out my orders. They were not otherwise part of my life. Maybe I needed Wee Jiffy as much as he had needed me. Whatever. The end result is that I have no-one to speak to. Apart from you guys, of course. And I really appreciate your coming.'

Pat assured him that they would continue to come. He smiled. 'Maybe Sarah could come on her own if I'm stuck. I do have other clients, you know.'

As they left after that visit Sarah was suffering from a feeling of panic. How could she possibly come to this terrible place on her own, without Pat's support? But then she had another thought: Frankie had said he was bored – was it possible that this hard man was not bored but maybe a bit frightened on his own?

On their way back to the office Pat was more practical; he explained what he had arranged about Frankie's dirty clothes. 'You know Mrs Collins? That's the woman across the landing who took in poor Maria Gilligan that terrible night. I've arranged with her to do Frankie's washing. She's quite a woman. The family haven't two pennies to rub together but at first, she wouldn't accept any money for doing the washing. I had to force her and it's now all agreed.' He suggested, 'I'll drop you off in the Gorbals and you can go up to see her with the washing and at the same time you can call in and see Mrs Gilligan? Tho' what good it will do I don't know.'

What he didn't tell Sarah was, that in thanks for the Collins' kindness that night, Pat had arranged, through a client of his, a good job for Mr Collins, one that would not be subject to the vagaries of the shipbuilding industry.

When Sarah knocked at the door Jessie Collins recognised her right away. She brought Sarah in, all the time apologising for the state of the house, which was, in fact, perfectly tidy. When she offered a cup of tea, Sarah, this time, accepted without any misgivings and she brought Mrs Collins – or rather, Jessie, as she wanted to be called – up to date with regard to Frankie and Mrs Gilligan. Jessie said she had a confession to make.

'A huvnae been to see Mrs Gilligan. Wi' ma Kirk background, not that a go, a just couldnae cross the threshold of a Chapel House. 'Is that no terrible? And that wee priest is just a caution. A met him in the street the other day and he told me a would huv' tae watch masel in case any o' ma neebours saw me talking tae him. An' he said he would huftae watch himself in case he's seen chattin' up a Proddy.'

Sarah laughed and agreed that Father O'Leary was, indeed, a character. There was no problem with Mrs Gilligan. In the state she was in, she wouldn't have recognised Mrs Collins anyway.

Jessie left Sarah in the flat as she went across to Frankie's to collect clean clothing – she explained to Sarah how it wouldn't be right for a young lady to be rooting about in Frankie's things to find clean kegs. (That was another new word for Sarah but maybe not one to be jotted down in her notebook).

After she left with the clean clothing, with profuse thanks to Jessie for all that she was doing (all brushed away by the woman) Sarah went round to the Chapel House to see Mrs Gilligan. If anything, she was worse than before. Most of the time she drifted off in sleep and the housekeeper said that this was how she had been for the last few days. Sarah was sad as she left. For whose benefit was she making the visit? Was it merely to make her, Sarah, feel better?

At Christmas time Sarah had three days off from the office and had to spend it with her mother in Edinburgh. Prior to that she received Christmas cards from Pat McLaughlin and his wife and from Callum Fraser. That was nice of Callum, she thought, but she also decided it would have been inappropriate for her to send him one. She and Miss Kinniburgh exchanged cards. When Sarah and Pat went up to see Frankie for the last time before Christmas, she took him a card, which she thought would help to brighten up his cell. And that was that for cards.

In Edinburgh Sarah 'had' to accompany her mother to Midnight Mass. That was not quite true. Despite Sarah having determined to turn her back on all that 'superstition' she could not have allowed Christmas to pass without taking part in some sort of ceremony celebrating the birth of Christ. And during the Mass, the candles and the prayers and the carols left her with an ache over something of which she was no longer a part. And there was still sufficient of her old feelings left to enable her to partake in the joy which the rest of the congregation felt in the feast. But she was glad to get back to Glasgow prior to the New Year, which, in any event, had never been celebrated in any major way by her family.

Between Christmas and the New Year, Pat, for the first time, asked Sarah to visit Barlinnie on her own as he had family commitments. She agreed without, she hoped, any perceptible show of reluctance but inside she felt totally insecure. There was the dread of approaching what she still regarded as that most forbidding place. On top of that, she had never been on her own with Frankie. When Pat was there, all she had to do was to add the occasional comment to what he and Frankie were discussing. What would she find to say on her own?

But needs must, as she remembered her father saying to her when she was a little girl. She took the tram out past Riddrie, then set out along the approach road feeling the prison windows glowering at her as she came closer. To her relief, the warder who let her in, recognised her and accepted without question that she was Frankie Gilligan's legal representative come to see him. There was an advantage in being a lawyer (Sarah didn't feel it necessary to disclose that she was not quite qualified) because there was no restriction on the number of visits. Also, with a normal visitor, a prison warder would always be in the room throughout a visit, but a legal adviser was entitled to see the client without anyone else present.

When Frankie was led into the room, he was surprised to see Sarah on her own, but clearly delighted that she had come. She found herself talking much more freely than she had anticipated, especially as Frankie, by virtue of his position, had little to tell. When she talked about her trip home to Edinburgh, and Jessie Collins, and Frankie's mother, she found what the staff in the office had found, that Frankie was a good listener. So much so that the time for the visit passed in a flash. When she apologised for talking so much, Frankie waved away her apologies. He had enjoyed listening to her news.

It was on this occasion that Frankie told her that he had nicknamed her 'Black Eyes' because she had such great (he was going to say 'lovely' but held back) black eyes. Sarah said that was fine, so long as he didn't give her one. She afterwards reflected that she had managed to share a joke with someone she had previously held in such dread. Still, she continued to address Frankie as 'Mr Gilligan'.

Thereafter, though, Sarah frequently went up to Barlinnie on her own. She also saw Jessie Collins on a regular basis, with Frankie's laundry, and began to enjoy the time she spent with her. If she was honest with herself, although she appreciated Jessie's kindness, Sarah had thought she had nothing in common, and wanted nothing in common, with this woman with her impoverished background and her speaking in a dialect which she had difficulty in following, especially at the speed with which the words poured out. But gradually Sarah came to appreciate the common sense of the woman; the way she fed and clothed the family with such small resources; the loving manner in which she looked after her children, and the ambitions she had for them; the way in which Jessie accepted her husband as he was, even though, as she said, like all the men, he always came home drunk on payday – a concept that Sarah, with her stiff Edinburgh background, found hard to take. Sarah, to be truthful, found Mr Collins little gruff but she accepted Jessie's saying he was a good man.

The more that Sarah talked to Jessie the more she came to admire her. With her academic background, Sarah had subconsciously absorbed her classmates' feelings, never overtly expressed, that they were of a superior sort, on a different level from those who did not have similar education and training. She now appreciated that Jessie Collins had qualities, not the same as those of Sarah's friends, but just as worthwhile. Sarah and Jessie were probably about the same age, but Sarah automatically looked on her as the elder, possibly because Jessie had a family and possibly because Jessie had lost whatever slimness she had possessed following the birth of her children and now looked quite matronly.

Jessie was from a poor background and, to aid the family finances, had left school as early as possible to take a job as a scullery maid in one of the big houses on Myrtle Park. She had met and married Alec Collins when she was still young. Sarah, with her naïve head filled with Jane Austen romances, and, she admitted to herself later, literally full of pride and prejudice, couldn't conceive of the concept of love when she thought of little Jessie and big gruff Alec.

Jessie never stood still. When she was talking to Sarah she would continue with her cleaning or cooking. When she sat down, she would mend or darn; or out would come the knitting needles for her to knit jumpers and socks and gloves for the children. She told Sarah she used to go across to Paddy's Market, where she could either get good second-hand clothes or buy some old knitted stuff and take it home to unravel the wool for further use. In the summertime she went by bus down to Lanark where she would pick strawberries to make jam.

These days, she had a part-time cleaning job in an office in the town and, with the wages Alec Collins brought in, they could make ends meet. Problems only arose when Alec was laid off because a ship was finished and there was no more work to be had. There were no savings to fall back on and that was when they had been so grateful to Frankie Gilligan, and now to Mr McLaughlin.

Jessie, too, had had her prejudices. She had thought that Sarah, this slim confident young girl who had entered her world so unexpectedly was very polite but aloof, unfeeling, entirely self-assured. Perhaps a bit condescending. But, as she got to know Sarah, she warmed to her. She realised that Sarah had her worries and her concerns just as Jessie had. It was simply that they were different worries and concerns. That made her more human, more approachable. Jessie became relaxed in Sarah's company, even able to do her chores when she was there.

Sarah came to be even more involved with the family after she found Jessie labouring with some aspect of the children's homework. Because Jessie, for all her qualities, could barely read or write. Sarah volunteered her services and she was glad that she had. These children had tremendous abilities, which would never have developed properly, but which blossomed under her care. And Sarah found she was a naturally good teacher. Nothing in her life up to that point had given her as much pleasure as seeing the progress the children made under her care. She never ceased to be amazed at how easily the children coped with what were now two languages they were living with: their mother's English and Sarah's

318

English. For example, they would arrive back from school and say, 'A cannae ge' ma heid roon the lessons when a' ge' hame; a'hm fair knackered,' but when Sarah would reply that they had to get their homework into their heads they accepted what she said without question. They moved effortlessly between the two forms of speech, effectively bilingual. And Sarah had the sense not to 'correct' them. She now looked forward to her visits to see the Collins family as the highlight of her week.

One thing Jessie did not admit to Sarah was that she had eventually screwed up her courage and visited Mrs Gilligan. She told her husband instead.

'Y'er daft,' he said.

'Ay. I'd knitted a wee pair of gloves for her. Ken, auld folk ay hae cauld hauns. But when a went tae the Chapel House a kept on straight past. A felt they were in there looking at me.'

'Daft,' repeated her husband, turning over a new page of his newspaper.

'But a turned back 'n made a sort o' go at it and rang the bell. It made a sort o' loud clanging 'n a nearly ran away, a was right feart. But the wummin who opened the door was jist a nice wee wummin wi' a great smile. Its jist a normal house inside, but big, ken. She took me through tae see puir Mrs Gilligan and brought me a nice cup a' tea. A showed Mrs Gilligan the wee gloves but a dinna think she knew whit they wur 'n she dinnae know me. The wee wummin said the gloves were lovely and she would make sure puir Mrs Gilligan would wear them. Ach, it's just a shame.'

'Daft,' said her husband again, but he was secretly proud of his wee wife.

But while Sarah's time was fully occupied, Frankie was often alone by himself and had much opportunity to think on what had passed and what was to come. He still had no misgivings about having killed Jaikie Houliston. He had to die. And he had to die in the manner that he had. But what lay ahead? Frankie was realistic. He was going to be found guilty of something, and the least he could expect was a long prison sentence, possibly life. That prospect stretching before him frightened him. He could cope with the rough and tumble of prison life but what else was there? At the very basic, no sex. In fact, no contact with girls, at all. No chance of family life. What could he do to fill the apparently empty void? In between the visits of Pat and Sarah he was subject to periods of deep depression from which he was relieved in some strange way by the prospect of the trial, which must come shortly. Then he would know where he was. In the meantime, he obtained some consolation from the thought that in his life to date he had never thought about what lay ahead for him. He had not, like Black Eyes, a career in front of him with University Graduation and then a fixed job. He had always lived day to day. And that was how he would continue.

45

Sarah would never forget that Monday morning. The University term had restarted after the New Year, with the main subject being Conveyancing, chiefly dealing with property transactions. Sarah found it just a bit dull because there was little of a contentious nature in the course, which was the part of law which Sarah found most attractive. In addition, unlike her colleagues, Sarah's main focus was on her office work and, in particular, Frankie Gilligan. She would have enjoyed sharing her experiences of a murder charge and visits to Barlinnie but, having learned from Pat McLaughlin that she should not discuss clients' business out of the office, she said nothing of what was going on and tried to involve herself with the others in discussing the completion of their course in May.

Her frequent trips to the Gorbals and to Barlinnie undoubtedly left her a little detached from the extra-curricular activities that were such an important part of the University experience. Callum Fraser voiced his concern that she was maybe feeling low, but she reassured him it was just continuing work in the office which was temporarily demanding her attention.

She had settled back into a comfortable routine revolving round University, office work and visits to the Gorbals and Barlinnie, when she came back to the office mid-morning after that morning's lectures to find the office in a turmoil. When she asked the staff what was the problem all they would say was that she should speak to Mr McLaughlin. She knocked on the door to his room which was normally left ajar, but to-day was closed. When she went in, Pat McLaughlin was seated at his desk, but it was not the bright Pat McLaughlin she had worked with the previous day. His hair, normally neatly parted, was totally dishevelled; his usual fresh complexion was sallow; he seemed to have lost stones in weight as he sat slumped in his chair gazing out of the window. Pat did not return her greeting, but merely motioned to her to sit down. Eventually he turned to her speaking in a hoarse voice.

'Frankie Gilligan has been served with the indictment. Here's a copy.'

Sarah, frightened by his manner, picked up the document. It read:

'The charge is that on12 December 1957 in or about Florence Street, Glasgow you did assault James Houliston by stabbing him with a knife a number of times and did rob him of a wallet containing One hundred Pounds sterling and did murder him. And such is capital murder within the meaning of the Homicide Act 1957 section 5(1) (a).'

Sarah, her heart sinking, realised the significance right away. The Homicide Act passed the previous year had done away with the death penalty for most murders, but the penalty was retained for a small number of murders, one of which was murder in furtherance of a theft. Frankie was facing, not life imprisonment terrible as that was, but death by hanging. Now she knew why Pat was the way he was. Still, she looked at him for reassurance, desperately wanting to be relieved of the burden which had fallen on her.

Pat shook his head. 'Frankie is many things. He has lived a violent life. But he's not a thief. Yet they have evidence from a witness who saw Frankie take the satchel, and the satchel was found by the police in Frankie's house, with his blood-stained fingerprints all over it. They also found the blood-covered knife with which the forensics say Frankie killed the guy. And the forensics say that there were more than ten stab wounds on Houliston's body. So much for self-defence.' Pat heaved a sigh, almost a groan as he rubbed his forehead.

Sarah said nothing. She was almost in a state of panic.

Pat eventually spoke again. 'You shouldn't be involved in this, Sarah, but you were a great help in visiting Frankie, and all that. I won't ask you to do anything further. It's not fair. I'll see it through to the end, but you can get on with work more appropriate for an apprentice.'

Sarah could feel tears coming but she managed to hold them back long enough to blurt out, 'No, Uncle Pat. Please. I've come to know Frankie and I think he relies on me. You can't ask me to abandon him now.' And then the tears did come.

Pat got up and, coming around the desk, patted her on the shoulder. 'We'll see, Sarah. We'll see. And you have been a great help.' He paused. 'I don't understand it. Frankie is no fool. He's not daft enough to hide things from us which we were bound to find out in due course. I just don't understand it. We'll just have to see what we can do. I'll go up to Barlinnie after lunch though God knows I have no appetite.' He hesitated again, thinking. 'And okay, if you're up to it, you can come with me. You're a great help in taking notes and keeping records for me.' Then he added, 'I presume that Frankie knows the significance of this. If not, I will have to tell him. Terrible. Terrible.'

As Sarah and Pat approached Barlinnie, her old fear of the place returned. In her frequent visits to see Frankie she had become more relaxed and had even felt at ease with the prison staff – apart from one unsmiling officer who job was to check the bags of those visiting to make sure that nothing forbidden was being taken in. Sarah had found she and Frankie shared a sense of humour, and an eavesdropping warden would have heard unexpected sounds of hilarity coming from the interview room, unexpected in a meeting of a prisoner on remand with his legal adviser. She also discovered a talent for mimicry and in a variety of accents told stories of University lecturers, her fellow students, and clients who came to the office, and, it must be confessed, the good Jessie Collins whose voice, Frankie said, Sarah had off perfectly.

One of the secret admittedly childish things, which Sarah had taken to doing, with suggestions from Frankie, was to put unusual things in her handbag just to see if she got any reaction from the warder who was checking. At various times she included a Sherlock Holmes pipe, a miniature Eiffel Tower, which one of the girls in the office had brought back from a visit to Paris, a figure of the Blessed Virgin Mary in a globe which had her covered in snowflakes if the globe were shaken, a mouthorgan (a 'moothie' as Frankie explained was the correct pronunciation), a shaving brush, some billiard chalk, some lacy knickers (Frankie's rather cheeky suggestion and which Sarah had to borrow from the Office Junior as her own were practical rather than decorative), and a set of false teeth. Not once, as Sarah watched his face, did the inspecting officer change the severity of his expression or make any comment, not even with the dentures.

But these light-hearted memories were far from Sarah's mind as she and Pat approached the prison. Once again, she was in terror of its shadow. The feeling returned to her that as they got to within fifty yards of the wall that songbirds ventured no nearer, to be replaced by the rooks with their savage beaks and their harsh cries. Once inside she felt the cold surround her. This time there was no funny item to be discovered in her bag. Waiting in the interview room for Frankie to appear, she felt the tension mount in her.

When Frankie was brought in, it was Pat and Sarah who were subdued. Frankie was his normal ebullient self and stretched forward towards them to urge them to take their seats.

Pat hesitated and then said, 'You've seen the indictment, Frankie. You know what it means?' Pat hesitated again. 'You understand you're now been charged not just with murder, but murder connected to a theft and that is a capital offence. Sorry, I mean an offence for which the penalty is – hanging.'

Sarah, covertly watching Frankie's face, was surprised at the lack of reaction to Pat's words.

When he replied, Frankie did so slowly. 'Mr McLaughlin, many years ago, when I was in the remand home, I remember talking to wee Father O'Leary about the death penalty. I told him then that I was in favour of it. An eye for an eye. And I haven't changed, no matter if the law has. But he looked directly at both his visitors in turn, 'this stealing thing is just daft. There's no way I would want to steal Houliston's bag. No possibility.' Pat tried to find the right words.

'But, Frankie, the police evidence is that his bag was discovered in your flat, with your fingerprints all over it. I remember you told me once that, when you get involved in a fight, you lose all sense of time and place. Is it possible you may have taken it when you were in that state, that night?'

Frankie leant forward and stared intently at Pat. 'Mr McLaughlin. That night *I killed a man*. Okay, it was Jaikie Houliston and he got what was coming to him. But killing somebody has an effect on you. I am crystal clear as to what happened from the moment I left Houliston's body. I did not take his bag. It has my fingerprints on it because I tore it off him in the struggle.'

Sarah had never seen Pat McLaughlin so hesitant and he again struggled with what he had to say.

'Frankie, I don't like to say this, but were you just as clear when you told us that you had killed Houliston in self-defence? The forensic report says that he was stabbed more than ten times. That's hardly self-defence.'

Frankie smiled a little sadly. 'Mr McLaughlin, you don't live in my world. That was a battle that night. A war. In a war you defend yourself by killing whoever is against you. If I had not killed Jake Houliston he would have killed me.' His look hardened. 'Quite apart from that, he deserved to die. He had killed Wee Jiffy. And they might never have been able to prove it.'

There was a pause, then, 'I'm sorry Mr McLaughlin. I'm sorry, Black Eyes. But that's it.'

Pat waited a little and then told Frankie that he would not go into all the detail at this stage. The purpose of the visit was to let him know that the charge against him had changed and to make him aware of the possible consequences. After that, Frankie addressed Sarah properly for the first time, asking after his mother. Sarah, her throat dry, assured him that she was fine or at least she was in safe hands. Then he asked her what she was writing in her notebook. He was astonished when she explained that she had been taking notes for Pat's benefit and intrigued when she showed him her shorthand jottings.

There was an awkward pause after that, so unlike Sarah's normal dealings with Frankie, and then they all gestured shaking hands and Frankie was led away.

Pat and Sarah said nothing while they were within the prison walls and, even afterwards, on the way back to the office, they exchanged only a few words before parting for the night, each full of their own thoughts over what had happened.

46

Sarah now knew what Pat had meant when he talked about the terrible effect of being involved in a murder case. It was with her, day and night: her last thought at night and her first thought in the morning. And that is if she had slept much at all

It was with a heavy heart that she paid her next visit to the Bar-L, as the prison was familiarly referred to. But, if she was subdued, Frankie was his normal self and did not appear to notice. And at least she had something practical to report. The police and the fiscal had completed their enquiries into Wee Jiffy's death and his body could be released for burial. As befitted Wee Jiffy's lack of importance the enquiries had been superficial; a number of potential witnesses had assured the police they had been engaged elsewhere in Glasgow at the time of Wee Jiffy's death. Then, when assured in private that they would not be charged with any offence, they were prepared – shocked by the senseless brutality of his death - to confirm, off the record, that they had seen Houliston kill Wee Jiffy. With Houliston subsequently killed, the authorities were content to close the matter.

What to do about Wee Jiffy's remains? The police, without making much effort, had been unable to trace any next-of-kin; it seemed nobody cared. Nobody, except Frankie, who was anxious that his wee friend should be properly dealt with. He told Sarah that he had thought the matter through. There was no point in having the remains buried because it would be a grave that no-one would visit. The alternative was a cremation, which ruled out any Catholic participation as cremation was still forbidden for Catholics but nobody knew if, indeed, Wee Jiffy had been a Catholic or any other religion. The solution for Frankie, then, was that it should be a cremation, presided over by whatever minister was attached to the crematorium, and thereafter Wee Jiffy's ashes should be scattered on spare ground in the Gorbals.

And that was what happened. Pat McLaughlin made the arrangements and some days later Pat and Sarah attended the cremation service at Linn Crematorium. It was the most depressing experience of Sarah's life. The presiding minister made a few observations and read passages from scripture, all of which sounded hollow to Sarah's ears. The Funeral Director's men were obviously anxious to get on to the next job, and it was all so lacking in any dignity, Sarah felt tears welling up within her. But how could she be crying for someone she had never met? Maybe Wee Jiffy deserved at least that.

Later Pat and Sarah travelled to the Gorbals and watched by a few curious ragamuffins, scattered the ashes as Frankie had requested. Pat said a few quiet prayers. Sarah wanted to but couldn't.

As they travelled back to the office Sarah felt she was surrounded by death.

47

A few days later Pat and Sarah were on the train to Edinburgh for a consultation with Senior and Junior Counsel on the basis of the Court papers that Pat had forwarded to them. They travelled First Class; Pat explained to Sarah that, when travelling on client's business, she should always go First Class. As they approached Waverley Station, Sarah felt her usual apprehension when returning to her native city. She dreaded meeting anyone she knew and for this reason, she kept her visits to her mother to the minimum. She cared about her mother but, arising from her mother's withdrawn behaviour following the death of her father, there was no strong bond between them. Even on this trip, she had only reluctantly gone along with Pat's suggestion that they should call to see her mother after their business with Counsel was completed.

Their meeting did not take place, as Sarah had supposed, in Parliament House but in Senior Counsel's grand terraced home in the New Town. The door was opened to them, not by some flunkey as Sarah had rather expected, but by James Galloway's wife, who showed them into what was presumably the dining room, while coping with two young children who clung to her - apparently her grandchildren. She explained that her husband had been delayed but would be with them shortly. In the meantime, she supplied them with tea and some scones she had just made.

James Galloway QC, when he came in, was not the tall dignified figure that Sarah expected, but a short round, bald-headed, middle-aged man, with a small moustache, still in Court dress, with what Sarah came to know as 'falls' rather untidily crumpled at his neck. He introduced himself and his Junior, Robert Simpson, who was formally but simply dressed.

Galloway seated everyone round the dining table and got down to business right away.

'What have we here, Pat? It's a serious business. Robert and I have been through the prosecution papers and we've also gone over your own observations. What we have is a man with a long criminal record and reputation, who admits killing this man Houliston, another scoundrel, but says it was in self-defence, and totally denies having taken Houliston's bag even although it was found in his flat.

'Gilligan is obviously a violent, sadistic thug who was a gang leader in his area because of his willingness to inflict serious injury on those who oppose him and his apparent imperviousness to fear of injury to himself.'

Sarah nearly broke in here to say that that was not the Frankie Gilligan she knew but wisely kept quiet.

'But from your comments, Pat, you think there is more to him than that. You and I go back a long time and I respect your judgement. I'll share with you the preliminary thoughts of Robert and myself all subject to review once Robert has had the opportunity of interviewing Gilligan.'

Pat nodded but didn't speak.

'There is no doubt that the prosecution can prove that Gilligan killed Houliston. They will have no witnesses to the fight. There were probably twenty people who saw what happened but I'm sure that not one of them would admit even to have been in the Gorbals at the time. The other evidence is overwhelming. The bloodstained knife, which forensics link to the wounds, was found in Gilligan's flat. The wounds were inflicted by a left-handed person like Gilligan. His shirt was covered in Houliston's blood. We can't deny it, especially as Gilligan himself freely admits that he did it. What is left to us?' He paused for a second. The room was silent.

'First of all, there is the question of self-defence. The number of blows struck in what was obviously a frenzied attack, militates against this. Gilligan says it was Houliston's life or his. He says it was a war and, in a war, you don't defend yourself by merely injuring your opponent. You try to put him out of action. We are all from Glasgow and more acclimatised to the rough edges of life on the street than our more effete Edinburgh colleagues, but, even to us, more than ten stabbings with a knife is way more than is required for self-defence. And we're used to tales of violence. What is the ordinary member of a jury to think? No, at this stage, I think self-defence is not on, unless we could follow the line that self-defence can be viewed not objectively but from the viewpoint of the person attacked.

'Another thing. If we led self-defence, we would have to have Gilligan in the witness box. And at this stage we don't think that is a good idea.

'Then there's the question of the theft. Gilligan denies, vehemently I understand from you, Pat, that he stole the bag. And you have told me that Gilligan is not a thief. That to me leaves three possibilities. One, Gilligan was so much in another state when the murder took place that he held on to the bag when he ripped it clear from Houliston's body and carried it home with him without thinking. Second, that there was a mix-up by the police, and it was inadvertently brought to Gilligan's house by a policeman who had picked it up in the confusion at the scene of the crime. Third, the bag was deliberately planted by the police.'

Sarah jerked forward at the mention of the third possibility. It had never crossed her mind.

Galloway noticed her reaction out of the corner of his eye. 'Yes, Sarah. It does happen. Just as prisoners have a regrettable tendency to fall down stone stairs when in police custody. The trouble is that ordinary members of the jury would react in the same way as you have done. The police would never do such a thing. So that is a route which we would have to pursue very cautiously.

'I think a different approach to the theft might be more worth exploring. The 1957 Act talks about murder 'in furtherance of a theft.' There is no possibility that, on that night, Gilligan set out to commit a theft. He plainly set out with his cohorts, pure and simple, to wreak damage on a rival gang. So, if there was a theft, the murder was incidental to it rather than in furtherance of it. That is a line we must pursue as it might at least save him from the noose. The difficulty is that the Act is too recent for any case law to be established. We will have to do some research on the studies which led up to the proposals for the Act, and in Hansard for the debates as it passed through parliament.'

Galloway stopped then and spread his hands palms upwards to indicate that there was nothing more to be said at this stage.

Pat McLaughlin thanked him for his analysis of the case, which Sarah thought was masterly, totally unlike what she expected from Counsel's untidy appearance.

Galloway glanced at his watch. 'Now, if you would excuse me, I'll grab my tea, then I have grandchildren to read a bedtime story to. Then I have to do more work on this appeal I am halfway through. In the Court today, the learned judges seemed impervious to the brilliant arguments I was putting forward. And you, Robert, know what our esteemed Lord Kilbrennan is like. Half the time he gives the impression he is thinking of his tee-off time at Muirfield rather than the case he's dealing with,' He smiled. 'Sorry, Sarah, don't let your fresh young mind be warped by the jaundiced comments of a cynical old practitioner. But it's been a hard day.'

The next step was for Robert Simpson to go through to Barlinnie to interview Frankie, for which Pat would make the necessary arrangements. Pat and Sarah then left and, after making a very brief visit to see Sarah's mother, took the train back to Glasgow. As she sat on the train Sarah, for the first time for weeks, felt a glimmer of hope. It had not occurred to her to analyse closely the wording of the Act but now, when she thought about it, she realised that here was a real possibility that Frankie could escape from the horror of the hangman's noose.

48

When Sarah went to visit Frankie, after the consultation with Counsel, the feeling stayed with her that there was some hope. As such, she was in a lighter frame of mind, despite having to tell him what she had done with Wee Jiffy's remains.

'It was so depressing,' she said. 'The whole crematorium thing. The minster and the crematorium staff and the undertaker's men. They were just going through the motions. Then Mr McLaughlin and I flinging the ashes about in a waste site in the Gorbals. It was as if Wee Jiffy was just a waste of space. Maybe he was. But I was sad.'

Frankie shook his head. 'You did right by him, but he wasn't a waste of space. I get a lot of time to think when I'm alone in my cell. None of us has any lasting importance. In forty years' time, who'll remember us? But at the time we're all important. Wee

Jiffy, for all he stuttered and was unsteady on his feet, and was always a bit scruffy, was a good friend to me. Maybe my only friend. He was part of the family, if you like. And he was Gorbals born and bred. It's right that his ashes were spread where he belonged.' He paused. 'I'm sorry I've gone on a bit. I'm too much on my own.'

Sarah smiled sadly. When she and Frankie met, they always mimicked a handshake, which was all that was possible across the broad table which dissected the room. Now, for the first time she stretched across the table between them and reached for Frankie's hand, not as a greeting but to show that she understood. Frankie leant right over so that it was just possible for their two hands to meet, and he unconsciously caressed the back of her fingers with his thumb. The stretch was uncomfortable, but they persisted.

And Frankie was immediately aware that something had changed.

It was like stepping from deep shadow into brightest sunlight. Abruptly. And Frankie knew that it had happened. One moment he was chatting to Sarah as he would to a close pal. The next, it was, strangely, as if she had moved away from him to become something infinitely more precious. To be cherished. No more someone to joke with and grin at. Now someone to bring smiles and joy. From that moment he stopped calling her 'Black Eyes'.

Without a conscious decision and without being aware of the change she was 'Sarah' from then on.

Sarah didn't pick up the new use of her name. They rather painfully untwined their fingers; conscious they might be seen by a patrolling warder glancing through the glass observation panels on the doors. They talked further until she had to leave. On her way back to the office she reflected as usual on her visit. She sensed that that there had been a change in the way Frankie acted. A softening. Perhaps it was his sadness when thinking of Wee Jiffy.

But it was the same in subsequent visits. For Sarah, the whole alteration in their relationship was less dramatic, more gradual, but still real, and time went on and she responded to Frankie's new warmth towards her. She did not contrast her new feelings with what had gone before, she merely felt a sense of happiness and contentment whenever she was now with Frankie and she did not ask herself why. Not that she called him 'Frankie'. When she discussed him in conversation with others, she referred to him, as they did, as 'Frankie'. But when speaking to him she still felt happier calling him 'Mr Gilligan'. Partly it had started as a bit of a joke; just as he had called her 'Black Eyes', but, subconsciously, it was a reflection of the respect in which she wanted to hold him, especially when others, including without malice, his own Counsel, referred to him as 'Gilligan'.

It was gradually, as her feelings deepened, the words 'Mr Gilligan' on her lips meant more and more, 'I love you'.

And now, as part of the routine of her visits, they always, at some stage, made a point of stretching painfully across the table to touch fingers so that, even for a short time, there was contact between them.

49

Ten days after the consultation with Counsel, Robert Simpson, the Junior, came through from Edinburgh to interview Frankie. Pat and Sarah accompanied him to Barlinnie, with Sarah poised to take notes. The trial was due to take place at the High Court in Glasgow on 21 May, but before that there was a preliminary hearing at which Frankie had to plead guilty or not guilty, and any special defences – such as self-defence – had to be intimated.

Robert Simpson was very much what Sarah thought Counsel should look like. He was tall with neat dark hair; about thirtyish, she imagined. He was dressed in black jacket and pin-stripe trousers, looking entirely out of place in the dingy surroundings. His manner in dealing with the prison warders was commanding and demanded the respect which they showed him. He was also firm and business-like in his dealings with Frankie, going over the evidence which the prosecution was going to produce in court and discussing with him Frankie's attitude to it.

'Now, Mr Gilligan,' (Sarah liked that), 'The question of self-defence. I've heard your version that you were engaged in a sort of war. There are certain rules of engagement in times of war when ordinary standards are set aside. But that only applies in an actual war which has certain defined limits. It does not apply to a street brawl, no matter how violent. My advice to you is that such a defence is, as they say in Glasgow, 'oot the windae'. It is your decision to make, you are the client, but to persist in it would merely expose you to the jury as a hardened criminal who lives outwith normal standards of behaviour.' Robert Simpson consulted his notes before continuing.

'The prosecution has not found any witnesses to the fatal stabbing. That is not unexpected. The people in your area, often for good reasons, are not fond of assisting a police enquiry. The prosecution case will, accordingly, be based on forensic evidence of the wounds which were inflicted, allied to the fact that, when you were arrested, you were still wearing a shirt covered in Houliston's blood, and the weapon which caused the wounds was in your possession. I understand that, in any event, you do not deny the stabbing. You will notice that I do not use the word 'murder'. It is for the jury to decide whether the attack on Houliston constitutes murder. Be that as it may, it is only fair to tell you that, although

344

we will attack every aspect of the evidence looking for loopholes, you must prepare yourself to be found guilty of the charge of murder.'

Simpson paused here to let his words sink in. Sarah concentrated her attention on the notes she was taken so as not to look at Frankie. Frankie said nothing. If Sarah had looked up, she would have seen Frankie mostly looking at the table but glancing at her in passing, almost looking for comfort.

Simpson went on, 'That leads us to the charge of theft and, in particular, to its connection with the stabbing. Now when–'

Frankie broke in, 'I did not steal that bag. What would I want with it?'

'Mr Gilligan, it was, to say the least, an unusual night. You had killed a man. You are known as a violent man but killing was something you had never done before. It must have had an effect on you. Am I right?'

Frankie looked into the distance before saying, 'Yes.'

'It had such an effect on you that you did not go into hiding. You went straight home, where you must have known the police would come looking for you. You, an experienced criminal, if I may say without giving offence, sat there still wearing the shirt which was spattered with Houliston's blood. You made no attempt to conceal the knife smeared with his blood, with which you had stabbed him. According to the police, it lay on the table beside you as you sat.'

Frankie concurred with a brief nod of his head.

'Mr Gilligan, is it not possible that, in the highly charged state of mind you were in, you had retained hold of the bag which you had torn from Houliston and brought it back with you to your house?'

Frankie broke out again, speaking forcefully, 'I did not steal that bag. Whose side are you on, anyway? Who saw me with the bag?'

'Mr Gilligan, I am very much on your side. The points I am making are the points we will have to deal when they come up in the trial. The witness who saw you with the bag was…' He checked his notes, 'Billy Morton.'

'That arsehole! Sorry, Sarah. That explains a lot. He tried to muscle in my patch when I was up for the policeman's death. When I was released, I sent him packing with a few reminders not to come back if he valued his skin. That McCulloch must have done a deal with him to overlook some pressing charges if he would testify against me. McCulloch has been out to get me since that other policeman's death. McCulloch was around that night. It was McCulloch who led the cops who broke down my door. It must have been McCulloch who planted the bag on me–'

Robert Simpson shook his head. 'I'll stop you there, Mr Gilligan. Juries do not believe that policemen are capable of being dishonest. You're an expert criminal. I am an expert lawyer, particularly in jury trials. You must believe me when I say that to pursue such an allegation is tantamount to sealing your fate. No. What we must do is to show that the removal of the bag was incidental to the stabbing. You did not set out to steal a bag. You set out to pursue a gang vendetta. The bag was an irrelevance.'

It was Frankie's turn to shake his head. 'I killed the guy. What difference does the bag make?'

'A difference that may save your life. And that's my job. To save your life.'

It was left to Frankie to have the last word as Simpson, Pat McLaughlin and Sarah left.

'I did not steal that bag,' he said.

'I did not steal that bag.'

These were Frankie's first words to Sarah on her first visit after the meeting with Robert Simpson.

'You believe me, don't you?' Frankie looked anxiously at Sarah and was visibly re-assured when she nodded.

'You see it's important to me,' he said. 'I'm not a thief. I know there's a wee kink in my nature. I don't know where it's from. When I'm in a violent situation, at a certain stage it's like the flicking of a switch or going over a cliff edge. I lose the grip of myself and become some sort of a monster, totally uncontrollable until it passes. That's why I was feared in my patch. They said in the papers that I was a psychopath. I thought they were saying 'cycle path' and couldn't understand it until Mr McLaughlin explained it to me.' This last was said with a grin, which Sarah managed to match 'But I am not a thief. And if I am going to go down, I don't want to go down on the basis that I am a thief. If I'm done for murder, I can't complain.'

Sarah smiled inwardly at the twisted logic of this man who had come to mean so much to her. How could she understand someone who could apparently kill callously, but was too proud to be called a thief? She could not understand it, but she could accept it. She reached across the table feeling for his hand. For a moment they stroked each other's outstretched hand before sinking back with a shared expression of relief from the pain.

After a pause Frankie said, 'When you were a wee girl, did you wear white ankle socks?'

'Yes, I did until I was about twelve or thirteen.' Sarah was surprised. 'Why do you want to know?'

Frankie shrugged. 'It's not important, I just wondered.'

But it was important. Frankie just could not find the words in his mind to describe how he felt about Sarah. Glasgow hard men do not do love; the word is not in their vocabulary. A girl is there to be enjoyed when needs be; a possession to be looked after like any other possession; to be valued when set against other girls; to be discarded if a better one appears. But Sarah was not like that for Frankie. The word now came to Frankie – she was a goddess. A goddess to be worshipped from afar. No, that was wrong. He wanted more than that. But to look for more was insulting to her. Frankie's mind was in a turmoil. He said nothing, but Sarah sensed the tension in Frankie's manner.

'What's wrong Mr Gilligan? Please tell me. We're friends. I feel closer to you than I've felt to anyone else in my life. We trust each other, don't we? You remember, last week when you thought I was looking very pale and I told you that I was having my period. That is something very intimate for a girl, but I felt I could tell you.'

Frankie looked down at the table, then at her, then at the wall, then again at her. Then he suddenly burst out looking straight at her, 'Ach, its daft. Here's me a thug and you an educated young lady from a polite background. I'm gallus, even to think about it far less say anything. But it's true. I'm feared that it will spoil things between us. Please not. I know you have been just been seeing me out of kindness. And it's not fair of me to repay you with this shite. Sorry, Sarah. You see what I mean. I'm not from a polite background. Sorry, Sarah. I should have just kept quiet. I've spoiled everything.' Frankie finished by throwing his hands almost helplessly on the table and looking at her with an abject expression on his face.

There was another long pause during which Frankie's face became, if anything, more frantic.

Sarah sat twisting her fingers with her head bowed over them. She gave a deep sigh and then an even deeper one. She frowned then looked up at Frankie. She had come to a decision about something which had been forming in her mind for weeks.

'Mr Gilligan, I know what I want to say but I don't know how to say it. Mr McLaughlin says that after a time as a lawyer you lose the ability to write a normal natural letter. It's the same with me now. I don't know how to say what I want to say except as a lawyer might say it. Right, it can't be helped. Firstly, I am not offended. My background in Edinburgh was just as low as yours. Secondly, I don't come to see you out of kindness.' She paused. 'Thirdly, I think – no that's too wishy washy – *I know,* that I love you.' She held up a hand as he moved to speak. 'Don't ask me to explain it. All I know is that you fill my whole life for me. I look forward to seeing you as the highlight of my week. I read that love is a spiritual thing but for me it is physical. I literally ache with the longing to hold you in my arms and hug you.'

Frankie couldn't speak. A couple of times he raised his arms as if to try to reach across the unbridgeable gap between them.

Then he pointed to his chest. 'In here. Hugs and kisses. Hugs and kisses.'

'Oh, yes, Mr Gilligan, hugs and kisses.'

Now that she had spoken, and Frankie had hinted at the love he hadn't been able to express, he found the words. 'Sarah, for me you are everything I ever wanted even when I didn't know I needed it. You are beautiful and lovely and pure and unspoiled and without shame and…'

Sarah held up her hand to stop him. 'Pure and unspoiled,' she said bitterly. 'There is something you must know.' The she hesitated for a long, long minute.

Frankie did not interrupt her.

'You know that I did my initial degree at Edinburgh University. It would have been normal to have continued with my law degree there as well. Something happened.'

Another very long silence during which Sarah sat with her fists clenched and her head bowed. And then in a rush, she said, 'At a final night party, I was raped by a fellow student.' Sarah, her face flushed, did not dare to raise her eyes to look at Frankie.

Finally, Frankie spoke. 'Sarah, look at me. Tell me that again but look straight at me when you are telling me and keep looking at me. You are not to be ashamed. You have done nothing wrong.'

Sarah told her story with many hesitations and many occasions when she tried to avoid Frankie's gaze and he had almost to force her to keep looking at him.

'He was a fellow student, a bit older than the rest of us. He had been in the army and had seen the world. I had no great feelings for him, but I admired him because he opened my eyes to new trends in books and art and to modern jazz. He had a problem with drink. Became a wild man, really out of control. But I prided myself that I could handle him. I was wrong. He got me alone and attacked me. He was a big strong man. I had no chance. I can't believe this myself, but I didn't cry out for help. I didn't want people to know what was happening. How Edinburgh was that?' Sarah swallowed hard and continued, 'After it was over, I escaped from the flat where the party was taking place without telling anyone. When I got home, I didn't tell my mother what had happened. I was too ashamed. I scrubbed and scrubbed myself trying to get rid of the uncleanliness I felt. I tortured myself by thinking that perhaps I had brought it on myself by maybe dressing too provocatively. I started to wear as dowdy clothes as possible. I was scared that other members of the class knew what had happened and kept away from anywhere I might meet any of them. Even walking in the street, every man I met seemed to me to be a potential attacker. My mother noted the change in me, but we were never really close, and she put it down to a failed love affair...

Love!' Sarah added bitterly. She had so far kept her composure but now she broke down sobbing, with tears streaming down her face.

Frankie, distraught himself, was prevented by the table to get to her, to console her.

'You know, Mr Gilligan – the worst thing? After I left school I gave up on religion. I thought it was all show. But despite this, there still remained in my mind the concept of the purity of virginity which the nuns had drummed into us. And that had been torn from me. I was spoiled goods. And that,' Sarah sighed, 'was why I reacted when you said what you said.'

Frankie jumped in as soon as she stopped speaking and he used the word which, up till then, he had been unable to use.

'Sarah Watson. Look at me. I love you. What you have told me doesn't divide us. It unites us. If you will let me say it. I love you. And I love you more because you trusted me to tell me what you suffered.'

After this, both Sarah and Frankie were emotionally exhausted and merely sat gazing at each other in quiet peace. When it was time for Sarah to go Frankie tapped his chest and Sarah tapped hers each saying 'hugs and kisses' with even greater intensity. Thereafter, they said it each time they parted.

After Sarah had gone, one of the warders who had supervised the visit said to his colleague, 'You know, it's all right this women's lib and saying women can be lawyers the same as men. But you wouldn't see a male lawyer during a meeting with a client, greetin' like she did.'

50

The next few weeks passed in a turmoil. Sarah had never taken alcohol or drugs, but an experienced user would have recognised the mixture of images and feelings which swept through her mind constantly, day and night, even when she was consistently busy. She had work to do in the office, independent of the murder case and, at University she had final exams coming up to enable her to take her degree in the summer. Despite her pre-occupations she had to force herself to take some part in the class social life, which was active because of the close-knit nature of the course. In this, Sarah found some solace in the company of Callum Fraser, in whose company she felt totally at ease. Her absorption with Frankie's case was obvious to him but he never pressed her on it and, of course, she did not disclose the true depths of her feelings for Frankie.

She still went to see Jessie Collins for a change of clothes for Frankie and continued working with the children on their schoolwork. She visited Mrs Gilligan on a weekly basis, although it was becoming ever clearer that Frankie's mother was fading away and was unaware of Sarah's visits. And looming over everything was Frankie's approaching trial, the thought of which was in Sarah's mind every hour of the day and frequently much of the night. She was aware that the case was affecting everyone in the office, right down to the office junior who always questioned her after her visits to Barlinnie. Pat McLaughlin was especially troubled. He had become distracted and tetchy, on one occasion reducing Sarah to tears by shouting at her and accusing her of lying, when she misplaced some notes he had given her. He did later apologise profusely to her, doing so in front of most of the secretarial staff, as they had been witnesses of his previous outburst. And, human nature being what it is, there were, maybe, some members of staff who were secretly pleased to see the blue-eyed girl being brought down a peg or two.

The only composed person in the office was old Mr Shaw to whom Sarah always spoke on his occasional visits. She found comfort just by being in his presence and sharing her worries with him, although never admitting her feelings for Frankie. She knew instinctively that he would disapprove, and she could not contemplate having that additional burden to bear. He happened to be in the office just after she had been attacked by Pat McLaughlin and she told him, through tears, what had happened, being quite open that she had been at fault. She never knew that afterwards he had spoken to Pat.

'Pat, I understand that you've been shouting at the staff again.' He paused with a twinkle. 'That's twice in thirty years. Just not good enough.' Then he grew serious. 'This case is killing you, Pat, but we're stuck with it now. I remember when we first became partners, what attracted me to you was that you were a Catholic – and there were many who thought I was daft – and you didn't think man was perfect but believed in forgiveness. That wee girl, Sarah, is a gem, but she is heartbroken, and I know you will do the right thing by her. Ah, I only wish I could do more to help you to carry the burden, but I would just be in the way. My dear friend.'

Pat stood up and lent forward to shake old Mr Shaw's hand. 'Craigie, you are a greater help than you will ever know.'

The minor difference between Pat and Sarah was thus easily forgotten. What Sarah could never forget for a moment was the terrible cloud hanging over her of her love for a man who, in a matter of weeks, could be sentenced to death.

Frankie, meantime, had little to fill the long hours of the prison day, from the early wake-up call to nightfall. He was kept apart from the other prisoners and had little inclination to speak to any of the warders. It was this, quite distinct from his personal feelings, which made Sarah's visits so precious. And it was during one of these visits that he mentioned casually, inspired by his school art teacher, he had once made some feeble attempts at drawing. On her next visit, Sarah produced pencils and paper, and, thereafter, he filled his time absorbed in sketching, strictly for his own viewing as he stressed to Sarah although eventually, after much pressure he allowed her to see some drawings. These she admired not out of politeness but because she thought they were genuinely good. He admitted that he was working on a drawing of her although he never allowed her to see it.

Of course, when Frankie told Sarah about his school art teacher, he did not mention their brief sex session on his last day at school but that, along with other sexual encounters, formed part of his nocturnal erotic imaginings. Thoughts of Sarah formed no part of those fantasies. He did not understand or try to understand it, but Sarah existed in a different part of his consciousness. It was a consciousness which filled his mind. In a way which would have surprised others he did not dwell on the outcome of his trial. What would be would be.

Frankie, above all, had the love of Sarah to sustain him.

51

Prior to the Gilligan trial there was a Preliminary Hearing at which Frankie's formal plea of Not Guilty was intimated. At that Hearing the defence required to intimate if they intended to make any special pleas, in particular if they intended to plead self-defence. From the outset, Counsel had expressed doubts that there was any possibility of such a defence being successful and they were anxious that in making it, Frankie would require to give evidence, which would expose him to being shown as a self-confessed thug who lived by violence. Thus, no plea of self-defence would be made. By the same token, after much debate involving Frankie, Pat and Counsel it was agreed, by Frankie reluctantly, that Frankie would not give evidence.

The question of theft was looked at from different aspects by Frankie and Counsel. Frankie continued to insist vehemently that he had not stolen the bag, despite Counsel pointing out time after time that, leaving aside the evidence of the witness, which they were confident they could challenge, the circumstantial evidence was that the bloodstained bag, with Frankie's fingerprints on it, had been found in Frankie's possession immediately after the crime. Counsel concentrated their efforts in trying to separate the theft from the killing. If they could persuade the judge to direct the jury that the killing was not in furtherance of a theft, they could save their client from the death penalty.

Although Sarah was present at all meetings, she had the good sense to confine herself to taking notes for Pat. She longed to interject that the Frankie Gilligan they were talking about was not the Frankie Gilligan she knew (and loved!) She was sure that if Frankie had the opportunity to present himself openly in the Court the jury would recognise that there was no question of Frankie being a thief and, indeed, the killing which had taken place was a necessary product of the violent culture in which Frankie had been brought up and could rightly be described as culpable homicide. But she held her peace. She didn't even discuss her views with Frankie in her meetings with him. She felt that it would be wrong to place some doubt in his mind about the defence team who were acting for him.

And who were straining every nerve to save him. In her naivety Sarah thought that experienced leading Counsel would take such a trial in their stride but, after one meeting, James Galloway and Robert Simpson had time to spare before catching their Edinburgh train and, at Galloway's suggestion they called in at a public bar close to Queen Street Station. Sarah, of course, did not drink nor, indeed, did Pat McLaughlin but both Counsel eagerly downed their whisky and relaxed a little under its influence. Although the talk was general, the trial kept on intruding into the conversation. Just before they were leaving Galloway turned to Pat.

'You know, Pat… Thanks for giving me this brief. But I don't know if I can handle any more like this. The thought that I, through some silly mistake, or wrongly expressed word, or failure to guide the case in the right direction, may cost someone his life, even someone as undeserving as Gilligan,' (Sarah didn't like that) 'bears heavily on me and I know Robert feels the same.' Robert nodded slightly. 'I spend all my waking hours and much of my so-called sleeping hours going over things in my mind in case I have missed something which would help us. Trying to put myself in the mind of a juror. What might influence him. Thank heaven the law has changed in most cases and I am sure will change again to exclude the death penalty completely.'

Pat said nothing, just listened.

'And you know, Robert has been researching the Parliamentary debates at the time the change in the law took place. To see whether we could get some insight, which could help us, into the phrase 'in the course of or furtherance of theft.' But it seems there was no great philosophical reason for it. It seems to have been inserted merely as a sop to those who were insistent that the death penalty should be retained in full. The kind of people who think the country has gone to pigs and whistles ever since the abolition of the death penalty for sheep stealing. So, we just have to concentrate on showing that there is no evidence of intent to steal in Gilligan's mind.

'And that takes us back to the decision whether Gilligan should be put in the witness box to speak to his state of mind on the night. But that exposes him to be shown to the jury as a career criminal to whom no sympathy should be shown. We can't take that risk.'

And with that, Galloway and Simpson drained the last of their whisky and left for the train.

As the day for the trial approached, Sarah was horrified to find that on the same date her final Conveyancing exam was due to take place. She spent a sleepless night worrying whether she should just miss the exam but fortunately she confided in Pat McLaughlin, who re-assured her that the morning of the trial would be taken up with formal matters like swearing in the shorthand-writers and

362

empanelling the jury This would take some time as the Defence was entitled to object to five of the prospective jurors without cause shown (just because he looked like a bit of a disciplinarian, as Pat explained) and a further number if the Defence could persuade the Court that there was good reason for exclusion. Sarah would be well clear of her exam in time for the real proceedings to start in the afternoon.

Sarah's pre-trial worries were intensified when, while buying her paper on the Sunday before the trial was due to begin, she spotted that one of the mass-circulation Sundays had a banner headline about Glasgow gangs. She bought a copy and was horrified to find the paper had devoted its front page and its centre spread to what it called 'a campaign to deal with the scourge of gang warfare in Glasgow which was returning the city to the lawless days of the Thirties'. It called upon the Courts to repeat the courage shown by Lord Carment, who had declared war on crimes involving razor slashing, and to punish the offenders with the harshest punishment available under the law. The spread bemoaned the fact that Parliament had just recently removed the death penalty for most types of murder, against the wishes of the vast majority of the paper's readership.

Sarah's heart sank as she read the article. She was indignant and frustrated, but what could she do? She spent the day alone with feelings of despair.

52

The day of the Trial (and of the Conveyancing exam) dawned. With thoughts of the trial Sarah would not have been able to sleep in any event but at least she was able to pass the sleepless hours by cramming into her head all that she needed to know about Bonds and Dispositions in Security and ex facie absolute Dispositions and Leases and tenement Title restrictions and boundary disputes… All of which she supposed would be her bread and butter in the future. (And which were so much less enthralling than the bare-knuckle law into which she had involuntarily become involved).

She managed to get through the Exam Paper somehow and afterwards Callum Fraser took her for some food in the Men's Union, before driving her down to the High Court building in the Saltmarket, just opposite the entrance to Glasgow Green. Sarah had passed the impressive sandstone building on a number of occasions on her way to the Gorbals, just across the river. Indeed, it crossed Sarah's mind that the Court was within half a mile of the area where the murder ('alleged,' she reminded herself) had taken place. There was a big crowd milling about at the entrance to the building but she quickly spotted Pat McLaughlin who had obtained the judge's permission for Sarah to sit in the well of the court, along with the other members of the defence team. Pat led her past the various policemen and Court staff into the building, and along corridors to what was called the Gown Room where James Galloway and Robert Simpson were waiting.

As they walked Pat asked how her exam had gone but she almost brushed the query aside in her anxiety about the progress of the trial. He confirmed that the morning had been occupied with the selection and the swearing in of the Jury and other procedural matters. They had successfully used two of their automatic objections to exclude one prospective juror who was a headmaster and one who was the managing director of a large firm. Pat explained how there was a belief among lawyers that those lower down the employment chain were more inclined to be sympathetic to someone who was more of their class. Whether that was true or not was another matter but at least the element of choice gave defence lawyers the feeling that they were doing something positive.

The three men sat idly, nervously, talking with Sarah listening, her mouth totally dry. She was suddenly conscious that her knees were literally knocking and was jerked out of her thoughts with a start as a bell high up on the wall rang. That was the signal that the Court was about to begin.

James and Robert donned their gowns and wigs and Pat and Sarah followed them along a corridor before an usher opened a door for them and she found herself in the Court chamber. As they were moving, Sarah had been conscious of a growing hubbub and when she entered the Courtroom she realised that the noise was coming from the excited exchanges of the packed ranks of spectators who were crammed into the public galleries.

The Courtroom was a high-ceilinged chamber, almost square. At one end there was a raised area, where the Judge sat at his desk, within a large rectangular alcove with pillars on either side. Immediately in front of the Judge, on a lower level, there was an area known as the well of the Court, consisting of a broad table occupied immediately below the Judge by the Clerk of Court, with the other sides occupied by the members of the prosecution team to the right of the judge and the defence team to the left. Immediately across the well of the Court, facing the judge and almost on the same level was the dock for the accused, which was accessed from below by a staircase hidden from the spectators. Behind that again were the public galleries. The jury sat in an area to the right of the judge looking across the well to the witness stand on the other side. Even had the chamber been empty Sarah would have been over-awed by its grandeur, but now, fully occupied, it left Sarah almost breathless with excitement and dread.

In the cells below, Frankie could hear the noise as a background to his thoughts. In his time in Barlinnie he had set himself to live in the minute and not be concerned about the outcome of his trial but, that morning, as he had waited to appear, the whole enormity of his position came to him in a rush and he could barely walk as he was escorted from the cell into the Courtroom. He had been taken aback by the size of the Courtroom and the number of people jammed into it. He was also conscious of being the focus of all eyes as heads craned to see him, as he felt, exposed in the dock between two police officers. His morning appearance had been short, while various formalities were gone through, but now the real trial was about to start and he steeled himself to keep his head up as he made the short journey from the cell once more back up into the dock. As he entered the dock with a policeman on either side, he saw Sarah with the rest of the defence team sitting in the well of the Court. He gave a little nod which she returned nervously.

The noise in Court rose even louder and then was brought to a halt as a hoarse, prolonged cry of 'Court' from the Macer announced the arrival of the Judge, Lord Melfort, into the Court. He bowed to the Jury some of whom bowed somewhat self-consciously in response, then to the Bar who all, including Sarah, returned his bow. He then took his seat and nodded to the Advocate-Depute that he should begin.

The Advocate-Depute, John Gilchrist, was a tall, spare, middle-aged man who carried out the examination of his witnesses in a quiet courteous way. The first witness was Frankie's old enemy, Superintendent Samuel McCulloch. He confirmed that he had attended (Sarah reflected that police officers always 'attend') the scene of the riot; that the information he received pointed to the accused as having been involved; that he had gone to the accused's house accompanied by other officers; that he had made a forced entry and, despite the noise which the forced entry had caused, had found the accused sitting at the kitchen table, wearing a bloodstained shirt and with a bloodstained knife lying on the table in front of him. The accused had allowed himself to be arrested without objection and the Superintendent, having arranged for the accused's mother to be taken to a neighbour's house, put a constable on duty at the entrance to the flat and had the accused taken to the police station, leaving the flat to be examined by the CID at a subsequent date. At the police station the accused was charged and made no reply to the charge.

Subsequently, the Superintendent was informed that a search of the flat had disclosed, in a drawer, a bloodstained bag containing £100 which was identified as belonging to Jaikie Houliston. Thus, the accused was, in addition, charged with theft.

The facts were so plain that James Galloway had little to work on in cross-examination. But he pressed the officer on Frankie's reaction to the second charge.

'You stated that the accused made no response when charged with the first charge.'

McCulloch nodded.

'Did he make any response when charged with the theft of the bag?'

'Not that I recall.'

'I think you do, Superintendent. To assist you, you might like to make reference to your notebook.'

McCulloch fished in his pocket for his notebook.

'Does it say anything there? And you will bear in mind that other officers can speak to what happened.'

'Gilligan replied, 'I know nothing about Houliston's bag'.'

'Strange, that this had slipped your mind, Superintendent. And is there anything else written in your notebook?'

McCulloch coloured and frowned. 'Nothing of consequence.'

'Let me be the judge of that, Superintendent. Let me assist you. Do the letters GTB appear in capitals? What do they signify?'

McCulloch glared at him. 'It's just something we used to put down after an arrest when we were young constables.'

'And what do the letters signify?'

When McCulloch paused, Galloway intervened. 'Again, let me assist you, Superintendent, because I know you are a god-fearing, upright man. Would you agree with me that they signify 'Got The Bastard'?'

Before McCulloch could respond, Galloway sat down.

The Advocate-Depute rose. 'Let me follow my learned friend in assisting you. Would you agree that the letters referred to, merely reflect, in graphic form, your understandable satisfaction at having arrested someone who had long been a thorn in your flesh?'

A relieved McCulloch nodded and was allowed to leave the witness box, casting, as did so, a malevolent scowl in the direction of Frankie.

The CID officers who had searched the flat confirmed that the knife shown to them was the one they had collected from the kitchen table. They also identified the blood-stained bag they had found in a drawer. They agreed with James Galloway, that apart from being in the drawer, there was no attempt at concealment of the bag which was the only thing in the drawer.

Galloway took more time in his cross-examination of Sergeant MacPherson who had accompanied Superintendent McCulloch when he broke into Frankie's flat and who had shepherded poor Mrs Gilligan to find refuge with Jessie Collins.

'Sergeant MacPherson, I believe you have served as a police officer in the Gorbals for many years?'

'Nearly thirty years now, sir.'

'And how would you describe your time?'

'I have enjoyed it. The Gorbals has a bad reputation but the vast majority of the people are good people. There are good things and bad things.'

'And I suppose you would call gang warfare one of the bad things.'

'It can be terrible. It comes and goes.'

'And what, in your view, provokes this gang warfare?'

'It's just the young men and boys. They have no jobs. They get by with various types of criminal behaviour. They grow out of it as they get older. Being in a gang gives them an identity. A feeling of security. They are mostly poorly educated with no prospects apart from prison. But in a gang and in their area, they feel they are someone. Mr Big. But every so often they rub up against another gang and their standing is threatened. People say that gang warfare arises because of dispute over territory. That's not true. A gang's territory is dictated by the streets in which the gang members live. That can't change. It's all about bragging rights. Why the enmity between two gangs comes to a boil is difficult to say. Sometimes it starts just because of a fight between two individual members of the different gangs. I think that this recent trouble may have started because of the result of a football match, but who knows. It's just an excuse to have a go at the other gang.'

Galloway was happy to allow Sergeant MacPherson to have his say without interruption. At one point the Advocate-Depute half rose to challenge the relevancy of the Sergeant's testimony, but he sank down again.

Galloway turned to the Sergeant. 'We have used the term 'warfare'. In normal warfare the dispute is about the acquisition of territory, but you have told us that in gang warfare territories don't change. In normal warfare the objective might by the taking of the other side's flags or the amassing of loot. Does this apply in gang warfare?'

The Sergeant smiled. 'Never, in my experience. They're just in it for the fighting.'

Galloway thanked the Sergeant for his evidence but the Advocate-Depute rose to his feet to re-examine. 'You will be aware, Sergeant, that a satchel belonging to Jaikie Houliston was found in the Accused's flat. You stated that property acquisition was not the point of these gang wars. But you wouldn't exclude opportunistic stealing?'

No. These things happen. I was puzzled that the bag was in Gilligan's house but that's what must have happened.'

When the Sergeant's evidence was finished, further evidence was given by various forensic experts. They established that Houliston had been fatally stabbed probably ten times, by a left-handed assailant; that the knife shown in court was the type of knife which could have caused the wounds; that the knife was smeared with Houliston's blood; that it was marked with Frankie's fingerprints; that the shirt Frankie was wearing was covered in Houliston's blood; that the satchel shown in court was smeared with Houliston's blood; that it also carried Frankie's fingerprints.

Galloway probed the testimony given by the experts, looking for a discrepancy of which he could take advantage but, to Sarah's dismay, nothing emerged that might have been helpful to Frankie's defence. On top of that Galloway had no contrary experts to produce who might have rebutted the prosecution evidence.

Following on the forensic evidence, the Court adjourned to the next day.

53

After the case was adjourned for the day, the legal team had a short meeting with Frankie and then repaired to The Western Club to discuss the day's events. Sarah was exhausted and curiously deflated. Pat explained on the way to the Club that the tiredness was a natural reaction to a day spent in Court, where one was totally concentrated on what was going on. It was the reason why criminal lawyers tended to be young because, for them, the day in Court was followed, not by relaxing as she could do, but by preparing for the next day's proceedings. Indeed, before they reached the Club, the first batch of the shorthand-writers' extended transcripts had already been delivered there, to be followed, within a couple of hours, by the remaining transcripts. Counsel would pore over these during the evening to determine whether there was anything in the reported evidence that they might have missed in the course of the day.

Sarah kept her disappointment to herself. She could not understand why Galloway had not attacked the prosecution witnesses more forcibly. With their evidence unchallenged, Frankie was bound to be found guilty of murder. Later in the evening Galloway explained. The fingerprint evidence was incontrovertible, as was the connection between the wounds suffered by Houliston and the knife found in Frankie's possession. So was the evidence of the young CID officer who had found the satchel. The evidence was clear and fair. Galloway and Simpson had listened to the evidence and would go over the shorthand transcripts that night to see if there were any gaps, any breaks in the chain of causation. Failing finding anything they decided that it would merely antagonise the jury against Frankie if they tried to cast doubt on witnesses who the jury would feel had given honest and fair testimony.

Galloway then said what Sarah desperately did not want to hear. 'As far as the murder charge is concerned, as they say in this part of the world, the game's a bogey. He is going to be found guilty. We must concentrate our efforts in taking the jury with us in agreeing that there was no question of theft and therefore no question of a capital offence. Our main point of attack is this guy, Billy Morton, who is the first prosecution witness tomorrow. He is the only person who says he saw Gilligan strike Houliston and take the bag. He is an obvious hood who has been put up to this by our friend Superintendent McCulloch, no doubt in return for other misdemeanours being overlooked. Morton hates Gilligan and we can attack his testimony on that basis. But it is a two-edged sword. When Gilligan was last in prison awaiting trial, Morton tried to take over his territory. When Gilligan was found not guilty and released, he took revenge on Morton by assaulting him to an inch of his life, including slashing his face with a razor. You will see the scar on his face tomorrow. The dilemma is, by highlighting this, we are exposing Gilligan to the jury as a hardened thug. The other 'slight' difficulty is that the crime of which Gilligan was found not guilty was the murder of a policeman. The jury are not supposed to know that, and we would prefer that it didn't come out.'

Before continuing, Galloway fingered his moustache, which Sarah had come to recognise as a sign of nervousness. 'We will be treading on very thin ice tomorrow, but Gilligan's fate may depend on how we handle it.'

After Sarah left the advocates to prepare for the next day she was in poor spirits, which stayed with her as she spent another sleepless night. She now had to face the fact that the very best Frankie could expect was life imprisonment. As dawn approached, she made the resolution that if such was the outcome, she would not abandon him. Her life would be dedicated to visiting him in prison until eventually he might be released. This gave her some consolation and enabled her to drop off to sleep at last.

Frankie, meanwhile, in his cell in Barlinnie, was little moved by what had passed that day. It was what he expected. He had no regrets about the killing of Houliston; he deserved to die, and Frankie would have done the same again. That was why he had made no attempt to conceal his tracks after the killing and had merely waited for the police to come for him. As he lay there, he thought back over his life and particularly his family; his father, sister and brother all long dead in various tragic circumstances; his mother, according to Sarah, barely hanging on to life. The thought of Sarah brought him calmness. He realised that, despite the threat of death he was facing, he felt, for the first time in his life, totally free from strain, surrounded by the warmth of her declared love. There was no point in looking back with regret. He had no future. Right now, whatever the circumstances, he was at peace. Before falling asleep he tapped his chest and said 'hugs and kisses' like a mantra, under his breath.

54

'COURT!' The hoarse cry of the Macer heralded the appearance of the Judge to open the new day's session.

But before that, after a restless night and before going back to the High Court, Sarah went into the office. In theory this was to tell the staff in more detail about the previous day's proceedings, but it was really to unburden herself to the female staff in a way she found impossible with the male defence team. With the women, she didn't have to hide behind a front of professional composure and they in turn were able to show their concern without restraint. When the inevitable question was put to her, all she could do was shake her head sadly. Like many of the girls, she was close to tears. Pat McLaughlin's secretary hugged her as she sat beside her. Frankie had been a popular figure in the office and, before Sarah left for the Court, the girls started to exchange stories about their experience of him. As Sarah made her way to the Court, she realised with a pang that it was just like a funeral.

In Court the Advocate-Depute, Gilchrist, called what was to be his last witness, Billy Morton. As Galloway had predicted, he did not cut a prepossessing figure. He was thin, almost gaunt, with the appearance of what Sarah was later to recognise as a drug user. His gaze shifted to anywhere in the Court apart from Frankie in the dock. When he gave his name in response to the Advocate-Depute's request he had to be pressed to repeat it more loudly and, in giving evidence, he gave the impression of not wanting anyone to hear him.

With some difficulty, accordingly, Gilchrist elicited from him that he had been present on the night of the killing, had seen Frankie stab Houliston, had seen Houliston's satchel dislodged by Frankie's blows, and had seen Frankie make off with it. The evidence was given in such a furtive way that Galloway felt sure he could show it to be unreliable.

Finally, the Advocate-Depute paused, fingering the papers on the desk in front of him. 'Would it be right to say that you and Gilligan are enemies? I ask this because I am sure that my learned friend is going to put it to you that your evidence is tainted by this animosity.'

Although she was some distance away Sarah was sure that she heard Galloway say under his breath, 'Bastard'.

Gilchrist continued, 'That's a bad razor scar on your face. How did you come by it?

Galloway was on his feet in an instant. 'My Lord, I must object to this line of questioning. It is not relevant to the case being tried here.'

The Judge looked over his spectacles at Galloway. 'It may not be relevant, Mr Galloway, to the case, but it must be relevant to the credibility of the witness's evidence. The Advocate-Depute is merely anticipating an attack by you on this witness's truthfulness and, if you like, is merely spiking your guns. Carry on, Mr Gilchrist.'

Gilchrist repeated his question to Morton, who stated that it was a result of a razor attack by Gilligan. At this Galloway again half rose from his seat but he realised that the Judge was not with him and contented himself with spreading his hands in obvious frustration.

'Why did Gilligan attack you in this way?'

This time Galloway rose so forcibly that he knocked over his chair. 'My Lord, I must protest. There is no evidence either before this Court or in any previous proceedings, that the prisoner attacked this witness. This is wild speculation having nothing to do with the veracity of the witness but designed to cast a slight on the prisoner's character.'

As the Judge hesitated Morton, who had no idea what was going on but felt under attack shouted from the witness box, 'He did it when I tried to take over his bit when he was up for the murder of that policeman.'

There was uproar. Galloway was on his feet blazing with anger. The Judge sternly reprimanded Morton to behave himself and demanded of the Advocate-Depute that he should control his witness. He then turned to the jury and told them to disregard the comments made by the witness. The Advocate-Depute sat with his eyes quietly cast down. The matter had come out exactly as he wanted. He said he had no more questions.

The atmosphere was tense as Galloway rose to cross-examine. He knew that juries did not like to have to deal with confrontation. He therefore departed from his intended line of questioning and said to Morton mildly, 'From what we have heard about bad-feeling between you and the prisoner can I take it that you were not part of his group?'

Morton narrowed his eyes, not sure where this was going, but nodded.

'And the information we have about your address would leave me to believe that you were not part of the rival group, the Calton Boys. Am I right?'

Again, Morton reluctantly nodded.

'Then why were you there?'

There was no response from the witness.

'If indeed you were there.'

Again, no response.

'I understand that the fracas, I'm sorry, *the fight* took place not in the street but on a piece of waste ground left where a row of dilapidated tenements had been demolished and where there was no street lighting. Is that right?'

The Advocate-Depute rose to object to statements being made by the Defence rather than questions being put to the witness, but the Judge was happy to allow Galloway to proceed, stating that it was probably a quicker way to get information from the witness.

Morton now confirmed that the fight had indeed taken place in the 'Wastie'. He was confused, however, when he was asked what the weather was like that night. As in the previous questions, he did not know what answer he should give to help his case.

Galloway offered to help him. 'It may aid your memory if I tell you that, according to the weather people it was heavily cloudy that night and you must remember that immediately after the fight broke up there was a violent thunderstorm. Does that ring a bell?'

There was no response from Morton, and Galloway turned to him again. 'How many people do you think were involved in the fight?'

Again, Morton was stuck for an answer. 'Getting information from you, Mr Morton, is like drawing teeth but I will again assist you. The police estimate was about one hundred people roughly fifty a side. Would you agree?'

Morton squinted over at the Advocate-Depute and nodded almost imperceptibly.

'How would you describe the fight?'

Morton shrugged his shoulders. 'It was a fight.'

Galloway smiled at the jury. 'That's the most you have spoken in the last twenty minutes. Can I be more descriptive and call it a mass brawl in semi-darkness, involving one hundred heavily armed men cursing and swearing as they tried to injure their opponents?'

'I suppose.'

'Of the hundred men involved how many do you think have come forward as witnesses to the alleged attack on Jaikie Houliston and the alleged theft of his satchel?'

Silence from Morton.

'I must again run the risk of my learned friend accusing me of putting words in your mouth, but I don't seem to have much success in getting words from that mouth. If I were to tell you that not one person, not one, apart from you appears to have seen the incident, would you be surprised?'

'I don't know.'

Galloway gave a derisive snort. 'You don't know. But I know that you are a confirmed liar who has concocted this story as an act of revenge against the prisoner. I won't waste any further questions on you.'

The Advocate-Depute stroked his chin but decided not to re-examine. There had always been the possibility that the witness would be as poor as he had turned out, but he was happy that the forensic evidence was more than enough to convict.

Morton's evidence had taken up much of the morning and, when Galloway indicated he would not be putting forward any defence witnesses, it was agreed the Court should take an early adjournment for lunch, leaving the afternoon clear for the closing statements for each side.

Although Galloway had a pretty good idea of what he was going to say to the jury, he preferred to be alone over the lunch break to finalise his thoughts. Robert Simpson, Pat and Sarah had lunch together where the talk kept on reverting to the likely outcome. Sarah longed desperately for one of the two experienced men to say something that would give her hope, but neither was possibly brave enough to say out loud what he was thinking.

When the Court re-assembled, the Advocate-Depute rose to his feet and turned to the Jury.

'Members of the jury, there have been many cases before this Court when evidence has been complex, and the jury has had great difficulty in getting to the truth. This is not one of those cases. There has been clear forensic evidence, which the defence has not been able to challenge, that Jaikie Houliston was stabbed, in a sustained and frenzied attack, at least ten times with a knife, causing his death. That the knife, or at least one like it, was found shortly afterwards in the possession of the accused, bearing extensive traces of Houliston's blood and also the accused's fingerprints. That the accused, when arrested, was wearing a shirt that was subsequently found to be extensively stained with Houliston's blood. That in a drawer in the house of the accused there was found Houliston's satchel again bearing the fingerprints of the accused and—'

At this point there was a loud shout from Frankie, jumping to his feet in the dock.

'I did not steal Houliston's bag.'

There was consternation in the Court. Galloway leapt to his feet in horror. There was uproar from the public benches. Sarah held her head in her hands. If there were anything which might turn the jury against Frankie, this was it. The Judge rapped loudly on his desk and turned on Frankie.

'You will remain silent. If not, you will be removed from the Court and the trial will continue in your absence. Members of the jury, you will ignore this outburst by the accused. He has chosen, as is his right, not to give evidence in his defence and he cannot make statements, especially in such a violent way, which the prosecution has no means of questioning. Please proceed, Mr Gilchrist.'

'As I was saying, members of the jury, Houliston's satchel stained with his blood and carrying the fingerprints of the accused was found by police officers in the possession of what you have now seen to be a violent and uncontrolled man. There can be no doubt that Houliston died as a result of blows delivered by the accused, who took the heaven-sent opportunity to steal the satchel. I ask you to find accordingly.'

It was now James Galloway's turn to make his final submissions to the jury. As he rose and turned to them, he fingered his moustache. He paused for quite a long period before speaking. 'Members of the jury. I am a bit weary and I am sure that you are also, because it is exhausting to concentrate for so long on a matter of such dreadful significance. But we, all sixteen of us, hold in our hands the fate of this young man who stands in the dock before us.

'I say 'young man' because, despite the attempts by the prosecution to paint him as some sort of monster, he is just a young man like any other. I have a son much the same age and no doubt there will be some of your number who also have sons very much like him. He is no different from them. But we are shaped by our environment. *Our* children grow up surrounded by love and care. Boys like Frankie Gilligan are left exposed at an early age to fight unprotected in a hostile environment in which only the toughest survive. Where our children achieve their standing amongst their peers by success at school or in the workplace young boys like Frankie make their name by being hard and they get to the top by being *the* hardest.

'Our sons bond by being part of, say, a football team, and there is always one other team which is the number one enemy. To beat them brings the greatest satisfaction. Frankie's team is the gang and the greatest pleasure is coming out on top in a clash with the neighbouring gang.

'For our sons, sport is a substitute for war and allows the fiercest competition to take place controlled by fixed rules. For gangs, there are no fixed restraining rules. Their clashes are rightly known as 'gang warfare'. In war, killing and maiming the enemy before he attacks you is a form of self-defence. No soldier waits for the enemy to strike before he shoots. But that is a form of self-defence which is only available in war. In a civilised society you have to wait for the attack before you react. Even though young men like Frankie think they are in a war situation, they are not. That is why it was not open to me to put before the Court a plea of self-defence. Frankie may have thought he was acting in self-defence, but he was wrong. All those other boys on both sides laboured under the same delusion, a delusion created for them by their environment. Our environment punishes that delusion, but I ask you to understand the world in which these boys live.'

As he paused for a second, Sarah marvelled at how he had tried to change the image of Frankie in the eyes of the jury; an image which had not been helped by Frankie's violent outburst earlier. He had linked Frankie with their own children. And he had made him more human by not referring to him as the accused or the prisoner but by calling him 'Frankie' throughout. Sarah smiled to think that she had taken a little offence during the preparations for the trial because Galloway had always called him 'Gilligan'.

James Galloway resumed. 'We have considered two violently contrasting views on the ethics of gang warfare but there is no such difference of opinion on the question of theft. Theft is theft. But one other thing is clear. In the context of gang warfare theft is an irrelevance. Sergeant MacPherson, a man with long experience of the Gorbals, emphasised that in his evidence. The clashes are about bragging rights or some perceived grievance. They are never, and I repeat never, about the acquisition of property belonging to the other side. It is a nonsense to suggest that Frankie set out on that fateful night to steal Jaikie Houliston's satchel. And yet it was found in Frankie's flat immediately after the fight. How could that be? Sergeant MacPherson confessed he was puzzled. I share his bewilderment. One thing I am not confused about. When Frankie was engaged in fighting with Houliston he was not doing so in order to lay his hands on his satchel.

'My learned friend has placed much emphasis on the forensic evidence but forensic evidence on its own has been found on occasion, to lead to wrongful conclusions in the past. So, what other evidence is there?' Galloway paused for a second and, rather theatrically, searched through his papers. 'Ah! We have the evidence of Billy Morton. I know why I overlooked it, because my learned friend did not see fit to mention it in his concluding remarks to you. And rightly so. In my long career I have come across many unprepossessing witnesses. But I have never seen a 'witness' – and I put quotation marks round the word 'witness' – who had so little to say for himself.

'If he was there, and I emphasise 'if', he could not explain *why* he was there, as he was a member of neither group. In a crowd of one hundred struggling men he was able to pick out Frankie Gilligan. In an area not covered by street lighting and on a night when the sky was covered by the heavy clouds that subsequently brought a thunderstorm, he was able to see clearly Frankie Gilligan stab his opponent and steal his satchel.

'You may have seen me shaking my head as the witness finished his testimony and I am sure you will have shared my disbelief. The witness may not have been lying. He may have made up his preposterous story and then believed it. One thing is certain. He was certainly not telling the truth.

'The prosecution brought forward Billy Morton to bolster their case. On the contrary, he has weakened it. The prosecution has to prove beyond reasonable doubt that Frankie Gilligan has committed the crime of which he is accused. I invite you to share with me the view that there is reasonable doubt and to acquit him of the charge against him.'

As Galloway resumed his seat, his Junior, Robert Simpson, leant forward and whispered, 'Well done' but Galloway did not respond. He sat with his head bowed and Sarah saw that his hands were trembling. She had read that advocates were like actors but actors, when they have finished their piece, are elated. Galloway was totally spent. Sarah had seen film coverage of runners collapsing at the end of a marathon and Galloway was like that. There was nothing left.

Meantime the Judge indicated that, as it was close to the end of the day, he would delay his charge to the jury to the next morning, and he adjourned the hearing until then.

Afterwards the defence team went back, as usual, to the Western Club, but Galloway excused himself from joining them for dinner. He was tired and would arrange for some sandwiches to be sent up to his room. After he left, Robert Simpson talked about the strain placed upon older members of the Bar when taking on murder cases. It was part of the ethos of the Bar that such a case would never be turned down, but the responsibility was enormous. Thank heaven, the death penalty was now rare. He enthused over Galloway's performance that day. He mentioned in particular something that Sarah had not even been aware of:

'The forensic evidence is incontrovertible. We all know that. But James ignored it in his final address. He devoted nearly all of it to the evidence of Billy Morton. He made it seem that Morton's evidence was the lynchpin upon which the whole prosecution depended. He wanted the jury to have Morton's evidence totally in the forefront of their minds so that, with the knowledge that it was rubbish, it would taint the rest of the evidence. I think it gives us a chance.'

At last some reassurance for Sarah. It meant that she slept more easily that night than she had before.

55

Sarah again called in at the office before going down to the High Court so that she could update the office staff on the previous day's proceedings. She was sufficiently encouraged by Robert Simpson's comments the night before to give them an optimistic outlook on what to expect. But that optimism drained away the closer she got to the Court and she entered it filled with dread. The exchanges between the members of the defence team were subdued as they waited the arrival of the Judge.

In his charge to the jury Sarah thought he was fair although she felt he laid too much emphasis on Frankie's outburst the previous day.

'You must ignore the comments made by the accused in interrupting the Advocate-Depute's closing address,' he instructed. 'It was open to the accused to give evidence on this matter but, as is his right, he chose not to do so. He cannot, having made that decision, make statements in court which the Advocate-Depute has no means of challenging or examining. It is still incumbent on the prosecution to prove theft, but no evidence has been presented to disprove it.'

He went over the remaining evidence that had been led, advised the jury of their responsibilities, and asked them to retire to consider their verdict.

After the Judge left the bench the defence team repaired to the robing room. Sarah said nothing. Even if she had any right to do so she was incapable of speech. Her mouth was dry. Her stomach clenched. She thought she might be sick. The men were also quiet, each with his own thoughts. At twelve o'clock an usher came in to say that the jury had requested something to eat so that their deliberations were obviously going to go on into the afternoon. The group was glad to accept his offer to bring in some sandwiches for them, although, when they came, Sarah had great difficulty in eating even one. The time wore on into the afternoon but just as it seemed that there would be no decision that day the bell high up on the wall rang, startling them all.

The jury was coming back.

The next few minutes passed for Sarah like a dream – or rather a nightmare. On looking back, she was not sure if she was fully conscious as she moved along the corridors to the Court. The noise from the public galleries was intense and only dropped when the Macer announced the Judge's arrival. Then there was total silence. It was broken when the door to the jury room opened. Even then the only noise was the sound of the jurymen's feet as they filed in to take their places. Sarah, almost like a little child who looks at a scary sight through splayed fingers, fearfully scanned the faces of the jurymen. They were subdued. One woman was sobbing quietly.

The Clerk of Court stood up and turned to the jury. 'Members of the jury, who speaks for you?'

A short stocky man in the front row stood up and said, 'I do.'

'What is your verdict?'

'Guilty of capital murder.'

There was immediate uproar. Sarah had no idea how the others reacted because she was fighting hard not to faint as she sat there. Eventually the court officials managed to restore order. The Clerk of Court who had remained standing turned again to the chairman of the jury. 'And is your verdict unanimous or by a majority?

'By a majority.'

The Clerk wrote down the verdict and read it back to jury before passing it up to the Judge. The Judge hesitated and then turned to Frankie.

'Francesco Gilligan, you have been found guilty of the charge of capital murder. The sentence of this Court is that you be taken from this place to the prison of Barlinnie therein to be detained until the Seventh day of July Nineteen hundred and fifty eight and upon that day within the said prison of Barlinnie between the hours of eight and ten o'clock forenoon you will suffer death by hanging, which is pronounced for Doom.' As the Judge pronounced the last words, he touched his wig with a black tricorn.

This time there was no perceptible reaction from the spectators, who seemed stunned into silence. Sarah knew that the word 'Doom' was used only in its archaic sense of 'punishment' but to her ears and to the ears of all the other listeners it had its modern sense 'final irretrievable damnation'. She had not looked at Frankie since the jury had come back into the Court but now, she dared to have a secret glance at him. He stood with his head bowed but with no obvious sign of emotion. When the police officers motioned to him, he turned and left the dock without looking at the defence team in the well of the court.

After the Judge had left, and as the court began to empty, the Advocate-Depute leant across to Galloway and said, 'Sorry, Jimmy', before he gathered up his papers and went out.

Sarah said nothing but she was aware of the three defence lawyers. James Galloway seemed totally drained as he looked but did not see the desk in front of him. Robert Simpson had his eyes closed almost as if he was praying. Pat McLaughlin appeared close to tears. Sarah suddenly realised why. For her, the verdict was a crushing blow to her friend... no, her beloved. But she had no part in the outcome. For the three men the verdict meant that they had failed. No matter how, logically, the evidence was weighed heavily against Frankie, it was their job to save him. And they had failed. They could, should, might, have saved him but they had failed.

The Court was almost empty apart from the Court staff tidying up before Galloway stirred and said they had better go and see Frankie. As they left the court, Pat held Sarah back and said with a trembling voice how sorry he was to have put her through this ordeal. Sarah was unable to respond but merely stroked his arm.

Shortly after they reached the interview room Frankie was brought in. He immediately came towards them with hands outstretched to thank them for their efforts. Galloway had, meantime, regained his composure. He expressed his dismay at the jury's verdict, which he was sure was wrong but said that their work was just beginning. As soon as was feasible an appeal would be lodged, once he and Robert Simpson had the opportunity to go over in depth all the short-hand writers extended notes and in particular the Judge's charge to the jury. There was still a long way to go. Sarah stayed in the background as they discussed what had to be done. When that was done all the men shook hands again and turned to leave.

Sarah could not contain herself any longer. She rushed forward and buried herself in Frankie's arms as, for the first time ever, they were able to embrace. She sobbed as he cradled her head against his shoulder, before Pat McLaughlin, sensing the reaction of the police officers, led her gently away. As she turned before leaving, Frankie tapped his chest and mouthed, 'Hugs and kisses'

Outside Sarah dried her eyes. Pat suggested going for a much-needed drink, but Sarah declined. She needed to have a walk by herself, and so decided to stroll over to the Gorbals to visit Frankie's mother. She crossed the river into the still heavily tenemented area and past the open ground where the fight had taken place. Some buildings had already been demolished and there were areas with building rubble strewn on the ground. There were signs saying 'Keep Out' but ragged children were playing in amongst the rubble just, Sarah imagined, as Frankie would have done.

When she asked for Mrs Gilligan, the housekeeper shook her head sadly but showed her into her room. For some time now, Sarah was sure that Mrs Gilligan had no idea who she was, but she seemed happy with visits. This time, Mrs Gilligan was sleeping – or possibly unconscious. As usual the staff had made sure that she was neatly dressed in her night clothes with her hair carefully arranged. She seemed peaceful. The housekeeper whispered that she did not have long to go, and suggested Sarah might like to say a prayer. Sarah wanted to but couldn't. She was too proud. She didn't believe in that anymore. But she so wanted to.

After she left, she wondered why she had bothered; but she was glad she had come. She did not realise that in wanting to comfort Mrs Gilligan she was comforting herself.

56

Sarah dreaded the thought of her next visit to Frankie. Her old fears of Barlinnie Prison returned as she thought that within these walls in a short time Frankie was going to be killed. She was, however, treated with greater respect by the prison staff. Now they knew that, although officially a legal adviser, she was much closer to Frankie than that. And Frankie, by being condemned to death, had been raised to a new level, entitled to a consideration not given to other prisoners.

She was fighting hard to keep back the tears when he arrived, but he was not as she expected when he came in. Instead of looking depressed, he seemed full of life and smiled his delight at seeing her. In response to her tentative question as to how he was he replied, 'Never better.'

Seeing her puzzled look, he went on, 'Ever since I killed Jaikie Houliston this was bugging me. This uncertainty. Do you know the worst thing which was hanging over me – oops! There is an unfortunate choice of words,' he joked in a way which almost broke her heart. 'The worst thing was the thought of life imprisonment. I could not have taken that, especially with the effect on you. As it is, in a twisted way, because I killed Jaikie Houliston, I met you and that has been the most wonderful thing that has happened in my life. No, please don't cry. For this short piece of time I have had your love and it has been complete and I would have hated to have it distorted by life imprisonment.

'And I want you to promise me something. I've been thinking about this. That you will always remember me with tenderness but that you will meet another man and that you will marry and have children.' He smiled. 'You can always call one of them Francis although that might give him a bad start in life.'

Sarah was unable to speak. She did not weep but her eyes were full of tears. If the metal table had not been between them, they would have hugged and that would have expressed what words could not. As it was, Sarah could just look at Frankie, but it was a look which conveyed to Frankie all the love which she had for him.

Then gradually they were able to talk normally and even laugh at the silly things Sarah used to put in her bag just to confuse the prison officer searching it. She also had him laughing at tales she remembered of the Collins boys whom she still continued to help with their lessons whenever she visited Frankie's mother. When Frankie asked about his mother, Sarah was prepared. There was no point in worrying him at this point in time. She merely said that she had been to see her, for which Frankie was most grateful, and that she seemed rested and peaceful.

However, when she got back to the office, she found that Father O'Leary had phoned and, on returning his call, she learned Mrs Gilligan had died peacefully in her sleep. Sarah was immensely saddened, not just for Mrs Gilligan but more for the effect on Frankie who was devoted to his mother and used to talk at length to Sarah about her Italian background. Now she was gone and with her the last remnant of Frankie's family. Sarah could only shake her head in horror at the tragic fate of the whole of that family. She spoke to Pat McLaughlin who confirmed with a sigh that he would deal with funeral arrangements. He did not tell Sarah this but it was one more thing he had to do, to fulfil his promise to his old school friend, Boxy, that he would look after his family; although Pat reflected sadly that he had not done much good. He did tell Sarah, however, that, as a condemned prisoner, Frankie would not be permitted to attend the funeral. He said that he would go up to Barlinnie to tell Frankie but agreed when Sarah told him that she wanted to do it.

Next morning Sarah was back in Barlinnie and, although it was unusual for her to visit two days running, Frankie seemed to be expecting her. As she hesitated, not knowing how to tell Frankie the bad news gently, he stopped her.

'It's all right, Sarah. I know. Bad news travels fast in this place. Oh Sarah, Mammy meant everything to me. The only blessing is that she did not know what had happened to me. She was spared that.' Frankie hesitated and looked down. There was a long pause as he struggled to control himself, and Sarah looked helplessly on.

Then he said, 'Sarah, can I tell you something which has stayed with me, my whole life? I don't want to burden you but, knowing that you love me, I feel I can share it with you.'

And Frankie, in fits and starts, told Sarah the terrible tale of him as an eight-year-old, frightened because he was alone in the house, long after nightfall, going out looking for his mother. How he had become disorientated and terrified in the badly lit streets. How he had panicked and fled crying from a man who had approached him in the dark. Then, turning yet one more corner there she was. Frankie hesitated with his eyes screwed tight then, with every word tearing him as he spoke, he said, 'She was standing in a shop doorway, pishing as she stood. You could see the pee dripping from her.'

There was a long pause. Sarah, her eyes filled with tears, said nothing.

'You know, Sarah, that didn't affect my love for her. I just wanted her to be safe. I didn't want anyone to see what I had seen. I didn't think that there was anyone around, but I had an uneasy feeling that there was someone there. Then she started off for home. Although she was drunk, she knew exactly where she was going. I kept my distance, but the daft thing was that, although I was trying to safeguard her, I only felt safe when I was near her.'

Another pause.

'On the night of the fight with the Calton Boys, when I met up with Houliston, he made a crack about Wee Jiffy who he had just killed, and I wanted him for that. And then he asked whether my mother was still pishing in shop doorways. He must have been the other person who I sensed was there on that night. And he had kept that to use against me for all those years. That's why I did what I did to him, for Mammy and for Wee Jiffy, and for me.'

'Oh, Mr Gilligan,' said Sarah. 'Now I know why you stabbed Houliston so many times. I'm so glad you told me this. We're a team; nothing held back between us. I had grown to love your mother as well, and what you have told me does not affect that. A love for a mother should be unquestioning.'

She told Frankie that he would be unable to go to his mother's funeral, but he seemed to know this already. He told her that she could go for him. That would just be as good.

They parted with their usual gesture of 'Hugs and Kisses', although this time with even more intensity than normal.

As Sarah made her way back to the office, she thought back to what she had said to Frankie about unquestioning love for a mother. Had she shown that sort of love to her own mother? Her mother had been difficult at times and Sarah had reacted to that. She had almost gone out of her way to avoid contact with her. Sarah had thought she was justified in so doing. But what right had she to judge? She felt she had learned a lesson from Frankie. She would make the effort to improve in the future. But should love for a mother not be natural and not determined? Sarah was still wrestling with that thought when she reached the office.

57

The next day the papers were full of the news of Frankie's mother's death. 'Killer's Mother Dead', screamed the headlines. As they had nothing current to go on, the journalists, as is their wont, had raked through their old copy and told the whole story of the tragic Gilligan family – two children already meeting violent deaths and the remaining one facing imminent execution. To Sarah's disgust one paper alleged that Mrs Gilligan had died of a broken heart because of the impending fate of her surviving son. Another stated, almost with glee, that part of Frankie's deserved punishment was that he would not be able to attend the funeral of his own mother.

'Do these people not know what they are doing when they print such hurtful rubbish?' Sarah was nearly crying in frustration.

Pat managed to console her. He had had many experiences of prying sensational reporters in the past. 'They will print whatever will sell newspapers and it works. People's worst instincts mean that they want to read that sort of thing, and will believe anything, the more outrageous the better.'

At Mrs Gilligan's funeral, which was held in St Francis Church, there were a few newspapermen and photographers lurking outside but, to Sarah's relief, nothing too intrusive. Father O'Leary said the Mass, but the congregation was small; Sarah was there along with Pat and his wife and there were some of Mrs Gilligan's old Italian friends. Jessie Collins was there, looked after by the parish housekeeper to whom she had become close because of her visits to see Mrs Gilligan. And Sarah was surprised but delighted to see, Alec Collins himself, looking very uncomfortable partly because he was squeezed into an unaccustomed suit but mostly because he found himself for the first time in a Roman Catholic chapel.

Maria Gilligan was buried in the same lair as her husband, Boxy, and afterwards Sarah took Mr and Mrs Collins for something to eat; Sarah and Jessie chatted happily away but Alec Collins still found himself grumpily ill-at-ease in the company of this confident young lady.

Later, when Sarah was giving him details of the funeral, Frankie smiled as Sarah told of Alec Collins's discomfort at being within a Catholic church – but still, he was deeply grateful for the effort made.

Frankie's pleasure at hearing small details like that puzzled Sarah. She, herself, was in a constant state of tension awaiting the appeal process but Frankie seemed unfussed even when a date was fixed for the hearing of the Appeal. It would be held in the High Court in Edinburgh; Pat originally decided to let his Edinburgh correspondent sit with Counsel at the hearing because, as he explained to Sarah, there was nothing he could add. It was just that an instructing solicitor had to be present. At the last minute, however, he decided to go through and Sarah thought she would accompany him to Edinburgh, not to go to the hearing but to visit her mother whom she had not been in contact with for some time.

As usual, when they met, Sarah was aware of her mother's inability to show her feelings. Molly's embrace was no warmer and no more extended that she might have given to a chance acquaintance, and her talk was brittle and ill at ease. Sarah, tense because of Frankie's situation, longed for a warm hug and understanding words, but they were not forthcoming. Although Sarah was happy in Glasgow, she had no close female friends there on whom she could have unburdened herself of her feelings for Frankie. And she didn't think she could ever talk about it to her mother; the very thought of it made the tension in her stomach even greater.

Then she remembered the conversation she had had with Frankie when he described his mother's drunkenness. They had agreed that love for a mother was absolute, non-judgemental... For the rest of her visit, Sarah made every effort to ignore her mother's awkwardness and to treat her with a love which her attitude did not seem to merit. And she thought her mother *did* seem to respond. When they parted their embrace was closer and seemed to have more feeling.

Walking back to Waverley Station to meet Pat, Sarah also felt more relaxed than she had been in Edinburgh since the trauma she had described to Frankie. She felt surer of herself, and walked with her head held high, not with her eyes downcast as had previously been the case.

As for Pat, he was pleased with the way the Appeal had gone. He expressed his admiration for the way James Galloway had presented the case and felt that there had been a positive reaction from the Judges.

58

It was all the more distressing when the news came through, about two weeks later, that the Appeal had been rejected. A new date for the execution had been fixed for 11 August.

When Pat told her the news, Sarah nearly fainted and had to sit down. He said that there was still one avenue to be explored - a Petition to the Queen to exercise the royal prerogative of mercy and annul the execution. Although technically the prerogative was exercised by the Queen, in practice the Petition was directed to the Secretary of State for Scotland who had the duty to take as much advice as he deemed necessary before responding. Sarah nodded blindly when Pat said work had already started on the Petition and she managed to get through the rest of that day without breaking down, although tears were never far from the surface. But when she reached the privacy of her flat her bottled-up emotion could be contained no longer and she let out a howl, as she thought later, like a she-wolf in the wilderness standing over the body of her dead cub. No words, just a long, sustained wail. And then the tears came flooding out of her, and as they did, she could feel the tension oozing out of her body.

That night she had the first long deep sleep she had enjoyed for weeks.

The next day she went to Barlinnie to see Frankie. She was full of trepidation, but Frankie seemed unmoved by the failure of his Appeal, about which he already knew. He was full of a visit he had received from Father O'Leary.

'You know what he's like, Sarah. Started talking the minute he walked in the door.' Frankie laughed, and mimicked the old priest:

How are you, son? Don't think much of your digs. It reminds me of the junior seminary I was in although I think this is more luxurious. And the warders are much more pleasant than the guys who controlled us in the seminary. Maybe they were trying to put us off. Nearly succeeded in some cases. Some of the boys came from a comfortable background and couldn't handle the change. Me. From the background I came from, this was a step up. But what I had was the love of a mother. And that's what you had. A lovely lady, your mother. She was peaceful at the end and we gave her a good send off.

Pat and Sarah were there of course and some nice wee old Italian ladies. And Jessie Collins, what a gem she is. And her husband, Alec. I think he sidled along the edges of the buildings, keeping in the shadows before darting into the church afraid in case anyone spotted him. But he was there. Good on him.

'I came today in case you felt like making your confession. No? No problem. The good book says that there is a great celebration in heaven when a sinner repents. But that's easy stuff. I think the big man up there has a special place for sinners who don't repent. He cares about the fall of a sparrow. He'll look after you. You loved your mammy, didn't you, and she loved you. That's enough to see you home…' Frankie ran out of steam, finally. 'And then he was up and away,' he added. 'He's some man. It was good of him to come and he was great with my mammy.'

What Frankie didn't mention was that, before he went, the priest must have spoken to the warder who let him in round Frankie's side of the table Father O'Leary placed his hands on Frankie's head, said a blessing over him and then left without another word. Frankie felt a sense of peace after the priest left, something he couldn't explain. He also couldn't understand why he didn't tell Sarah about the blessing, but he didn't.

Sarah was still too affected to make much of a go at conversation, but it didn't seem to matter to Frankie. The priest's visit seemed to have had the effect of awakening a flood of memories and he spent the rest of Sarah's visit talking about his relatives, especially the Italian ones, and about his growing up in the Gorbals. The only slight smile came to Sarah's face when she thought that Frankie was speaking just like Father O'Leary with one

412

topic running into another, one anecdote triggering off another, often with little connection – as far as Sarah was aware. But to be truthful Sarah was not paying much attention to what Frankie was saying. All the time her mind kept jumping to the fact that Frankie, her Mr Gilligan whom she loved, was days, *yes, days*, from execution, death by a means of which Sarah had learnt the precise details from her ghoulish lecturer in Forensic Law. Try as she might she could not banish the images from her mind, and she was actually glad when it was time for her to go. On her own she was able to wrestle with her thoughts without having to put up a show of interest and enjoyment in Frankie's reminiscences. Like someone nursing a toothache she wanted to be alone to concentrate on her pain.

59

The final blow, when it came, was not declared in open court in a dramatic fashion. Rather it was contained in a letter delivered by a short, stout, self-important man dressed in morning coat, pin-striped trousers and a bowler hat. Having to visit the depth of squalor, which was his view of Glasgow, was bad enough, but the lift was having one of its off days and the messenger felt it was far below his dignity to have to climb six sets of stairs to what appeared to be the dingy office premises of Shaw McLaughlin & Co. He tried to convey his displeasure as he handed over the envelope to Rose, the office Junior, and demanded a receipt. His importance was, however, lost on Rose who merely signed the receipt before turning her attention to other matters, leaving him to make his way back down the stairs, carefully avoiding contact with walls or banisters for fear of contamination.

Normally, Rose would have opened the envelope there and then, but there was something about the weight of the envelope and the word 'URGENT' on the outside that made her take it unopened through to Pat McLaughlin to whom it was addressed.

As soon as he saw the envelope, impressed with the seal of the Scottish Office, Pat knew what it was. His fingers trembled as he held it for a moment, unopened, in his hands. He said a silent prayer. Then he reached for his paper knife, slit open the envelope, took out the letter and unfolded it. All done so slowly as if he was in a dream.

The letter read:

'Sir,

I am directed by the Secretary of State to inform you that after careful consideration of the case of Francis Gilligan he regrets that he is unable to find sufficient grounds to justify him in advising Her Majesty to interfere with the due course of the law.

I am, Sir,

Your obedient servant,'

It was signed by an official at the Scottish Office.

Pat's reaction was one of deep, deep dejection. But also of fury. Was the fate of this man so unimportant that it could be dealt with in such a brief, cold official way? No reasons given. And not even signed by the Secretary of State himself. He must have been too busy and had given it to some flunkey to deal with. Was that an indication of the care he had devoted to the Petition?

Pat's office door was always open, but he rose and closed it before returning to sit at his desk. He thought of his friend, Boxy Gilligan. On his deathbed he had asked Pat to look after his family. How terribly Pat had failed: Boxy's son and daughter suffering violent deaths; his wife, lost to reality, subsiding into oblivion; and now, Frankie, about to be executed by a vengeful state. There must have been something he could have done, Pat agonised. Had he been too passive, not wanting to interfere?

He thought of Sarah. He should never have exposed her to this ordeal. He had meant to give her some experience of an unusual case, and then she had become useful with her shorthand and typing skills. But she had become involved in a way he had not anticipated. (Being, in fact, much more deeply involved than Pat suspected).

Pat sat a long time on his own. In the main office the staff discussed anxiously what could have happened; Pat's door was never closed and in addition, he had asked for no telephone calls to be put through. When Sarah returned from her usual duties at the Ordinary Court, her cheerful smile faded as soon as she entered the typists' room. Something had gone wrong. The girls all had their views but when Rose told of the delivery from the pompous little messenger, Sarah immediately knew what that envelope contained.

She almost collapsed into a chair. As the girls watched her fearfully, she managed to explain hesitantly what the envelope would have been, and that it must have contained a rejection of Frankie's Petition, his last hope. He would be executed in ten days' time.

Sarah stayed with the girls for a long time. Some were tearful; some sat saying nothing; some exchanged some quiet words. Frankie was not just a name in the papers. He was someone they knew well. Someone they liked.

Eventually Sarah summoned up her courage and, going along the corridor, knocked on Pat's door. When she went in, Pat, standing at the window, held out the official letter but she did not need to read it to learn the bad news. Pat was gaunt, almost shrunken. The hand holding out the letter was shaking. Without thinking what she was doing, Sarah went round to Pat and put her arms around him and held him while he fought to control himself and she wept.

After a bit they separated, and Pat seemed to square his shoulders.

'Right, I must go up to Barlinnie and tell Frankie the news. He's better to hear it direct from me rather than vaguely though the prison grapevine. No, I'll go on my own this time, Sarah. You can see him tomorrow. But thank you for your support, Sarah. You have been wonderful through this. You can tell the girls what has happened, but I suspect they already know.'

60

Sarah passed the next few days in a state of confusion. On the one hand she wanted to fully occupy her time so that she was less aware of the terrible ache which afflicted her constantly. On the other hand, she wanted the days to Frankie's execution to stretch out as long as possible.

After the first torrent of misery, she no longer cried. She had read somewhere that recently widowed women went through a period when the tears just dried up. That was what she experienced. She was numb. She reacted when people spoke to her but it was if they were coming from a far distance. At least they occupied her. It was when she was alone that she could not escape the pain. Sleep was just a succession of short losses of consciousness ended by a quick jerk back to harsh reality.

Because of prison regulations she was able to see Frankie only twice in the period leading up to his execution. On the first occasion she was surprised that the tram taking her up to Barlinnie was so quiet because it was normally full of children from St Aloysius College on their way to their way to their sports ground at Millerston. Then she realised that the schools were on holiday. When she thought of the school, she reflected on the fact that were it not for a fatal flaw in Frankie's father's character, Frankie, as a boy, would have been one of those off to the sports ground, rather than struggling for survival in the back courts of the Gorbals. In later life that feeling of random unfairness never left her.

On that first visit, they were both quiet. They didn't spend time discussing the rejection of Frankie's petition; he had had expected it to fail. They didn't talk much: sometimes lovers don't feel like talking, they are content to be in one another's company. The fact that they can be happy with that, is a token of their love.

Prior to the second visit, which was to be the last one, Sarah was overcome with grief but also tortured by the feeling that she must not impose her torment on Frankie.

He was immediately aware of her distress, however, and tried to comfort her. 'Sarah, you are the best thing that ever happened to me. I cannot regret anything that has happened because it has brought you to me. I have been thinking how perfect it is. We would normally have never met. Even if we had, we might have enjoyed our time together and then drifted apart. What future would there have been together for a rising young lawyer and a hoodlum from the Gorbals.

'No, don't stop me, Sarah, I've had plenty of time to think this out. In the midst of all this squalor and these terrible surroundings we have created our own perfect world. And when it ends it will do so when our love is still completely true.'

Frankie had to stop there because Sarah, who had thought she would never cry again, was convulsed in tears.

Frankie waited until she had at least partially recovered before going on, 'Do you know the only flaw in my happiness? Yes, happiness, Sarah. It's that you will be distraught at my death. Please don't, Sarah. I want you to be happy as well. Between us we have created this perfect jewel. It will never be lost. I want you to cherish it. It will never go away even after I'm gone. But don't spoil it by wishing that it could go have gone on longer.' Frankie paused again as Sarah struggled to produce a tearful smile. 'Mr McLaughlin was up to see me. He's a lovely man. Our family has given him a lot of trouble, but he has always remained faithful. I think he was very fond of my father.' He hesitated again. 'Would you believe that I made a will when he was here? Me making a will?

When Mr McLaughlin asked me to think about it, I realised that I had a wee bit of money. I haven't left any of it to you.'

Sarah, with a mixture of gestures and garbled words, made it clear that she would not have accepted any money.

'You know that I would give you everything, but what we have is more precious than money.' Frankie confirmed. 'Now take a deep breath and tell me that you love me. You have no idea how good that makes me feel.'

Thus encouraged, Sarah did tell him that she loved him and added various other expressions of her love. In doing so she gradually recovered her composure and the time to the end of her visit passed in quiet contentment. At least until she had to go.

Frankie shook his head as she then began to break down again. He tapped his chest. 'Always hugs and kisses.'

And Sarah was able to recover herself sufficiently to respond with the same words and gesture.

She left with her head held high, too enwrapped in her own thoughts to appreciate the gentleness shown her by the prison staff as she was taken out. Once outside, going back up the long avenue to the main road, tears again overwhelmed her. She decided she could not be seen in the tram in this state and, after one last look back at the prison, set off on foot a distance of some four miles back to the office.

The walk steadied her and she was able to keep her composure when the office staff crowded round her for her news. The head typist told her that in her absence they had all decided to request permission to take time off, to go as a group to Frankie's funeral.

Sarah sadly shook her head. 'There's no funeral. After the execution,' how hard it was for her to say that word, 'Frankie's body is immediately taken and buried within the confines of the prison. The minimum of ceremony. No mourners.'

The girls were downcast. They had so wanted to show as a group that the man whom the public at large regarded as a villain, was their friend and that they wanted to stand by him.

Sarah left them talking amongst themselves and went to her own office where, luckily, her fellow apprentice, Alastair Clarke was not there. She had become used to him, but he was not the type of person in whom you could confide your innermost feelings. Her chat with the girls had brought forcibly to her mind that she had to make her own decision. What was she going to do on the morning of the execution? She did not want to be alone. At the same time, she did not want to be involved with other people. Then it came to her. She knew, because Pat McLaughlin often went, that there was a Mass for office workers in St Aloysius at 7.45 every morning. That was just a quarter of an hour before the execution. Of course, she did not believe in that sort of thing anymore, but it was an environment where she could be alone but still part of a group.

It occurred to her that some of the girls, those who were Catholics, might want to do the same thing and she went back along the corridor to tell what she was doing. After she left them, there was a lively debate because, while Mass might suit the Catholics, they had wanted to do something as a group. The upshot of the discussion was that the girls decided that they would all go to St Aloysius, where the Catholic girls assured those who were not, that they would look after them so that they did not feel out of place. Jean Munro confided to her friend Ina that she was happy to go but that she would not let her husband know, as she suspected that he would not approve.

61

The morning of 11 August was a beautiful morning. The day had been bright since the early hours. Sarah knew because, although she was dressed in her night-clothes, she had been up pacing the floor most of the time. But now, as she looked down on the early traffic in Sauchiehall Street, she felt strangely calm. As the time came, she dressed in sombre clothes before leaving to climb up the hill to the church. Outside the church, the office staff gradually gathered before going in as a group. The girls, especially the younger ones, were overawed by the splendour of the interior, with its lofty decorated roof and marble panelled walls and altar. Sarah sat a little apart from the other girls. A few rows in front of her she saw Pat McLaughlin already in place, with his head bowed over his missal. Sarah had chosen her seat deliberately because, unlike other churches, there was a clock high upon the north wall and Sarah could see it from where she was.

Those in the church were not the only ones who had Frankie in their minds.

Robert Galloway, preparing for a day's walking in the hills, struggled to free himself from the terrible feeling of guilt from which he would never escape, that he could have saved Frankie Gilligan's life if he had handled the case differently.

Jessie Collins had been up early preparing her husband's piece before sending him off to work with a kiss. She was now chasing the children to get ready for school; preparing their snacks; always busy. She had the wireless on in the background, and in the recess of her mind, no matter how she scurried around, was the thought that Frankie Gilligan was about to be executed.

In Camden Town in London, a young trainee television producer thought back to the days of her childhood when, with her neat ankle socks, she had played games with a boy called Frankie who was now a man about to be hanged.

Constance McLaughlin knelt by her bedside and prayed; for Frankie Gilligan but even more so for her husband Pat, whom she had seen age twenty years as the terrible case went on. She was not sure if he would ever recover.

Father Tony O'Leary said his usual eight o' clock Mass that morning. When it came to the prayers for the dead, he added a

425

special prayer for Frankie Gilligan: 'In Thy mercy, O Lord, hear my prayer for Thy departed son Frankie. May he find peace at last in the shelter of Thy love.'

Superintendent Samuel McCulloch snored peacefully in bed beside his little wife. He had no regrets about what he had done. Gilligan should have hung for the murder of that police officer from McCulloch's own station. He'd got away with that one. McCulloch was quietly satisfied that he had fixed it so that Gilligan didn't get away with the Houliston murder. Justice had caught up with Gilligan in the end. There was a symmetry to that which pleased the Superintendent.

Sarah knelt with her head bowed. She longed for there to be a God so that she could talk to him and ask him to intercede on behalf of Frankie, whom from long habit she still thought of as Mr Gilligan. She did a thing she had not done in years. She talked to her father. Was it possible to send thoughts through the airwaves? As the minute hand on the clock moved inexorably towards the hour, she strained to send messages mentally across the miles from the church to the prison:

'I am with you. I love you. Hugs and kisses. Oh, Mr Gilligan…'

But the deepest messages were those which could not be expressed in words.

Having deliberately chosen her place so that she could see the clock she now averted her gaze from it as if that would somehow stop it. She redoubled her efforts and, with her eyes tightly closed, strained to transmit her love. She was shaken out of her intense concentration by the sound of the altar bells signalling the Consecration of the Host, followed by the gong sounding as the priest raised the Host high above his head.

Involuntarily, Sarah raised her head and, without thinking, caught a glimpse of the clock on the wall. It was past eight o' clock.

It was all over.

Epilogue

Many years later, Bobby Smith, who had been a prison officer present at a number of judicial executions, took part in a documentary about his experiences. When asked about condemned men's reactions as they approached the execution chamber, he described a wide range, from hysteria to dumbness. One he remembered in particular was Frankie Gilligan who was very calm and very appreciative of the efforts of the officers involved. When asked about any last words, Bobby said that some shouted and swore, some cried for their mammy. Frankie Gilligan, he recalled, kept muttering under his breath the same few words, like a mantra. It sounded like 'hugs ma misses'.

I, FRANCIS GILLIGAN residing at Eighty-two, Cumberland Street, Glasgow in order to settle the succession to my means and estate upon my death do provide as follows:-

ONE   I appoint as my Executor Patrick McLaughlin, Solicitor, Glasgow whom failing, James Armstrong, Solicitor, Glasgow (hereinafter referred to as 'my Executor')

TWO   I direct my Executor to make payment of my lawful debts and funeral expenses and of the expenses of winding up my Estate.

THREE   I direct my Executor to give effect to any writings granted by me, however informal they may be provided they are subscribed by me, dated after the date hereof and are clearly expressive of my intention as to which my Executor shall be the sole judge. Any bequests so made shall be free of interest, delivery expenses and government taxes unless otherwise stipulated.

FOUR   I bequeath to Alec Collins and Jessie Collins, equally between them the flat they currently rent from me at Eighty-two Cumberland Street, Glasgow together with the sum of Two Thousand Pounds Sterling.

FIVE   To my beloved Sarah Watson, I bequeath my Auntie Barbara's sewing machine together with such of my sketches and drawings as she thinks are worth keeping. I have not left her any money because the jewel which we shared is worth more than any money could buy. I know she understands that.

SIX   I direct my Executor to transfer the whole residue and remainder of my means and estate to the Franciscans of St Francis' Church, Glasgow to be used by them for the benefit, welfare and education of children in the Gorbals area of Glasgow prior to them going to secondary school, and I express the wish that Sarah Watson, if she is willing, should be involved in any decisions about the use of these funds.

SEVEN   My Executor shall have the fullest powers of retention, realisation, investment, appropriation, transfer of property without realisation and management of my estate as if he were the absolute beneficial owner and shall be entitled to act as solicitor or agent in any other capacity and shall be entitled to the

430

same remuneration to which he would have been entitled if not an Executor

EIGHT   I declare that my domicile is Scottish.

LASTLY   I hereby revoke and cancel all prior Wills and testamentary writings made or granted by me: IN WITNESS WHEREOF these presents are subscribed by me at Glasgow on Fifth July Nineteen hundred and fifty eight before these witnesses William Crawford and Alexander Mackay, both prison officers, Barlinnie prison, Glasgow

ABOUT THE AUTHOR

John Francis Hart is a retired lawyer based in Scotland.

This is his second novel, the genesis of which was the writer's experience in joining a legal office which was still deeply affected through acting for a client who was hanged for murder the previous year.

His first novel, The Burton Sisters, was published in 2019 and tells of the struggle by two sisters to become medically qualified set against Victorian prejudice. The Burton Sisters draws on the report of an actual court case which he came across while preparing for the defence in another litigation.

Printed in Great Britain
by Amazon

60834647R00260